Maxwell slowly bent to the side and lightly kissed Christine.

"I know you were expecting that. I didn't want to disappoint you."

Christine was skeptical, even though her heart lurched. "Be honest. You mean you couldn't help yourself."

He arched a brow as the elevator stopped on the sixth floor. Christine walked out slowly and turned to face him. He continued to stand in the elevator, watching her, bemused.

Christine sighed. "Thanks again."

The door started to close and at the last possible moment, Maxwell stepped easily into the hallway. She realized she was waiting for him. Then he came closer . . . and they were in each other's arms.

Christine met his kiss as if this had been the game plan all along. Everything else flew out of her head as she closed her eyes and let Maxwell hold her against him. She let him kiss her thoroughly. It was, to put it simply, wonderful.

Realizing they were in the hallway, she pulled away and stared into his eyes.

"Was . . . was that a . . . goodnight kiss?"

Maxwell's gaze swept over her. He shook his head. "No."

Christine closed her eyes and shook her head as if to clear it. "My . . . goodness."

Maxwell reached to touch her mouth. "Yes."

SENSUAL AND HEARTWARMING

SANDRA KITT
Suddenly

PINNACLE BOOKS
KENSINGTON PUBLISHING CORP.

PINNACLE BOOKS are published by

Kensington Publishing Corp.
850 Third Avenue
New York, NY 10022

Pinnacle, the P logo, and Arabesque are Reg. U.S. Pat. &
TM Off.

First Pinnacle Books Printing: June, 1996
10 9 8 7 6 5 4 3 2 1

Printed in the United States of America

I wish to thank Narvice Overton, Inhalation Therapist, for her information and assistance. A special thank you to Maxine Frere, Senior Research Nurse/Coordinator of The Family Care Center/Pediatrics at Harlem Hospital, who allowed me to see where, why, and how. I have great admiration for these two professionals, and others like them, for the difficult work they are performing.

For . . . my best friend, Laurie Clark, who is also my other sister.

Prologue

Saturday, May 12th

"Excuse me . . . are you Christine Morrow? The model? I saw you on a television commercial the other night. Wasn't that you?"

Christine ignored the voice for a moment, staring across the table instead at one of her dinner companions. The beautiful blond woman facing her raised her brows as if to say, 'How tiresome'. But they were seated in a prominent place in the popular Tribeca eatery just so they would be noticed—she and the other three models who'd planned a champagne dinner together to celebrate their return from Europe and a series of fabric shows. The restaurant was noisy and small . . . but allowed them to be the center of attraction.

Christine took a sip from her champagne and slowly turned her head. She gave the eager man standing next to her a long look, the kind that used to say, 'Are you talking to me?'. But Christine had learned to accept the inevitable and make it work to her advantage. She was going to be recognized no matter where she went. It was part of the price she paid for having become one of the top models in New York, Paris, and Rome.

So, instead of saying something cutting and rude,

as she'd known other models to have done . . . as she herself had done on occasion . . . she turned her charm on the young man. The other people at her table hid their amusement . . . and cynicism . . . and watched to see what she would do.

"Yes, I am. How sweet of you to notice me," Christine said and smiled in calculated surprise.

He blushed. "You're even prettier than your pictures," he said guilelessly.

"You're seeing the real me. No makeup."

"You don't need any," he replied, patting his pockets in search of something to write on. Realizing he still clutched his linen dinner napkin, he thrust it out to her. "Could you sign this for me?"

Christine arched a brow as she heard the suppressed laughter behind her. "You mean, you're going to steal one of the restaurant's napkins just so you can have my autograph?"

He blinked. He hadn't thought of that. "Well . . ."

She took the napkin and smoothed it on the edge of the table. "Never mind. I can't begin to tell you how many napkins leave this place because Robert DeNiro or Whoopi Goldberg decide to have dinner here." Taking the proffered pen of one of her companions, Christine signed her name in a sprawl over the center of the napkin and gave it back to her fan. "There. Just remember you can never wash it." Laughter finally erupted behind her.

"Don't worry. I'll probably frame it." The young man beamed, nodding as he turned away.

"Well, you know you've *really* made it when you're framed on a dinner napkin," her handsome companion said with a chuckle.

"You should talk, Dano. I saw you take that waitress's phone number," the blonde said.

"She's also an actress," he said defensively, as if

that made a difference. But his attention was immediately drawn to a ravishing young woman who smiled at him even while holding the hand of her date.

"I'm ready to go," the blond woman pouted, flipping her hair carefully over her shoulder. Half the men around her turned to notice. "Let's go over to The Monkey Bar."

"I don't feel like that tonight," Christine said, shaking her head and allowing the rest of the champagne to be drained into her glass. She was already feeling a little buzzed. "Let's go over to The Blue Note. There's a great jazz combo playing tonight. We can catch the last set."

The tall, black actress sitting next to her scoffed. "Show-off. You only want to go there because you know the musicians. Didn't your brother-in-law used to play with them?"

"I know why she wants to go," Dano said, winking at Christine. "She found out there's a private party tonight for Mizrahi and *he* knows a lot of cool people."

The blonde laughed. "You'd better be careful who you flirt with. Keith might find out."

Christine grimaced prettily, sipping more champagne even though her head was beginning to throb. "Keith and I are not joined at the hip."

"What if Cade is there?" the actress asked slyly. "I know you two used to have the hots for each other."

Christine shrugged indifferently as the name of the handsome athlete was mentioned. They'd been an item for a fast minute, but that was before Keith. And before she'd found out about the string of groupies surrounding baseball star Cade MacMillan.

Besides, she didn't want to be in the shadow of someone more well known than she was.

"So what are we going to do?" Dano asked, looking around at his female companions.

"I want to go dancing," the blonde persisted.

"Why don't we just go somewhere for a drink?" the black actress suggested.

"We just split two bottles of champagne," Dano exclaimed. "As it is, I'm going to have to spend three hours at the gym tomorrow."

Christine grinned and put down her empty glass. She glanced up at a trio of men seated at the bar, looking at her in rapt attention. She graced them with a sultry stare, then crossed her legs in the black one-piece cat suit which daringly emphasized and outlined her lean long body, knowing that her brown skin and green eyes only added to her allure. She smiled as she turned back to her table. Ignoring her headache, she decided she wasn't ready to go home yet, and Keith was still out of town. "Let's do all of it. We have all night."

The actress frowned at her. "Don't you have a show tomorrow or something?"

Christine shrugged. "I do. Are we ready?"

Dano signaled for the waiter and signed the tab. As they got up, every eye in the restaurant was on them. Normal conversation became a sort of sighing hum as they trooped through the room toward the door. The blonde grabbed the last unopened bottle of champagne and randomly selected a table, giving the bottle to the startled couple. Christine brought up the rear, exiting as grandly and deliberately as she'd entered earlier, leading the quartet in for dinner. She half expected applause to break out, but settled for the awed silence.

They went out into the calm spring New York

night, squabbling noisily over who should sit where in the waiting limo.

"What difference does it make?" Christine asked, getting in first and securing the seat she wanted. "We're all going to the same place."

"Where to, please?" the driver asked.

Christine waved her fingers airily. "Just drive. We'll let you know when we get there . . ." She settled back and let the nonsensical conversation drift around her. She glanced out the tinted window at the rest of the world and slowly began to smile.

Beauty and rank *definitely* had its privileges.

Saturday, May 19th

"Hello," Christine said into her telephone in a tone both breathless and annoyed. The word was not spoken as a question of curiosity, but a bark in response to the ringing of her phone. The noise made her head hurt.

There was a deep male chuckle on the other end. "Did I interrupt something?"

Christine immediately checked herself as her sense of being bothered dissipated. "Oh, hi, Parker. Hold on a minute?"

"Take your time," he said agreeably.

Christine put the receiver down and casually padded barefoot back to her bathroom, carelessly dripping water from her wet hair and body onto the carpeted floor. The bathroom was still steamy from her shower, and smelled of shampoo and scented oils. Christine used the end of a towel to wipe moisture from the mirror and peered critically at her image, turning her head slowly from side to side. A quick scan showed clear brown-sugar skin without blemishes or signs of sleep deprivation. The only real sign of her lifestyle was a gnawing pulsing at the back of her head . . . the start of another headache. She automatically reached for the bottle of aspirin in the medicine cabinet and shook three into her palm. Glancing into the mirror again, Christine could see that her green eyes, her most dramatic facial feature, were only slightly red, but she knew that eye drops would take care of that. At least, for the evening. Filling the bathroom glass with water, she quickly downed the aspirins.

She wrapped a towel around her head turban-style, tucking in loose strands of hair. Then she wound a second towel around her slender body, fastening the ends over her breasts. She then returned to her bedroom and climbed onto the bed, curling her legs to the side before picking up the phone once more. She closed her eyes and relaxed against the pillows.

"Hi. I'm back."

"You know, when I said I'd hold a minute I didn't mean the rest of the night," Parker said calmly.

"You caught me in the shower. I ran naked to answer the phone."

"I guess I should be glad you weren't in any other compromising position."

"Then I wouldn't have answered the phone," Christine said sweetly.

"We haven't heard from you for a while. Thought I'll check and see how you were doing."

Christine smiled. "Translation . . . where was I last night and who is he?"

Parker chuckled. "That's your sister's voice you hear over your shoulder. Your father and I know you'll call sooner or later, otherwise you're okay. George seems used to your woodsy ways and doesn't even blink when he doesn't hear from you for a week. But my folks are complaining they haven't spoken to you recently."

Christine sighed, although she knew there was no criticism in her brother-in-law's voice. That wasn't his way. Parker never got on her case when she was forgetful or rude or late or anything. He merely pointed out other people's reaction to her behavior . . . or lack of it. And that only succeeded in making her feel more guilty.

"Well, you and Daddy understand me better than anyone," she said. "I promise I'll call Mama Kay and Uncle Ward tomorrow. I hope they don't think it's personal, Parker. Your parents are really great and they treat me like a daughter, but I've been so busy. I got back from Europe just last Saturday and I've been booked solid this whole week. I have a campaign fundraiser tonight . . ." She sighed dramatically. "I don't want to go but I owe Marcus Del Vecchio a favor. He got me the cover of the Paris and U.S. *Vogue* in the same month and he's not going to let me forget it."

"Don't expect any sympathy from me. That's why God invented the telephone and the FAX machine. So you don't have to make your family worry. Why didn't you call to let us know you were back?" Parker asked reasonably.

Christine rolled her eyes heavenward. "You're right, you're right. I was bad."

Parker chuckled, as if he was listening to the guileless explanation of a wayward child. "Did you knock everyone's socks off in Italy?"

"You know it," Christine said demurely. She quickly changed gears and became excited. "Oh, Parker, I brought you back this fabulous jacket from the Ferragamo show, and I got Alexandra this darling voile wraparound, although she won't be able to wear it until next summer . . . oh, my God! I didn't even ask how she's doing."

"When you left for Europe she was a week over-due. How *should* she be doing?"

Christine blinked and held her breath. Her eyes widened as she sat forward on her bed and stretched her long legs straight out. "Do . . . do you mean . . ."

"I mean your sister gave birth about two and a half hours ago. You're an aunt, but you'll under-stand that I didn't call you immediately . . ."

That was all Parker got out before Christine squealed. He winced and held the receiver away from his ear.

"I'm an aunt, I'm an aunt . . ."

She scrambled onto her knees and, in the middle of her bed, began to bounce up and down. The towel on her head fell away, as did the one around her body. Bare as the day she herself was born, Christine expressed her genuine joy with wild, un-restrained exuberance. Anyone seeing her just then would have thought her demented . . . but magnifi-cent.

"Oh, my God . . . oh, my *God!* Alex is a mommy! And you're a daddy! And . . . and Daddy is a . . . a granddaddy!" Christine continued.

Parker was laughing hysterically. "Yeah, we know. We got all of that, Christine."

She stopped pouncing and breathlessly sat cross-legged in the middle of the destruction. "I can't believe it."

"Alex was pregnant for nine months. To hear her talk, it felt like a lifetime. You better believe it."

"What I mean is, you and Alex have been married

more than six years. You certainly waited long enough to start a family."

"We thought we'd take some time to settle into marriage first, and spend some time with each other. And I was still touring a lot at the time. Now I'm ready to be a father."

Christine grew reflective as she tried to catch her breath. "Is she okay? Is it a boy or a girl? What did you name him . . . her? Did you stay with Alexandra in the delivery room? Did it hurt a lot? I don't know if I could do that. Everyone says it hurts so bad . . ."

"Alex breezed right through. She was only in labor two hours. And it's a girl . . ."

Christine gasped and then sighed giddily. "A . . . girl . . ."

"We're calling her Lauren Shani Harrison."

"Shani. That's so pretty."

"It's Swahili. My mother suggested it and Alex and I liked it."

"Lauren Shani . . . it's a mouthful. She's *got* to have a nickname."

"You think about it. In the meantime, I want to get back to Alex and my daughter."

"Your daughter . . ." Christine repeated, softly to herself. "Parker, I'm so happy for you and Alex."

"So when are you coming down to D.C. to meet your niece?"

Christine frowned. "I . . . I don't know. There's a shoot next week, and I'm filming a commercial . . ."

"Whenever you can work us into your calendar, let us know," he said dryly.

"Parker?" she began. "Who does she look like?"

He chuckled. "Alex says she's definitely a Harrison . . ."

Christine grinned. "Poor thing . . ."

"But she's got that beautiful Morrow mouth . . . and Alex's lungs."

Christine nodded. "Maybe we'll have another singer in the family. I better let you go. Tell Alex . . . I'm very happy for her. And I'll call her tomorrow after some of the excitement dies down. I promise. Kiss my niece for me, Parker. And . . . congratulations."

"Thanks. Good luck with your thing tonight. Make us proud."

"Bye . . ." Christine murmured as she hung up the phone. She sat holding the receiver, staring at it.

The sudden quiet in her large co-op apartment after the excitement of the call and her brother-in-law's news made Christine feel instantly alone. The space and soundlessness seemed to engulf her, threatening to shrink her into insignificance. The euphoria of a moment ago upon hearing the news that she was an aunt and her older sister was a mother vanished, replaced with a kind of sad introspection.

A little girl . . . Alexandra and Parker's daughter.

After a moment Christine got off the bed. Pensive, she picked up the damp towels and headed toward the dressing room. Now she wished more than ever that she didn't have to get dressed to play the vamp tonight in front of a cast of thousands . . . all strangers. She wished she could just get on the next flight to D.C. and slip into the ordinariness of her family. Yet, even that thought made her frown. It wasn't often that she really thought of being back home in D.C. She'd made a very good life for herself in New York. She was happy for Alex and Parker, but maybe she could never go back again. The thought made her feel somewhat frightened, like she didn't belong anywhere.

Christine deposited the towels in the hamper and listlessly dug through her closet, not even seeing the dozen upon dozens of gorgeous dresses and ensembles hung nearly wall to wall. She had been able to afford such riches as a result of being a highly paid print and show model, and a favorite with the top designers. But right at that moment it all seemed so excessive.

She pulled out a simple black Donna Karan slip dress and hung it on the garment hook behind her closet door. It was the kind of dress that didn't cling but suggested and hinted at the shape beneath the expensive fabric. It was the classic garment that left the details to the imagination. But if she had decided on a potato sack, Christine would have felt just as excited about getting dressed. She suddenly couldn't focus, her headache a continuing dull pain. The prospects of the evening ahead made her all the more irritated. And then, something else took over.

She glanced into the full length wall mirror in the dressing room and examined her body pretty much the same as she had her face in the bathroom. Only this time it wasn't with a critical eye toward weight gain or muscle tone—it was to try and imagine herself pregnant and growing larger and ungainly. For the life of her, nothing materialized from the fantasy, and it began to dawn on Christine just what her sister had accomplished . . . and how fortunate Parker and Alexandra were. Her sister would regain her lithe shape, go back to teaching music, perform now and then when Parker talked her into it . . . and she would still have her child, a little girl.

Christine frowned and realized she had no sense

of what that must be like. To have someone to love her especially, someone *she* could love and take care of. Having been the baby in her own family for so long that everyone . . . Alexandra, her father, even Parker to some extent, had taken care of her. She found it a little difficult to realize that she could no longer claim that honor. Now all Christine could see was herself. Alone with a closet filled with wonderful clothing, a lifestyle that by any standard would be considered abnormal but to be envied. With a face and body that the camera and fashion designers loved.

Men had been known to lose their cool and become foolish over her. She had broken a few hearts and had had more than her share of proposals. But no one had ever said that they loved her and meant it. Not with the fervor and sincerity Parker Harrison had declared for her sister, Alexandra.

Christine let out a startled little sound of surprise as if something significant had just occurred to her. She sat down on the vanity stool with her back to the mirror.

And she suddenly began to cry.

One

"When Clint came on the set we all tried to be cool like . . . hey, what's the big deal? But you know everyone was kind of watching him out the corner of their eye, and pretending like it was no big thing. But when he talked, *everybody* paid attention. It was really something. He's okay. Down to earth, no airs or attitude like some of these dudes."

"Ummmm," Christine murmured as she jotted notes on a short shopping list of things she needed to get the next day. Cotton swabs, toothpaste, shampoo . . .

"Anyway, after the scene he comes over and hangs with us for a while. He made some observations, but not like he knew everything. He was just being friendly."

"Uh-huhhh," Christine nodded, closing her fat daily calendar with its endless scraps of paper and business cards. She bent forward to drop it carelessly into her leather tote, which also contained her makeup pouch, several different combs and brushes, extra nylons, a hair blower, and a curling iron. Aspirins.

She glanced out the tinted windows of the car, idly scanning the thousands of pedestrians and tourists that overflowed the streets of New York now that it was May. Average people who did average things.

Like eat at fast food restaurants and shop at the malls
and go to movies in cineplex theaters. When she'd
first come to New York, Christine had sworn she'd
never do any of *those* things. She was going to live in
a building with a doorman, never have to cook, travel
everywhere by taxi, and become famous and rich.
She closed her eyes for a moment, against the lives
of the rest of the world, against the one Keith talked
so enthusiastically about, wondering when she had
begun to feel like she belonged to neither.

"I thought his best work was that picture that
came out last year. He acted his age, know what I
mean? Didn't try to be some young jock who always
gets his man and the girl . . . even though he did."

Christine pulled a small vanity mirror from her
purse and looked at herself. She blinked rapidly.
The eye drops hadn't helped very much. On the
other hand, she had to admit that it defeated the
purpose to clear up the red only to start crying
again as she'd done nearly the entire time she'd
dressed and put her equipment together for the
fashion show. *The hell with it,* she thought peevishly,
snapping the compact shut. She didn't care if people thought she'd been up all night or had been
out drinking. She was being used to show and sell
clothes . . . not justify her personal life. Such as it
was. She frowned as she quickly flashed through a
mental list of people she knew, things she did, and
places she went. It startled Christine to discover that
most of her life centered around her career.

But the thing that was most bothersome was not
being able to understand why the news of her
niece's birth had made her an instant emotional
wreck. Why the thought of her sister and brother-
in-law's happiness made her suddenly aware that her
own personal life left much to be desired.

What personal life? she asked herself.

The words settled in her brain but she couldn't conjure up an image of what they meant. It was a blank, with no details other than the acknowledgment that she had a great apartment and a beautiful car. That she had an endless supply of designer clothing and enough money literally to do whatever she pleased. But Christine experienced no particular feeling of happiness at her list of perks. There was only the sensation of being enclosed in a glass box looking out at the rest of the world—untouchable and unreachable and all alone.

But that was nonsense, she thought, taking a deep breath and remembering the birthday party she'd attended just the night before, when a contingent of notable young Hollywood stars had come to her table specifically to introduce themselves and praise her beauty and style. The night before that she'd been a guest for dinner at the home of a late night TV talk show host. She'd met the producer of a record company there who definitely seemed interested in her, except Christine knew he was married with kids. And she'd encountered an old beau who made it clear he was still interested.

Christine let her mind drift back to the voice of the man next to her in the driver's seat of the smoke grey Mercedes 500 SL.

"Woman, I bet you haven't heard a word I said," he complained.

"You want to test me? Go on, ask me a question," she said pertly.

He chuckled. "All right, I believe you. But you still seem awfully quiet. Is it something I did? You break a fingernail? PMS?"

Christine poked him sharply in the ribs with her elbow.

". . . Did you get some bad news?"

She crossed her long legs as she shook her head. She began to rock her foot restlessly. "My sister had her baby."

"Hey," Keith drawled. "That's cool. Congratulations. You're an aunt."

Christine cringed. There was something very different about the way Parker had said it. Although she knew that Keith Layton was sincere in his good wishes, they made her feel isolated and disconnected as if it had nothing really to do with her. Like there was something she'd lost . . . or maybe never had.

"Thanks," she murmured and found to her great annoyance that tears threatened once again. She rubbed a hand over her forehead. "Oh . . . damn . . ."

"What's the matter? Forget something? I sure hope you don't want to go back to your place, Christine, or you're going to be late." He tapped the horn as a couple of young boys roller-bladed across the path of the car.

Christine let Keith think her words had to do with the evening. She shook her head and took a deep breath, clearing her mind. "It's nothing important. Just a slight headache . . ."

Keith readily accepted her response. "I got a callback from TriStar, so I'll be flying out to California at the end of the week. Why don't you take some time off and join me?" he asked, his hand stroking her thigh gently and intimately.

The caress was familiar and evoked a stirring of warmth in Christine. She turned her head to study his handsome profile as the question slowly registered in her distracted mind. Keith was dressed in a tux, although she'd told him it wasn't necessary. But he knew what he was doing. For all of his pretense of being laid-back and spontaneous, he had an agenda and it called for him to be noticed, too. Keith was devastating in the black suit with contrasting white formal shirt.

For a quick, flashing second, Christine again experienced that same sense of appreciation she'd felt upon seeing Keith Layton for the first time. She'd never seen such a beautiful black man. Of course, that was by industry standards. Away from the business, folks might regard Keith with some suspicion because he didn't look like everyone else, even though he walked the walk and occasionally talked the talk. But then again, Christine remembered with irony, she'd always been told the exact same thing.

She'd been with a crew doing a shoot on a beach in the Cayman Islands two years ago. Keith had appeared, a near-perfect specimen of manhood, right beside her in the shallow water of the bay. She was posing in a swimsuit and a wide-brimmed straw hat, the blue-green water lapping at her thighs.

Christine smiled at him now as she recalled the exact moment he'd risen from the water, scaring her silly and completely ruining the shot, which had taken an hour to set up. Keith had been like some improbable chocolate god from the sea, and she'd stood open-mouthed as he'd surfaced in scuba mask, respirator, and fins, the water cascading down his hard, brown body. He was tall . . . taller than she was . . . and athletically built with a dazzling smile and even white teeth. *Male model,* Christine had thought instantly, prepared to dismiss him. But that hadn't been the case.

She could still evoke the physical thrill she'd felt when he appeared at her hotel room that night. Christine couldn't recall, however, if anything had been said between them the whole long night they'd made love.

"Let me think about it," she finally said in answer to his question, aware of her lack of enthusiasm. That alone made Christine wonder what was the matter with her.

"Come on . . . we'll chill out and have some fun for a few days. My agent is lending me his Malibu house . . ." he coaxed with a charming, seductive grin that had always worked in the past.

Christine resisted, nonetheless. Yeah, it would be fun. Keith knew how to show a woman a good time. But she wasn't sure if just having a good time would do it for her. "It sounds great, but I need to wait for a few days . . ."

He arched a brow at her, easy and not offended. "In case a better offer comes along?"

"Well, you know what that's like. Business opportunities happen on the spur of the moment."

"You know, sometimes even when there's a better offer you have to make a decision about what you really want."

Keith's words had a curious ring of truth and wisdom. "Ooooh. How philosophical."

He laughed. "So, who's going to be at this bash tonight? Anybody interesting? Anyone I should introduce myself to?"

She shrugged lightly and sighed, already bored with the evening's prospects. "Just the usual suspects. Political types all wanting to rub elbows with the powerful. Party crashers and wanna-bes."

Keith's hand stroked her leg again. He cast a brief glance in her direction. "Why don't we just forget it and go back to the Sherry Netherland. We could order up some champagne . . ." His voice dropped to a seductive growl. "Do the wild thing . . . go to Lutece or Arizona later for something to eat . . ."

Christine pursed her full lips. "Who's paying the bills this week?"

"The folks at GQ. I did a layout for them last week with Mario and Wesley and they need to do a reshoot. I told them if they wanted me to stick around they had to put me up somewhere."

She shook her head ruefully. "One of these days you should think about actually getting your own place instead of having clothes and possessions all over the country, begging favors from people. When are you going to settle down?"

"You know what my life is like. Here this week . . . gone the next. It doesn't make sense to go to the expense of maintaining an apartment I'm never in. Besides, I like living light. I don't want to be tied down with stuff."

"Or with any one person," Christine added.

"Except you," Keith said seriously. "There's no one like you."

"I know there isn't," she said baldly, "but I couldn't live the way you do, Keith."

Keith's jaw began to tighten reflexively. "Is that why you won't marry me?"

Christine made a face. "You don't really want to get married. You just want someone to be seen with. A playmate. If I ever said yes you'd have a heart attack."

"Okay, let's not go into that again. I'm here in New York right now because of you and because I found some good-paying work. Next week I could be in California if I get a role or a TV shot. Next month I could be on location in Saudi Arabia. But I always come back here to you. What more do you want?"

Christine frowned, knowing that Keith was right.

But it still sounded unsatisfying. It still seemed a shallow answer. And it didn't make her feel any better. She'd never believed that any of his proposals were to be taken seriously. Especially when sent by FAX from someone else's office while he was on location, or said in a rush as she was about to board a plane. Christine knew that there was no question that she always had the best time with Keith Layton. He was irreverent and fun. A daredevil and a risktaker. He was an exciting lover, playful and inventive. Tireless . . . exhausting. But he lived totally in the moment. And she wasn't even sure she was all that interested in getting married, but if and when she did she knew she'd want what her sister Alexandra had. A husband like Parker Harrison—talented, good-looking, smart . . . and mature.

Nonetheless it sat uneasily with Christine that she had found Keith and his life acceptable because he was so handsome and charming. Together, they turned heads. Any social setting, with any group of people, was smooth and comfortable because he got along with everyone. No one could say no to him and it was clear he could have just about anything he wanted. Any other black man who lived the kind of life he did . . . wayward and moment to moment . . . would be considered irresponsible and a lowlife. But no one had ever suggested such a thing about Keith.

And it wasn't as if he took advantage of people . . . exactly. He simply made the best of any given circumstance. To *his* own advantage, of course.

"You never used to complain about my life. Hey, how much different is it from yours?"

Christine could think of several ways, but her temples were beginning to throb and she decided there was no point in arguing. "Let's change the subject, shall we? Anyway, I can't back out of this evening. I told Lillian Paskow I'd be one of the models in the runway show. All the clothes were given by designers who want a favor from this political candidate. They want some serious improvements on Fashion Row. Better lighting, paved streets, police presence to prevent their shipments from falling off the back of delivery trucks, if you know what I mean."

"Well, politicians make me nervous. I don't trust any of them."

"Who does?" Christine responded. "I don't even like the candidate this fundraiser is for, but I don't have to vote for him, either. I'm only showing off some great clothes for people willing to pay a lot of money for them." She turned to regard Keith's profile. "You know what these things are like. I don't have to stay. After the show we can leave. How's that?"

"I can do that."

Keith dropped her off at the front of the Sheraton Hotel and Towers while he parked the car. Christine stepped into the entrance with a certain carriage and majesty that came to her naturally, but which she'd cultivated over the years for maximum affect. She moved as if everyone around her were invisible, although she was quite aware of the stares she drew. People knew who she was, recognized her but weren't sure from where . . . or guessed that she must be famous since she certainly acted as if she was. A doorman appeared through the throng, tilting his head and smiling in greeting while obviously enjoying the privilege of being acquainted with her.

"Miss Morrow. It is good to see you again," the much shorter hotel employee nodded, reaching to take her heavy leather tote.

Christine smiled slightly, automatically mindful of

the image she wanted to project. "Thank you, Eduardo."

"You will be showing in a different place than usual. The designers wanted the big ballroom tonight."

"The ballroom. Are they expecting that many people?"

"Oh, yes. Maybe a thousand. Just follow me."

He hurried before her, struggling with her bag.

Christine swept through the lobby, leaving people agape. She let Eduardo lead her to the elevators and the banquet floor two levels up. On the short ride up she sighed and turned to the pleasant hotel worker who, although he behaved toward her with polite deference, did not mince or condescend.

"I hate huge audiences. Are there a lot of people already?" Christine asked.

Eduardo nodded. He was a veteran of the many affairs at the hotel which drew the social elite. "Hundreds. I saw the mayor. He came and went. And there's a couple of senators. There are many important people here tonight, Miss Morrow. But a lot of them . . ." he made a face and shook his head sadly. "They are not as nice as you are."

Christine laughed lightly. "I wouldn't spread that around if I were you. You'll ruin both our reputations. I bet you've seen quite a lot going on over the years, Eduardo. Some day you should write a book."

"Aye . . . Dios mio . . ." he moaned, rolling his eyes toward heaven.

As soon as the elevator doors opened onto the banquet floor, Christine could hear the artificial and distorted sounds of a band playing. Loud conversation and laughter spilled from the Grand Ballroom out into the corridors. A few people meandered casually in and out of the room, dressed in formal wear and sipping glasses of wine or champagne.

Christine opened her purse and pulled out a ten dollar bill. "Where is the dressing room going to be?"

"In the Marquee and the Paris Salons. They opened up both rooms, one for men and one for the women. I'll take your bag back."

"Thank you," she said, handing him the bill. "Let them know I'm here. I'll walk back in a minute. And could you get me a glass of water?"

"Of course, Miss Morrow," Eduardo said and nodded. "Is there anything else I can do?"

Christine struck a pose, pivoting expertly on the balls of her feet to show off the understated black crepe dress.

"How do I look?" she asked.

Eduardo chuckled. "You will put the other women to shame."

Christine winked. "Eduardo, I think I'm in love with you." She watched him blush as, shaking his head in amusement, he walked away.

She then turned her attention to the ballroom, trying to pull together some enthusiasm for the next few hours. Christine realized, as she hesitated and felt her reluctance take hold, that she really would rather be someplace else. But she didn't know where. After all, *this* was her life, what she did. Still, she didn't expect it to be a fun night. She didn't particularly care very much for being part of an evening's entertainment, but she was a professional and as she'd already indicated to Keith, this was a job. Christine took a deep breath, tilting her chin up to give her features a look of cool indifference. It was her trademark in the industry. It kept most people at bay, but curious.

Christine quickly let her eyes roam over the crowd. She'd been to these events before—corporate evenings, testimonies, society charities, museum benefits, symphony galas. Sometimes for no reason at all, other than an excuse for people with lots of money to get together to party and be seen among the rich and famous . . . and those who aspire to be.

She caught a glimpse of a well-known, handsome young publisher of a trendy new magazine about the club scene. He was known to pursue any woman who interested him despite the fact that he was married. He looked her way now, and gave Christine the kind of confident smile that said he never regretted his attempts to corner her. She returned the smile.

"I know someone we can hit for maybe a couple of thou. I'm telling you, this is a sure thing . . ."

Christine didn't even bother looking in the direction of the boastful voice. They were either talking investments . . . or drugs. She walked a little way along the wall, feeling a sudden sense of unreality. She knew people just like the ones here . . . and she wondered why.

"Honest to God, she has the worst taste. Someone told me she paid almost three thousand dollars for that dress. And did you see that awful outfit she was wearing at the Mayor's reception? And her husband is such a . . ."

Christine sighed and turned away.

In this arena of ornate chandeliers, alabaster pillars, and wild rose Prussian carpeting, Christine could recognize men and women, black and white, who were willing to plunk down $2,500.00 for the evening. In return they would have the privilege of being schmoozed by a politician who would, if he won the next election and gained sufficient power, eventually extract much more from them. Christine raised her brows and grimaced cynically. These were the very people who made corruption possible. It suddenly made her feel very odd inside, disappointed perhaps, that she *could* recognize the type. But she had been in New York for seven years in a high profile business in which only the toughest survived. Christine knew she was, if nothing else, a survivor.

And she had been witness to or privy to enough acts of professional sabotage, character assassination, jealous rage, vicious gossip, and pointless attempts at hurt and manipulation . . . all in the name of professional advancement . . . to be suspicious of every single smiling, well-dressed person in the room. And to wonder, more recently than ever before, just what the hell *she* was doing here.

A sudden wave of unrest washed over Christine and all she wanted was to leave. Keith's suggestion to duck away began to sound good, except she didn't want to spend the evening with him talking about Hollywood. Christine knew that with the millions of people that inhabited New York, and even with all the people she knew, it was entirely possible to feel very alone. Parker and Alexandria and their new daughter came to mind. The conversation with her brother-in-law had done something to her, Christine realized. She thought that maybe what she wanted to do was be home with her family.

"Beautiful . . ." a male voice murmured softly as he brushed past her with two drinks in his hand.

Christine didn't even bother sparing the man a glance. She actually didn't focus on any one person, but let her eyes keep moving as she stood still, drawing everyone's gaze to herself. This is what she did at the start of nearly every event. Now it was second nature, instinctive. Work the room and generate curiosity, leave them guessing so when she made her appearance on the runway, she knew she'd have their undivided attention.

But her eyes did notice someone different. Her attention lighted on a man who was immediately separated from the others by the sheer force of his presence. He had to be six feet three since he appeared to be at least three inches taller than she. He was broad shouldered and, she had to admit, stunning in formal wear. His face was chiseled with planes and angles that gave his features a decidedly masculine quality. It was a hard face, with the eyes and mouth of someone perhaps not so much cynical as experienced. His skin was dark and he was clean shaven. The prominence of his cheekbones and jaw, the subtle flaring of his nostrils and full wide mouth made his face appear more square than it actually was. Christine wasn't sure she would consider him particularly handsome—he had the kind of face many people might dismiss as average. But on the other hand, she was used to a much more specific look in a man—remarkable and almost perfect. Photogenic. Yet this was a man you couldn't ignore. Leaning against a pillar, the whiteness of the marble making him seem even taller, broader, he stood staring right back at her.

It was clear to Christine that he'd been watching her for some time. His intense, dark scrutiny made the muscles of her stomach quiver. She was certainly used to being looked at and admired, but his eyes held something much different. His attention didn't strip her naked as some men were wont to do but seemed more intent on probing into her soul. Christine didn't blink. She'd played this game before, too. The idea was to satisfy her own inquisitiveness about him while completely ignoring his for her. But she waited too long and before Christine could act further, the man pushed away from the pillar, turned, and abruptly disappeared into the crowd. For a moment she was stunned. She'd *never* gotten that kind of response before from anyone.

"Christine! I didn't know you were doing this show." She finally did blink, then smiled genuinely at Patrick Ferris and waved at him over the heads of the other guests.

"Pat, what are you doing here?" Christine called out so she could be heard over the noise.

The tall, handsome man with his ash blond hair and startling aqua eyes was slender and elegant in black slacks and black crew neck sweater, worn with a black and white herringbone sports jacket. People in fashion were usually the first to break the rules, remake the conventions. Pat *never* dressed formally for anything. He laughed lightly and shook his head as he pushed his way through the thickening crowd to reach her. He put his arms around her loosely and kissed her European fashion, on both cheeks.

"I know. I swore if I ever stopped modeling I wouldn't be caught dead at an affair like this. But . . ." He stuck a finger in his ear and winced.

Christine pursed her lips. "There's someone here you want to meet," she finished easily.

"Yeah, there is. I came up with a book proposal and my agent has it circulating the houses."

"Another tell-all of the modeling scene?"

He mimicked silencing her. "Not so loud. No one's ever done it from the male point of view. I especially want Kathy Cresswell to take a look at it. She seems to have a talent for finding potentially hot projects . . ."

"And making everyone a mint of money because she's also smart about promotion and marketing."

Patrick chuckled. "You always could read my mind. Maybe that's why we worked so well together at the trade shows."

"It was more than that," Christine said, taking his arm and hugging it affectionately. "We used to cause a near riot when we modeled together, posing like lovers."

"But it was spectacular and it worked. Black and white together, in living color. We were in every major publication from here to Europe, made a lot of money, and started a fashion trend."

"And you still left it all behind," Christine reminded him, staring into his handsome face. There had been many people who assumed that she and Patrick had been lovers, just because they'd appeared so often in print ads.

Patrick shrugged, looking around uncomfortably at the crushing crowd. He had to lean in toward Christine to be heard. "I got tired of the hustle. I began to feel like, get a life already."

Christine arched a brow. Where had she heard that before? "And you think becoming a writer is more legitimate?"

"Maybe not. But I'll respect myself in the morning. I don't have to work at being handsome just like you don't have to work at being gorgeous. God was *very* good to both of us. But I'd like to do something with my life that really required some use of my grey matter."

"I hear your midwestern upbringing loud and clear. But you always were a lot smarter than the rest of us."

"Hey, Cynthia Mallory stopped at the height of her career as the top full-figured black model and decided to go back to school for an MBA. She's here, too. I saw her with her fiancé."

"Her . . . fiancé . . ." Christine repeated blankly. Again she began to feel like her world was changing before her very eyes. Something was happening to everyone she met and she had a disturbing sensation of being left behind.

"Excuse me!" a voice said crisply behind them.

Patrick and Christine turned to locate the voice, and found a flash going off, momentarily blinding them.

"Come on . . . smile. This is for *Vanity Fair*," the photographer said, adjusting his camera and aiming once more.

Patrick slipped his arm around Christine and held her against him. She automatically tilted her head toward Patrick and smiled vaguely up at him. The flash went off again in quick succession. Their presence and the fact that they were being photographed began to draw a circle of onlookers. One man, already a little the worse for alcohol, sidled up to Christine and nudged her with a familiarity she found distasteful.

"You must be a model, right? You sure are tall and leggy," he said audaciously and laughed at his own humor.

Patrick groaned. Christine glanced down at the man with a confused but innocent smile. "I'm not so tall. You're just very short for a man."

There was a momentary silence before someone cackled and it slowly spread around her. The smile vanished from the man's face as it turned red. He was embarrassed but apparently not sure how Christine meant her barb; he silently turned away and meshed into the crowd.

"Listen, I'm going to circulate. Is Keith with you tonight?" Patrick asked.

"He'll be here in a minute."

"Great. I'll just hang around with him."

"I think I've caused enough of a stir. I'd better get back to the dressing room and see what they have lined up for me."

Christine walked out of the ballroom in the direction of the two salons Eduardo had indicated. As she walked the length of the corridor, her steps silent on the carpeting, the man from the ballroom came to mind. The one who had given her such a frosty stare, and then dismissed her. *He had some nerve,* she thought, unreasonably annoyed with a perfect stranger with whom she hadn't even exchanged a word. But by the time she'd reached the cramped and chaotic room where the models were to dress and change, Christine had convinced herself that he had done her an injustice and she wasn't going to forget it.

There were twelve females in the small space, all in various stages of undress. Some were in robes sitting with damp rollers in their hair while having makeup applied. Others were already being zipped, tucked, and pinned into their first garments. Laughter and loud talk mixed with the whirring of hair blowers and shouted instructions from the dresser and her assistants. Christine knew most of the models and greeted them briefly as she found a stool for herself and located a quiet corner for her tote bag. She quickly stepped out of her dress and shoes and carefully put them aside. Eduardo had left the water and the first thing she did was take several more aspirins.

She stood in front of the mirror, staring critically at her reflection, finger-combing her hair, pushing and pulling at it as she tried to decide what style to go with for the show. For years she'd worn her naturally curly hair short, no more than an inch all over her head, which made her stand out as most of the other models wore theirs long. But recently Christine had grown it nearly to her shoulders. She sometimes styled it straight, but it still had a wild fullness that had been dubbed *ethnic* by the industry watchers, and widely copied by black and white models alike. She knew it was doubly effective with her green eyes and a berry-colored lip gloss that emphasized the shapely curve of her mouth.

"Christine, I'm glad you're finally here. I've given you all the Anne Klein and Karan outfits. You have the most experience so I've instructed the girls to follow your lead. This is not a Missoni or Kenzo crowd so I don't want anyone coming off like a brainless teenager out there. No showing off."

Christine smiled at the short, middle-aged woman who looked habitually harassed and dressed as if she never paid any attention to fashion herself. Her hair was an improbable red and frizzy. Christine didn't think that the highly respected stylist and self-professed housemother to 'the girls' was even five feet tall. But she commanded more respect and attention than anyone Christine had ever met during her entire career as a model.

"Hi, Lillian. You're going to stunt your growth," Christine suggested, pulling the cigarette from the woman's mouth, taking a puff herself, and returning it.

"Now you tell me. Listen, I got a new girl here to break in. Calvin found her and really likes her. Thinks she's going places. I said I'd give her a try tonight and see how she does." She looked around

and beckoned toward a tall, skinny girl. "This is Antoinette Holiday . . ."

"Tonee," the girl corrected, "with two e's."

"That's cute," Christine murmured dryly. She gave the girl a vague smile and shook her hand, looking her over quickly but thoroughly. *Naomi Campbell clone,* Christine thought immediately. The girl was tall and thin as a rail, leggy, wearing one of those very short floral baby doll dresses with spaghetti straps that Christine hated. They made just about *everyone* wearing them look very silly. But the girl, who couldn't have been more than eighteen, had a face that reflected a kind of youthful innocence. Christine also knew she could be destroyed in a heartbeat in this business, but the girl had very old eyes. Christine had seen that before, too. Girls who were so focused, so desperate to break into modeling that they would do almost anything. But Antoinette . . . Tonee . . . wouldn't have to do much at all. She had a natural grace combined with what was, no doubt, an iron will that was going to get her exactly what she wanted. Ultimately, what she deserved.

The lanky young woman stood staring into her face. Christine was a little taken aback. Tonee Holiday was bold and forward.

"Your contact lenses are a great color. I have a pair that make my eyes look yellow like a cat."

Christine raised her brows. "These aren't lenses. This is my natural eye color."

"Yeah?" Tonee uttered, clearly skeptical, and then just shrugged. "You're so lucky. I bet you get asked to do print ads all the time because you have pretty eyes."

Christine slowly turned away and grimaced in annoyance. Tonee Holiday was probably going to be a great model, but she was *not* going to qualify as a scholar.

"Okay, ladies," Lillian rasped over the noise. "The candidate is giving his opening remarks. When he's done the music will start and that's our cue to be at the start of the runway. It's makeshift, so don't stump too much or you'll end up in someone's lap . . ." There was some laughter. "You each have five outfits—they're color-tagged so there's no mix-up about who wears what. Okay, let's finish dressing for the first line . . ."

Christine stood up and reached for her first garment from a clothing rack she was sharing with another veteran model and Tonee, who was applying her makeup. A quick look showed Christine that she knew what she was doing, and had the right color blends for her skin tone.

Christine put on her outfit, a cocktail dress with matching jacket, and sat again to do something with her hair. She dug in her tote for accessories, pulling out scarfs, felt and knit hats, costume jewelry. She held a pair of oversized pearl clip-ons to her ears to see if they worked with the silk suit.

"Hey, girl . . ."

Christine turned at the sound of the down-home voice and beamed at the woman weaving her way through the maze to reach her. She was very attractive and beautifully dressed in a tailored outfit that complimented her large shape.

"Cynthia! Patrick told me you were here. What is this? A gathering of retirees?" Christine stood halfway up as they air-kissed each other and were jostled as another model reached over for a hairbrush.

"I guess so," Cynthia said in bemusement. "Or we just know the right places to hang out. How you doing? I thought you were going to call me last week."

Christine wrinkled her nose. "I know, but I was in Europe. I just got back."

"How was it?"

"Just what you'd expect. Hectic, crowded, and a bit dicey. You know what goes on behind the scenes." Christine looked around at the chaos. "Just like this."

"I hear you," Cynthia said dryly, glancing around. "Boy, I sure don't miss all of this."

"So what are you doing these days?"

"I'm in school, believe it or not. I have a few small business ventures I want to start." She held up her perfectly manicured left hand and wiggled her chubby fingers. "And I'm engaged!"

Christine experienced momentary envy. "Congratulations," she said, admiring the glittering diamond set in white gold. "Who's the husband-to-be?"

"James Weston. He's a doctor."

"A doctor," Christine said in surprise. "How did you meet him?"

Cynthia made a face. "Well, it was one of those days when I thought I should lose weight. James is the cardiologist sharing office space with my nutritionist. He introduced himself and said I didn't need to lose a pound! One thing led to another and eight months later, here I am. What about you?"

Christine shrugged. "Still here." She averted her gaze, concentrating on fastening a necklace while trying to hide an expression of wistfulness. What did Cynthia have that *she* didn't?

Cynthia looked around at the madness and grimaced. "Girl, I don't know how you stand it. I don't know how I did it for so long."

"What are the options?"

Cynthia cackled. "Almost anything. Marry Keith." Christine pursed her lips and checked her makeup one final time in the mirror before standing up. "I don't think so . . ."

"I want you to meet James. Maybe we can all get together some time."

"Fine. Just give me a call," Christine answered vaguely, turning back to her preparations.

As Lillian lined the women and men up for the start of their program, Christine stood silently waiting, reflecting on her very first runway show. The excitement of being center stage, knowing that more than a hundred important people in the industry were focused not only on what she was wearing but on her ability to show off the clothing, was heady stuff. The cameras clicked constantly in little white bursts of light. Her pictures in the trade papers, and eventually in magazines like *Glamour, Essence, Bazaar,* and *Vogue.* Popping up in the gossip columns paired with some actor or author or athlete. The endless round of parties and travel . . . and attention.

She thought it would never end. At twenty she didn't want it to. But Christine thought now of Tonee with her flexible body and her apparent talent for drama and exhibitionism, for that, too, was part of being a great model. Tonee showed great potential—energy, excitement, and youth. She was part of the next generation of superstars. And Christine was beginning to wonder just what that made her . . .

She checked the outfit in the full-length rollaway mirror and forgot about everything for the moment but what she was supposed to do, what she had been very good at for seven years.

Christine stood poised for her entrance. The music was pounding, the beat keeping time with her persistent headache. She reminded herself to take

a few more aspirins when she came off to change
for the next number. She lifted her chin and pulled
back her shoulders, then tucked in her pelvis, which
automatically flattened her midsection. Christine
touched her hair, which was pinned up and exposing her long graceful neck. She moistened her lips
and tried not to squint when she stepped through
the curtain and the stage lights hit her dead on.

"Okay, darling, you're on," Lillian said, patting
her shoulder and stepping back.

Christine stepped through the curtained partition
and went into her routine. She knew that there was
an audience out there, but she couldn't really see
them past the lights. Just a few faces staring up at
her. She kept her posture and remembered her strut,
opening the jacket of her two-piece ensemble and
putting her hands into the seam pockets of the dress
underneath. She came to the end of the runway and
pivoted while at the same time quickly shrugging the
jacket from her shoulders and letting it slide down
her arms. She caught it by the collar and, swinging
it out of the way, turned so that the back of the garment was revealed. There was an appreciative gasp
from the audience. The dress scooped low, nearly to
the waist, exposing Christine's bare back. She exited
to the sound of enthusiastic applause.

"Hurry and get into number two," Lillian said
laconically as Christine passed along the corridor
back to the dressing room.

But Christine didn't hurry. She walked slowly as
she realized her stomach was churning and she had
a feeling of slight nausea. When she got back to the
salon she sat for a long moment with her eyes closed.
The activity and noise around her made Christine
feel dizzy and overheated. She finished the rest of
the now-lukewarm water that Eduardo had left for

her earlier. Then she got slowly out of the first outfit and began to dress for her second appearance.

"That's a great outfit," Tonee said behind her. "But it's probably too old for me, right?"

Christine merely smiled at the younger woman in the mirror as she adjusted the neckline of the halter-topped navy jumpsuit with its contrasting white collar. "That's what being a model is all about. You're supposed to make everything look good."

Tonee shrugged as she carelessly tossed her first outfit over the bar of the clothing rack and reached for her next dress. "I wish we were wearing bathing suits. I look *great* in swimwear."

"I bet you do," Christine murmured absently, wondering what else she could take that would calm her stomach down until the show was finished.

As she followed Tonee back to the ramp for the second line-up, Keith suddenly appeared. Tonee slowed her steps and gave him a fetching smile and tilt of her head.

"Hi," she whispered in a breathless young voice that would make any listener think she was shy. She continued walking slowly but coquettishly, holding Keith's surprised gaze for a long moment.

"Hi," he respond automatically before he turned his attention to Christine with a curious grin. "Who was that?"

"Her name is Tonee Holiday . . . with two e's. Another sweet thing looking to make it big. Cute, isn't she?" Christine asked rhetorically.

Keith chortled. "I'd say Ms. Tonee Holiday is on her way."

"Yeah, but where? What are you doing back here?"

Keith looked regretful. "I gotta cut out of here. My agent just beeped me. He cornered a director who's casting his next movie and Stu wants me to meet them for dinner down at Odeon. I only have an hour to make a pitch for myself."

"That's great . . ."

"Christine! We're waiting . . ." Lillian said in a stage whisper.

"Are you going to be okay? Can you catch a cab later? Meet me back at the hotel."

She frowned and shook her head. "I don't think so. I just want to go home afterward. My stomach is acting up. Good luck tonight," she said, holding out her cheek for Keith to kiss. Instead he held her lightly by the waist and kissed her on the mouth.

"Yeah, thanks. I'll call you tomorrow, okay?"

Christine nodded as he hurried away. She pressed her hand against her stomach, her concern growing as she continued on to the holding area. The music began to clang in her head.

It was on her fourth trip down the runway that Christine wondered in a kind of hot haze if she was going to make it through. But there was no choice. She'd worked shows when she had head colds, and cramps, so she wasn't going to let her upset stomach stop her now, even though she felt worse with each passing minute. She longed for the show to be over.

Preparing to change into the last outfit, she realized that the remaining dress was not the one allotted to her, yet there was no time to look for it. She quickly got into the remaining dress, even though the color was all wrong with her skin tone. The beige was too close a match, making her seem washed out. She would simply fade right into the fabric. Nevertheless, Christine returned to the staging area dressed and ready for the last time. Lillian spotted her and gestured impatiently with her hand.

"You can't wear that."

"Tell me about it," Christine murmured peevishly. "But there's nothing else back there so I didn't have much choice."

"Maybe we shouldn't send you out there . . ."

"I'm a professional," Christine said airily. "I can do this. But someone is wearing my outfit."

"I know, I know," the woman nodded, urging Christine toward the platform. "Marilee already told me about the mixup with her and Tonee. You got what was left. Just go. Make it look fabulous . . ."

At the last instant Christine grabbed a wide-brimmed floppy hat that someone had left on a chair. Even as she began the walk she placed the hat on her head and worked with it, her movements drawing attention away from the dress. She played with the brim, bending and flipping it, twisting the hat at saucy angles. She made her steps lighter, playful, even though her stomach heaved and she feared she would be sick right in front of the audience. She kept swallowing, her expression calm and a flirtatious smile on her rouged lips. Then she felt perspiration begin to break out on her forehead and chin.

Christine made her turn at the end of the platform and headed back toward the curtain. Delighted applause followed her exit, but immediately after the curtain closed behind her she sagged and stumbled against a wall. She closed her eyes and tried to breathe deeply, but quickly stopped because the stale fumes of perfume and wine, makeup and hairspray were only making her feel worse.

All the models were assembled, waiting for the final parade when they would all prance out once more, not posed but natural, to wave to the audience and encourage bids and sales on the items.

But Christine didn't join them. She couldn't. She heard Lillian ask with a worried frown if she was okay. Christine mumbled and kept on walking, concerned only about getting to the dressing room where she could stretch out on the sofa and close her eyes for a moment. But when she realized she might not make it, that little white dots were appearing before her eyes and growing bigger and bigger, she wanted to stop and lie down right where she was. She continued to walk slowly, trying to stay in focus, breathing deeper . . . holding on to the wall as the space began to spin around her.

There was someone standing near the elevator. A man. Tall and dark. Christine thought she might know him, that she had seen him before. He looked at her and just stared. She wanted to reach out to him but didn't even have the strength to lift her hand. Besides, it was shaking. Maybe he will help, Christine thought to herself. He'd find her a chair. Quickly.

"Please . . . I . . ." she murmured, her voice echoing in her head. The room began to tilt until the man seemed to be slipping onto his side and the floor was swinging up to where the elevator should have been.

The man suddenly jerked forward and began to move toward her. His fast movements made Christine's stomach roil. She was aware that her legs had given out beneath her. Her hand suddenly touched the floor. It occurred to Christine, in that last instant, that her head was going to hit the floor as well. But it never did.

And then she couldn't remember anything.

Two

He was surprised at how light she was.

Even at dead weight she seemed ethereal. Her head fell back against the crook of his arm as he knelt, half supporting her limp body, so she didn't slump to the floor. She was breathing deeply through slightly parted lips, as if she couldn't get enough air. He could see that her forehead and chin were a little damp with a soft sheen that made her skin look like silk. He couldn't help staring, wondering if it was as soft as it looked. She moaned quietly, a kind of innocent mewling sound. It was in direct contrast to her voice which earlier in the evening had held so much assurance and attitude. Her expression was even different, unguarded and open; she didn't seem like the same woman who had made such a grand entrance into the ballroom. But she was.

He felt the way her body pressed against him, unaware of his presence. She wasn't underweight, as many models appeared to be, just very slender and soft. For a moment he could let himself believe that she might be vulnerable and even in need of protection. But that was fleeting, especially when he recalled that anyone willing to prance and parade in front of total strangers could hardly have an ego problem.

She wasn't completely unconscious, he realized, as

he felt her faint struggle to regain control of herself. He pressed his index and middle fingers firmly against the pulse at the junction of her jaw and throat. Rapid but not erratic. Suddenly he found himself slowly spreading his fingers, just enough to touch her skin and feel that it was slightly cool . . . and unbelievably smooth. He pulled his hand away abruptly, annoyed more than embarrassed by the liberty he'd taken. He leaned over her as he watched her frown and try to speak.

"I feel . . . so . . ." she murmured in a soft slur.

He tilted his head closer. No smell of alcohol. Instead, he found himself engulfed in the gentle aroma of a perfume that seemed to float around her like a cloud. It was pleasing and made his nostrils flare. He looked at her more closely, feeling a little disoriented. The music from the banquet hall was softer. The lighting in the corridor was subdued. He stared at the woman in his arms, allowing fantasy to take over for a brief few moments as his imagination played games and he thought he was holding a sleeping beauty.

He had to admit that he was.

He looked at her differently now, at the outfit she was wearing and how it covered her. It was a wrap-style garment of thin fabric. It showed a lithe body as befitted her profession, and long, shapely legs. It also displayed enticingly rounded breasts. For an instant he could imagine . . .

The elevator door opened and a man stepped out, nearly tripping over the huddled bodies of the two people in the hallway. He gasped.

"*Que pasa?*" Eduardo asked with concern, hurrying over to hunch over the two. "Is Miss Morrow sick?"

"I don't know yet. Looks like it." The man looked around the hallway. People were starting to wander out of the ballroom, a few staring in curiosity. He slipped his arms completely beneath her back and knees and stood up in one fluid motion. Her body slumped against him and with another moan of confusion her head dropped to his shoulder. Her hair brushed feather-light against his mouth and chin. It tickled. A shaky hand came up to press to her forehead.

"What . . . what are you . . . doing?" she asked, slightly agitated.

"It is all right, Miss Morrow. I will call the doctor," Eduardo said anxiously, hurrying off to a hall phone.

"I *am* a doctor," the man said impatiently. "Is there a room where I can take her?" he added briskly.

"Oh, yes. This way . . ." Eduardo nodded, pulling a ring of keys from his pocket and hurrying around a corner to a short corridor with several closed doors. He quickly opened one room and turned on a light before standing back to let the tall man enter, carrying Christine in his arms.

"Eduardo? What's . . . going on? Put . . . put me . . . down," Christine croaked, regaining sensibility and pushing feebly against her captor's chest.

The man ignored her question and gently placed her on the sofa, then sat on the low coffee table, facing her. He took her wrist, placing his strong fingers against her pulse while he checked the rate against his watch.

"What are you on?" he asked flatly, his deep voice impersonal and hard.

"What?" Christine asked, trying to pull her hand free. Her eyes fluttered open and she focused on his face. *Him* again. The man from the ballroom. The one who had stared at her so coldly. He was still regarding her with an expression that bordered on contempt and indifference.

"What drugs have you been taking?" he asked again, still measuring her pulse and ignoring the expression on her face.

"Excuse me?" Christine asked incredulously, trying to regain possession of herself.

"Oh, no. You are wrong," Eduardo spoke up defensively. "Miss Morrow, she no take drugs. Never."

"She's on something," the man insisted. He looked up from his watch and into her face. For a moment he couldn't say anything more.

In the ballroom earlier he couldn't help but notice her. After all, that had been her intention. He'd literally zeroed in on her across the crowded room, inexorably drawn by her mere presence. She was tall and stunningly dressed . . . and she *was* beautiful.

He stared into her eyes, unable to resist their hypnotic pull, fascinated by the emerald color. He quickly discovered that it was not cosmetic but her own color. And he could see . . . could even feel . . . how easy it would be to sink into their depths.

His jaw tightened and he lowered his gaze to her dress. He began to loosen the tie around Christine's waist, which held the flimsy dress in place.

"What do you think you're doing?" she moaned.

"This is too tight. It's restricting your breathing."

"Leave it alone!"

He ignored her and the dress loosened as he pulled at the ties. "I want you to try and stand up. Start walking around." He turned to Eduardo and saw the suspicion and doubt in the man's face. He reached into an inside pocket of his formal jacket and pulled out a small white card. He handed it to the Latino man. "Can you get me a glass of milk?"

"Milk?" Eduardo repeated blankly, reading the information on the card. But when the man glared at him he nodded and turned to the door. "Yes, sir. Right away."

"I'm fine. Stop it," Christine demanded, pushing away the man's hands as they roamed over her with quick, efficient movements, but also with a distraction that she found inappropriate. Still, she didn't exactly feel threatened—she was acknowledging to herself that his hands were very strong, but careful, and his exploration had a surprising soothing affect. As if he knew what he was doing. As if she could trust him. But his touch was also decidedly male . . . and provocative.

Christine looked into his face, to see if maybe he was just being fresh after all, but found an aloofness, a closed expression which was at direct odds with his thorough movements. He suddenly placed his hands around her waist and hoisted her into a sitting position. Her senses spun as Christine grimaced and held onto his arms for support. The loosened dress did allow her to take deep breaths that went to her stomach. He stood up, still holding onto her as she balanced on her own feet. He stepped back a little, but kept one hand firmly around her forearm.

She looked into his face, and the stone hardness of his features and expression belied the attention he'd given her. It was confusing. She wanted to say she was fine and didn't need his help. She wanted to tell him again that she wasn't high on some kind of drug, but just felt overheated. Christine opened her mouth to speak . . . and then couldn't. She swallowed, feeling the stinging, bitter essence of bile creep up her throat. She swallowed again. Her eyes blinked with sudden distress. They pleaded, filling with embarrassment and a need that superseded any thought of protecting her ego.

"Oh . . . oh, my God . . ." she murmured, her fingers touching her lips.

He didn't even hesitate as he accurately read her body language. "In here . . ." he said quickly, propelling Christine before him into an adjoining room, and through another until he'd located the bathroom.

Decorum and grace were thrown aside as Christine dropped unceremoniously to her knees in front of the commode . . . and was promptly sick to her stomach. She clutched at the sides of the porcelain bowl and her body convulsed with the awful involuntary contractions as her system purged itself.

"Go with it. Let it happen. Let it all come up," he said, squatting behind her. His hand was on the back of her neck and unconsciously massaged the base of her head gently. His other hand rested on the curve of her waist.

Christine gasped and moaned, struggling through the violent upheaval in her body, soothed by the sound of his voice even though his tone remained remote and unsympathetic. When the cleansing had ended she shifted positions and sat on the floor, too weak and exhausted to move.

He stood up and soaked a washcloth in cool water in the sink, wrung out all the excess, and then turned to her. She sat on the floor with her eyes closed, looking helpless and fragile. The dress draped loosely around her and he could see the top of her breast inside the opening. She wore no bra but the soft folds in the fabric prevented any further exposure. He inadvertently squeezed the wet cloth in his hand and water dripped on his shoes.

"Here," he said, holding out the washcloth.

Christine briefly opened her eyes. Her embarrassment was complete. She felt humiliated, but still she was going to thank him for his kindness. Then she glanced covertly into his face and saw neither sympathy or concern. Christine snatched the washcloth from his hand. "Thank you," she said sharply.

He slipped his hands into the pocket of his slacks and leaned casually against the bathroom door frame, watching her with detached interest. His jaw began to work reflexively again, and his brows drew together. "I probably should report you for substance abuse. For your own good. You should get some help."

Christine sucked her teeth in annoyance and glared at him. His intimidating and imperial attitude annoyed her even more. She wiped her face, smearing her makeup on the once pristine white cloth. "I'm not on drugs and neither is anyone else in the show. Just where do you get off accusing me of something like that?"

"It's pretty obvious you've been taking something. Your system is slightly toxic. That's why your pulse was too fast. You were sweating. You became dizzy and nearly passed out. Vomiting . . ." he reminded her bluntly. "What should I think?"

She tossed the cloth into the sink. "Why should I care what you think?"

"I seem to recall that it was you who reached out to me for help by the elevator. I could have just left you there, gone on about my business."

Christine grimaced as she tried to stand up. He made no effort to help her this time as she lowered the top of the toilet seat and sat down. "I would have reached out to Godzilla if I'd thought he could find me a place to sit down," she said dryly. Christine held her head in her hands and mumbled, "I'm not on anything. I don't do drugs. I'm not stupid."

"So, you're telling me that for no reason you simply got nauseous and had to . . ."

She threw a look of dislike in his direction. "I'm telling you I haven't taken anything. Not even something to eat." She blinked and hesitated. "Well . . . the only thing I had was . . ."

"What?" he prompted.

"Aspirin. For a headache."

"How many?"

She shrugged indifferently, trying to pull her clothing to rights, awkwardly retying the front of the wrap dress. She wondered what he was thinking as he'd loosened her clothing. "I don't know. A few. I had some this morning, and then I think this afternoon. I took some before I came here, and . . . and . . ."

"Go on. How many more?"

"After I got here and just before the show. What difference does it make?"

He stared at her, not answering right away. He noted with interest the subtle flush on her cheeks, the petulant, almost innocent, expression on her face now that all the blusher and lip gloss were gone. Her thick hair was a profusion of twisted curls that looked like loosened dreadlocks. It framed her face to accent her features. Large, expressive eyes aided by their extraordinary color. A mouth that was full and well-shaped . . . and enticing. He shifted positions against the door.

"It makes a lot of difference. Unless you're trying to kill yourself. In that case, I'm sorry I interrupted," he drawled. Slowly, he stood away from the doorway, pivoted, and retreated through the bedroom and back into the sitting room.

Christine sat staring after him, her mouth open in shock. "Hey!" she yelled, struggling up and following unsteadily behind him. "Just who do you think you are?" she asked, catching up to him. He turned to regard her with total indifference. "I wasn't trying to off myself, you fool. I told you, I just don't remember how many aspirins I took."

He opened the door to the suite, prepared to leave. He turned briefly back to face her, impatience and annoyance in the stiff broad sweep of his shoulders, and in the drawn eyebrows and hard glower of his dark eyes. "Look, you're a grown-up . . ."

Christine blinked at him, hearing the distinct sarcasm in his tone.

"You're free to do whatever you want. You seem to be okay now so if you weren't trying to do something crazy then it doesn't matter what I think. If I were you I'd still see a doctor and find out why you need so many aspirins in the first place. They don't cure anything."

Just then Eduardo slipped through the opening in the door, a glass of milk in his hand. He looked at Christine and the tall, imposing man in the doorway, then back to Christine again.

"Ms. Morrow. Are you feeling better?"

She took a deep breath, frustrated by Eduardo's interruption just as she was about to give this arrogant somebody a piece of her mind. "I'm fine, Eduardo."

Awkwardly Eduardo held out the glass to the man at the door. "Here. This is the milk you wanted."

The man nodded at Christine, his attention still focused on her. "It's for her."

Eduardo turned to Christine and slowly approached her. He nervously looked over his shoulder at the man, sensing, uncomfortably, the tension between him and Christine.

She shook her head stubbornly. "I don't like milk."

"If you don't want to get sick again you'd better take it. It will coat your stomach and keep the queasiness down until you can get something decent to eat. Besides aspirin."

Christine narrowed her eyes. She fought the pain that was gaining momentum behind her lids. The rumbling was starting again in her stomach. But she was not about to give him the satisfaction of seeing how terrible she was still feeling. "You have a nasty bedside manner."

His gaze swept leisurely over her, making note of every detail. But his expression gave nothing away beyond the aloofness he wanted her to see. A slow, cynical grin lifted one corner of his mouth as he nodded to her and pulled the door open. "You don't want to know what I think about you." He pulled the door quietly closed as he left the room.

Christine watched him leave, deciding against pursuing a confrontation with the stranger. The minute the door closed she dropped wearily to a side chair, feeling her knees wobbling beneath her and her head pounding again. She glanced at Eduardo, who stood looking confused. Christine tried to smile at him.

"Don't worry. I'm not on drugs, Eduardo. Thank you for standing up for me."

Again he held out the glass. "He said you drink this."

She stared at the glass. "I should have had something to eat . . ."

"I can get you something."

Christine shuddered in distaste and reluctantly took the glass. Food was the very last thing on her mind. What she really wanted to do was go home and crawl into bed. "No, thanks. But you can do me just one more favor and go to the dressing room.

Tell Mrs. Paskow that I'm not feeling well and I'm going home. Have someone throw my things together in my tote and bring it to me."

"Do not worry," he said and sighed with relief. "Eduardo will take care of everything."

Christine frowned into the glass, scrinched up her nose, and took a tiny sip. She stuck out her tongue and shook her head. "Ugh!" She stopped Eduardo as he was leaving her. "Eduardo, do you know who that man was?"

"Oh, sí," he nodded, taking the card from his pocket and giving it to her.

She squinted over the printed information. "You're kidding. That obnoxious man is a . . . a doctor?"

"That is what he said. Is something wrong?"

Christine shook her head absently, reading the details. "No," she murmured. "It's just that . . . he seemed more interested in killing me than curing me."

But it was more than that, although Christine was not about to discuss it with Eduardo. She was surprised that the good doctor had been so abrupt and curt with her, not appreciating her physical misery. His indifference was odd and made her uncomfortable. She was stunned that he had such a cold persona.

And she was not used to having *any* man so openly dislike her.

"Wait a minute, I'm coming," Christine croaked irritably as she stumbled half-asleep from her bedroom. Her stomach protested the abrupt change in her body from deep sleep to upright movement before she was fully awake. Christine didn't bother with a robe, certain she could get rid of whoever had the nerve to ring her doorbell at seven A.M. It had to be a delivery person, someone at the wrong apartment, or building management. She didn't bother looking through the peephole, which would have told her who it was immediately. Instead she unlocked the door, yanked it open, and found Keith standing there, looking handsome, cheerful, and wide awake.

"Morning," he said, stepping into the apartment at the same time he slipped an arm around Christine's waist and gave her a kiss as she tried to stifle a yawn.

"Oh, my God, Keith. How could you?" she asked in annoyance, squinting at him. "It's barely light out. Couldn't you wait a few more hours?"

He chuckled as he secured Christine's door and followed her into the living room. She collapsed onto the sofa, curled into a fetal position. She closed her eyes again as if to sleep.

"No, I couldn't wait. I had to see you as soon as possible." He sat on the edge of the sofa and began stroking her shoulder and back through the gossamer fabric of her nightgown.

"I'm not flattered," Christine grumbled, her words muffled by the thick cushions.

"I'm serious." He shook her gently. "Christine, wake up."

When she didn't answer, Keith stood up again and slipped his arms beneath her and lifted her from the sofa. He turned and carried her back into the bedroom.

It felt strange to Christine. Keith never picked her up, even playfully. But she had a sensation, a memory of being in someone's arms and transported like this just recently. She'd felt very light and safe. Last night, as a matter of fact. But somehow Keith carrying her was different. He always smelled sort of heated and athletic. Very physical. But last night there had been another man with a scent that was calm and cool in a way, like someone in control and sure of himself. Christine frowned. She didn't want to think about *him*. But she moaned softly because Keith's gait made her stomach heave.

Christine felt herself being lowered to her bed. She reluctantly opened her eyes and looked into his face. She admired his handsome features in a kind of clinical way, aware of the beautiful, strong shape of his mouth, the classically cleft chin. She remembered when she thought she and Keith were a perfect couple. Now the thought seemed trivial and meaningless.

Keith grinned as he leaned over her, half reclining on the bed next to her. He kissed her mouth again. "So, how was the bash last night? Did I miss anything?"

"Not much," Christine murmured, seeing no point in telling him of her malady and the rest of her adventure. She certainly wasn't going to tell him about the doctor. And there was no point in making comparisons. "What about you? How did the dinner go?"

"I bagged it. I got myself a deal," he said, trying hard to keep the boastful excitement out of his voice.

Christine blinked when she realized what he'd said. "Keith, that's great! Do you mean you already have a role and you're definitely going to be in a film? Or do you have to audition?"

"Yes," he nodded. "Both."

"Well, why didn't you call and let me know?"

"Because it was late. We talked until almost one in the morning. And then I had things to do . . ."

She frowned. "At one o'clock in the morning? Like what?"

"Pack."

"Pack?"

He nodded. "Umm-humm. I'm leaving for California this morning. It means I'm going to have to cancel that shoot for *GQ*, but I think the stakes are higher in L.A. I'm goin' for all the marbles."

"You've been waiting for this," Christine responded quietly, digesting the announcement and its implications. "I'm really happy for you."

Keith suddenly stretched out on top of her, pressing her into the bed. The fabric of his jeans and shirt, his suede jacket, rubbed roughly against her skin. "Yeah, but it means I'm going to be away longer than I thought."

"Hey, you're not going to the Arctic Circle or Timbuktu, just California," she murmured.

He stared into her face. "Are you going to miss me?"

"Of course I will," she reassured him.

"Come with me?"

Christine sighed and ran her fingertips along his jaw, across his brows, staring into his handsome face. "No."

"Why not? You can put off a show for a couple of weeks. You have the clout."

She shook her head. "Keith, I can't. This isn't a good time for me," Christine said. "Besides, this is your trip. And I hate L.A. This is what you wanted, isn't it?"

Keith began kissing her face. "Sure. I just don't much like the idea of leaving you."

"You're not leaving me. You've made a decision to go and I've chosen to stay. We're even."

"Dammit, Christine," Keith growled in annoyance, even though he was beginning to get stimulated by the softness of her body beneath his. "You don't even sound like you're sorry we're going to be apart."

"We've been apart before," she said, beginning to return his kisses, enjoying the way Keith's mouth manipulated hers in a teasing manner. Evoking in that moment the pleasure they'd always enjoyed together physically.

"What if we were married? What if someone offered me the role of a lifetime and it meant you had to come with me to the west coast?"

"I'm . . . not going . . . to play *what if* . . ." Christine said in between responding to the growing aggressiveness of his kisses. "Don't you trust me? Don't you think I'll be here when you get back?"

"You're so beautiful. There are lots of men who'd love a chance to come on to you."

Christine made an impatient sound with her teeth and tongue. "I'm not public domain. I'm not up for grabs. I'm . . . I . . . Keith . . ." she whispered as his hand pulled up her nightgown and closed around a bare breast.

She still wasn't fully awake, but his kisses and caresses made Christine feel languid and lazy. Her nipple responded to the flicking of his thumb across the bud and she sighed when he began to kiss her deeply, his tongue exploring her mouth. His body undulated, against her as his arousal began to escalate.

But something felt wrong about this.

Christine began to think about what they were

doing . . . what she and Keith were *about* to do . . .
instead of just going with it.

She didn't feel like making love.

"Keith . . ." she tried to get his attention, but he
was trying to shrug out of his jacket.

Keith groaned. "Christine, it's . . . going to be a
long time," he suggested.

It was, Christine reasoned. The least she could do
was send him off with a happy smile on his face.
Then she could go back to bed.

They both jumped when the intercom buzzer
sounded. Keith cursed softly under his breath.

"I have to get that," Christine told him, pushing
at his chest to make him move. Keith rolled off her
and lay flat on his back with his eyes closed, breathing deeply.

"Don't bother. I know who it is. It's my ride to
the airport."

Christine sat up, pulled down her gown, and
turned to him in an attempt to comfort. "Bad timing. Sorry."

"So am I."

The buzzer sounded again. Keith reluctantly got
up from the bed.

"I'll call you as soon as I get settled." He kissed
her briefly and headed back toward the door with
Christine padding on bare feet behind. Once there,
Keith turned and pulled her into his arms, squeezing her tightly and burying his mouth and nose into
her neck. "I'm going to miss you."

"You better hurry or your luggage will be alone
on that flight to L.A.," she teased, hugging him.

Keith kissed her one final time and looked long-
ingly into her eyes. "I love you, Christine. Don't you
forget that you belong to me." He winked and hurried through the door, jogging to catch the elevator.

Christine silently watched him go, keeping the contradictory emotions coursing through her in check. She closed the door and covered her mouth delicately as she yawned. She returned to her room, climbed back into bed, and within a minute was soundly asleep again.

"I can't believe you're home already. What's the matter? Couldn't afford the stay?" Christine teased her sister, two hours later when she'd awakened again.

Alexandra chuckled quietly. "They get you out of bed and out of the hospital as soon as possible these days."

"But . . . aren't you sore, or anything?"

"I didn't have an episiotomy or stitches, if that's what you mean. Lauren came too fast for that. Hers was a very easy birth. I was lucky."

Christine drew her legs up and twisted them to the side as she reclined in a corner of the sofa, cradling the phone between ear and shoulder. She sighed to herself. *Yes, you are,* she thought silently, still trying to imagine her sister as a new mother. Of course, that wasn't really such an impossibility. After all, Alex had mothered her for years, putting up with some pretty outrageous behavior and attitude, Christine recalled ruefully. "How does it feel to have a baby of your own? Does she cry all the time? Are you going to breast-feed her . . ."

"I love it. No, and yes," Alexandra responded with amusement. "I'm also tired all the time and a little bit scared . . ."

"Scared? How come?"

"Christine, this is probably the most important thing I've done in my life," Alexandra murmured seriously. "I've brought another human being into the world who's completely dependent on me for everything. It's an incredible responsibility. I want to do it right. I want my child to be healthy and happy and to grow up to be brilliant."

"Well with you and Parker for parents she's certain to become a musical genius. Did he run right out and buy Lauren her own baby grand yet?"

"No," Alexandra laughed. "Just a carload of stuffed animals. And you should see Daddy with her, Christine. It's so sweet. He just sits and grins at her from ear to ear. He said he never thought he'd live to see this day . . ."

"Well, if he'd waited for me he might not have," she responded dryly.

"Don't say that. Daddy just means he's happy to be a grandfather. Besides, you're not ready for this yet."

Christine blinked and then frowned. No, she couldn't really imagine herself with a baby, either. And, she realized now, she'd never really given any serious thought to having one. Of course, it would also mean finding a man whom she cared enough about to want to have a baby with. She mentally scanned through a short list of men she'd known in the past five years . . . and easily discounted every one of them as potential daddy material. Even Keith. No way. As a matter of fact, Christine surmised, she hadn't met anyone recently who was even interesting and different. No . . . that wasn't true. There was that man . . . Dr. Chandler.

She fidgeted and played nervously with the ends of her hair, rolling strands of it between her fingers. "What do you mean, I'm not ready? There's nothing wrong with my hormones," Christine muttered defensively.

"Hon, your hormones are not what I'm talking about. Look, Christine . . . you live a crazy life. It's not normal. It's not even approaching normal. You're never home. You probably have more frequent flyer miles than God! And you have relationships with men who are . . . are . . ."

"More self-centered and unavailable than I am."

Her sister sighed. "That's not what I was going to say. But the fact is, you're very focused on your career. That doesn't make you selfish, it just means your priorities are different. You're having fun, and you don't have time for kids."

"But you wanted to be a famous singer. You wanted to do light opera. Now you have Lauren and Parker and you might never fulfill your dream," Christine reminded Alexandra.

"Oh . . . but I have," Alex said quietly. "I have everything I've ever wanted. And fame is fleeting, anyway. It can't hold a candle to something as precious as Lauren and my husband."

"Then it's a good thing Parker is so famous. Someone has to pay the bills. I hear he was invited to play for the Queen in June at some jubilee. And he was asked to write the score for a new musical."

"Yes, but he says he's not doing a thing for the next month. He wants time with me and Lauren."

Christine didn't answer right away. She stared off into space, picturing her sister nursing her niece and Parker watching lovingly. She shifted in the chair once more and experienced a funny upheaval in her stomach, but not like the night after the fashion show. This wasn't a physical discomfort so much as a hollow feeling.

"I have to admit this week has been almost perfect," Alexandra added.

Suddenly, without any logical reason, Christine

found herself irritated with all of this unbounded joy. It seemed excessive. It seemed unfair. Alexandra had inherited their father's musical genius; she could play the piano and she had a wonderful voice. She had found a strong, smart, talented, *and* kind black man who adored her and who had given her a daughter. Everyone admired Alexandra; she had taken on the responsibility of an elderly, ailing father and also taught music to children unable to afford lessons. Her sister, Christine grudgingly admitted, had always been there even for her, despite the fact that she could be difficult and a general pain in the . . .

"I'm so glad you called. I feel like I haven't seen you in months."

"You haven't," Christine said and grinned.

"So, how was the show last night? Parker tried to explain that it had something to do with a politician and raising money, but you'll understand if I was preoccupied," Alexandra chuckled.

Christine felt her stomach tense. She recalled, for a brief instant, the episode when she'd almost fainted but had ended up, instead, in the arms of a stranger. She could recall his brusque tone with her, but she could also remember the warmth of his body as he'd cradled her, and then carried her into the suite. The experience had come back to her later that night after she'd gotten to bed. It came to her in a dream in which every time she turned around, that man was there silently watching her. She hadn't been so much angry as excited and curious. Only this morning had the anger taken hold again. He was rude and impatient and a bully. She resented all the space he was taking up in her thoughts.

"It was a fundraiser," Christine finally responded.

"The fashion show was okay. I don't know if anything was sold."

"Did you get anything for yourself?"

Christine frowned as she smoothed down the fabric of her Calvin Klein robe. "No. The last thing I need is another dress in my closet."

"Is this the real Christine Morrow I'm listening to?" Alexandra teased. "The one who would kill for a Christian LaCroix or Emmanuel original?"

Christine ignored her sister's gentle sarcasm. "I didn't stay until the end. I went home because I wasn't feeling well."

"What's the matter?" Alexandra asked at once.

"Oh . . . I had a headache and my stomach was upset. And then I got so dizzy I . . ."

"Christine!" her sister said in mild alarm.

"It wasn't anything. I probably took too many aspirins on an empty stomach and that made it seem worse."

"I don't like the sound of this. Are you telling me everything?"

"Yes, Mommy," Christine mimicked dryly. "I drank a glass of milk and that helped until I got home last night."

"Well, that was smart thinking. At least you did that. Maybe you should see a doctor. I don't recall you being sick since you had the measles at twelve . . ."

Christine grimaced and felt her stomach react again. "I don't need to see a doctor."

"Christine, I'm serious. Why are you suddenly having all these headaches? You mentioned getting them before you left for Europe. And why are you running around without eating properly? And fainting . . ."

"Stop fussing," Christine muttered impatiently. "I shouldn't have said anything. Now you're not going to stop until I agree to go see some doctor. There's nothing wrong with me. At least not physically. I'm just ticked off because Keith woke me up at the crack of dawn this morning, and I think I lost my appointment book."

"Well, I'm sorry about your appointment book, but that can be replaced. I do want you to see someone. And if you won't listen to me I'll put Parker on."

"You think that's going to make a difference?"

"Yes," her sister answered succinctly. "The one person you seem to respect is Parker and I'll sic him on you in a heartbeat."

"So now you're comparing your husband to a dog?"

"Girl, you know what I'm talking about. Look, why don't you come home? Dr. Johnson is still the family doctor and he'll be happy to see you again."

"No, thanks. Dr. Johnson is very sweet and he's very old."

"Chicken. Well, come home anyway. We haven't seen you in a while . . . and, quite frankly, you sound like you could do with a break."

"Maybe," Christine prevaricated.

"Daddy asked when you were coming down again."

"Unfair. Don't use Daddy to try and get me down to Maryland."

"Fine, Christine," Alexandra said patiently. "When you're ready we'll be here. Just take care of yourself."

"Give my love to everyone," Christine added, hanging up the phone.

She sat for a long time listening to the silence in her apartment, and even to her own breathing. She realized that she was beginning to get a headache again, and frowned. She hated to admit it but they were becoming troublesome. She rubbed at her temples, feeling the tightening in the back of her neck and the pinched sensation behind her eyelids. *I'm just tired,* Christine told herself. But the idea of spending the day at home suddenly had a curious appeal. She didn't want to have to make appearances today. But she'd intended to have her nails done and get a massage. She'd promised to meet some friends for lunch. Yet when she thought about it she realized that she just wanted to be alone for the day and tune out.

She climbed off the sofa and went into her room, where the bed was still unmade and the contents of her tote had been dumped in the middle in her latest attempt to find her date book. But it wasn't in the things she'd brought home from the hotel the night before. Christine sighed in exasperation and sat down on the side of the bed. Her head pounded. She didn't know what she was going to do if she'd lost her book. It would take her forever to duplicate all that information, not to mention appointments she needed to know about for the next week or so.

Futilely, she swept her hand through the scattered items. A small white card flipped in the air and settled on top of her wallet. Christine frowned as she picked it up and smoothed out the bent edges with her fingers. She looked at the information and her eyes narrowed.

D. Maxwell Chandler, MD.

"Humph!" Christine uttered in disgust. "D for despicable."

But she kept staring at the card, recalling her sister's words. More than that, remembering how concerned she'd felt after she'd gotten home the night before, knowing she'd come close to losing consciousness. What if it happened when she was alone? What if she hadn't had that glass of milk to settle her stomach? What, exactly, had gone wrong the day before to bring her to near collapse?

Christine gnawed thoughtfully on the inside of her jaw and continued to examine the card. The address was up in Harlem, on Strivers Row. It was an historical two-block area of landmark brownstones belonging traditionally to professional blacks. The surrounding neighborhood may have become blighted over the years, but Strivers Row maintained its reputation as a desirable place to live. But still, the Harlem address gave Christine pause. She'd never been up there and, its history and notoriety notwithstanding, she was suspicious of a doctor who couldn't afford a better location.

She blinked at the train of her thoughts. Why was the location Dr. D. Maxwell Chandler chose to conduct business any concern of hers? He was probably a crackpot or a lousy doctor anyway, she mused. But she fingered the card and read the information over and over again. She was able to conjure up an image of the stern Dr. Chandler as he'd summarily dismissed her the night before as if she was not worth his time and attention.

That did it.

Christine went back into her living room and picked up the cordless phone. Making her way slowly into the kitchen, she began to dial his number. The call was answered on the second ring by a brisk female voice.

"Dr. Chandler's line. How may I help you?"

Christine hesitated. She hadn't really thought about what she wanted. Dialing the number had been purely spontaneous. But there really was a doctor and he really did have an office . . . and this was his secretary.

"Hello?"

"I . . . I want to make an appointment," Christine finally spoke up, surprised at how nervous her voice sounded and how her hands gripped the phone.

"Are you one of the doctor's regular patients?"

"No, I . . ."

"Well, let me see what's open for next week."

"Next week? Can't I come in today?"

The woman on the other line laughed incredulously. "I'm afraid not. Dr. Chandler is booked clear through until 3:00 and his office hours are usually only until noon on Saturday. Unless this is an emergency . . ."

"This *is* an emergency," Christine improvised imperially.

"What's wrong?"

"Well . . . I don't know. That's what I want him to tell me. I was at a function last night and Dr. Chandler just happened to be there when I . . . I fainted. He said I needed to see . . ."

"Oh . . . so you *do* know him," the nurse-secretary filled in.

"Yes, that's right," Christine went along, hearing the pages of an appointment book being turned. In the background she could also detect the excited, high-pitched sounds of toddler voices.

"It's really tight today," the woman murmured absently. "But if he said he wanted to see you . . . can you make it here in an hour? I can try to squeeze you in between two other appointments. One of them is usually late anyway."

"Yes, I'll be there."

"Good. Your name?"

Christine gave the assistant all the information,

feeling an unexpected build-up of excitement and anticipation. She hadn't forgotten for a moment that Dr. D. Maxwell Chandler had blown her off. Well, she had news for him. She was famous and sought after. Magazine articles had been written about her, she'd been photographed by Avedon and Lebowitz, film deals had been offered . . . and all of them turned down. Christine knew she could have just about anything she wanted. No way was she going to let D. Maxwell get away with dismissing her.

Just who the hell does he think he is? Christine snorted, working herself into a frenzy of indignation. She poured herself a cup of decaf and made two slices of dry, fat-free toast.

And wondered what she was going to wear.

Three

Christine paid the cab driver as she noted, with some amusement, his furtive glances around the street, as if expecting someone to jump out of an alley and mug him. Worse . . . to demand to be driven somewhere. It was clear to Christine that the driver wasn't used to this part of the city, and may even have refused her fare had he known she was headed to the center of Harlem. Nonetheless he'd brought her here without complaints or excuses. When he pulled away from the curb, Christine secured the strap of her tote on her shoulder, adjusted her sunglasses, and looked around.

The street was actually very quiet. There was no one around. The exquisite architecture of the turn-of-the-century four-storied buildings spoke clearly of a bygone era. Christine remembered that there were similar structures in parts of Washington D.C., where she'd grown up, but that they, too, as with most urban centers, had fallen on hard times. The buildings in D.C. were not quite so large, but with the same flavor and details. But just a block in either direction, everything changed. She was shocked by the amount of deterioration and decay so close to the peaceful and orderly street. Why had Strivers Row survived where many other parts of the community had not?

Christine tried to imagine D. Maxwell Chandler in this setting . . . and the image didn't fit very well. On the other hand, she had no real idea of the kind of man or doctor he was, other than that abrupt experience with him in the hotel. She also had to admit to herself, albeit reluctantly, that sheer curiosity had brought her here today, which had her wondering what she was going to say when she walked into his office.

Christine took a deep breath and repeated the address to herself as she searched the numbers on the nearest building. She walked past the next two houses until she found the right one. There was a small white sign attached to an old-fashioned wrought iron post which announced the office of D. Maxwell Chandler . . . and Frances Grimes, OB-GYN. Christine stared at the sign in surprise . . . and confusion. Did that mean that Chandler was an OB-GYN, too? The very thought of him being a doctor who would know the female body in intimate detail was unsettling. She recalled the way his large, strong hands had held her, had roamed over her limbs, pressing and touching. Christine swallowed and frowned when she recalled that when he'd loosened her dress she'd felt a flash of breathlessness, even though she hadn't known fully what was happening to her. When he helped her stand up to find the bathroom, the strength in his hands and arms had been impressive . . . and seductive. She felt oddly protected with him. Despite his clear abhorrence of her, when she needed his help, he *had* been there.

Christine decided she was trying to save herself the trouble of confronting Dr. Chandler by suddenly instilling heroic characteristics in him. But the very idea made her want to laugh.

She walked down the short entrance stairs to the door, just below street level, and rang the bell. It brilled deep within the structure and echoed. A buzzer sounded, releasing the outside door, and Christine pulled it open and entered. The foyer was brightly lit and led to a reception area where a woman sat answering the phone. While she waited, Christine took a moment to look around the room. It was not very big, but the lighting was bright. The furniture was not the modern cloth-and-chrome structures typical of reception areas. There was a sofa and loveseat, soft enough to relax in. There were pillows on the sitting surfaces, and pillows on the floor. Two ficus plants reached almost to the ceiling, and flora and fauna prints decorated the walls. It was not so much cheerful as soothing.

There were four other women in the room, and several children sitting on the floor with toys or quietly reading books. One woman held a sleeping infant.

"Can I help you?" the assistant at the desk asked as she hung up her phone.

Christine approached the desk and removed her sunglasses. "I have an appointment to see Dr. Chandler. I'm Christine Morrow."

"Yes, I spoke to you earlier," the woman nodded, reaching for a clipboard and pen as she stared at Christine. "I've seen you somewhere before," she murmured, studying Christine intently. "What pretty eyes you have."

Christine merely smiled. "Maybe I remind you of someone you know."

The woman chuckled silently. "Honey, *none* of my friends looks like you. And I mean that as a compliment." She passed the clipboard to Christine. "Just fill these out and I'll see where I can find an opening for the doctor to see you." She beckoned behind Christine. "Mrs. Turnbull, Dr. Grimes is ready for you now . . ."

The woman with the infant got up and called another of the children to her side. She left the waiting room and proceeded through a door to the left of the assistant's desk. Christine took the vacated seat and settled herself to fill out the medical form. She was aware that the other women were staring. Even one of the older children sat mesmerized, watching her. Christine found the scrutiny uncomfortable, as if she was an oddity or some alien species. One of the little girls, about five or so, put down her toy and approached one of the seated women to lean against her arm as she stared almost transfixed at Christine.

Christine tried to smile at the little girl, but she felt funny doing so because she wasn't used to meeting, let alone communicating with, someone so young.

"Mommy . . . she's pretty," the little girl stage-whispered to her mother as she gnawed on a finger she had stuck in her mouth.

Christine pretended not to hear because she didn't know how to react. The mother pulled the girl's finger free and whispered back.

"Stop staring. It's not nice."

That caught Christine's attention, too, although she still didn't indicate by gesture or expression that she was aware of the aside. Still, it was a strange sensation to be in the presence of people talking about her as if she was invisible.

"She looks like a movie star," the little girl added. She suddenly left her mother's side and moved to stand directly in front of Christine. "Are you a movie star?" she asked guilelessly, tilting her head and twisting her body back and forth.

"Kenya, *get over here!*" the mother instructed her daughter, reaching to grab the child by the arm and yank her back.

"It's okay," Christine said when she finally found her voice and smiled awkwardly at the woman. She glanced at the little girl and shook her head. "I'm not an actress, I'm a model," she said simply. Yet, even as the words left her mouth it occurred to Christine how silly it sounded. It was like saying she got paid for having her picture taken, or that she wore other people's clothes for a living, or that her job was just to be beautiful.

"Valerie, you go on in," the woman at the desk instructed.

Christine watched as the curious little girl and her mother got up to enter another room. Christine turned in her finished form and began to leaf through an issue of *Black Elegance* magazine. She stopped when she came across a photo of a young black model. She squinted to focus and realized it was that young girl who was at the show just the night before. Tonee something-or-other.

The ad was for a cigarette company. It was usually an easy first assignment to get for an untried model, but not politically correct, as many quickly found out. Such advertising was not good for a model's image if she was perceived to be endorsing something that wasn't healthy. But all that aside, Christine could see clearly, in the beautiful smile showing perfect teeth in the creamy brown of her face, in the flirtatious tilt of Tonee's head and the provocative arching of her back that thrust her small breasts forward, that the girl knew what she was doing . . . knew how to pose. And if attention was what she wanted, then there was no question that the eyes of the world were going to find her sooner or later.

Christine grimaced, put the magazine aside, and picked up an old issue of *Ebony*. The cover story was on the top twenty-five African-Americans to admire. She turned to the start of the article and scanned the photographs. She played a mental game with herself to see how many of the men and women she actually recognized or had heard about. Christine stopped at a small black and white insert image of a man. When she read the caption it was to find the name of Dr. D. Maxwell Chandler printed beneath.

"Miss Morrow? Will you follow me?"

Christine closed the magazine. She started to return it to the stack on the table, but instead she stood to follow the assistant and stuck the magazine into her bag. She found herself in a narrow corridor that had additional doors on either side. The nurse entered one room and stood aside as Christine entered behind her. The room was small and cramped and functional. There was an examining table covered with a length of stiff white paper. Besides the table there was a low stool and stainless steel sink. A cabinet of supplies and towels. A cart with glass jars containing tongue depressors, Q-tips, cotton balls, tapes, and Band-Aids . . . and lollipops. Christine blinked at the multicolored candy, finding it totally out of place.

"Take off your things, and the doctor will be right in. There's a gown on the table . . ."

Christine turned quickly to the nurse and frowned. "But I just wanted to talk to the doctor about what happened to me last night."

The woman smiled kindly. "He won't be able to

answer any questions until he's examined you." She frowned thoughtfully at Christine. "When was the last time you saw a doctor?"

Christine felt the warmth of blood rushing to her face. Not in years. Not since she was a teenager and wanted birth control pills. No, more recently than that. Three years ago when she wanted to have a mole removed from the inside of her left thigh. She *never* allowed her picture to be taken in lingerie or swimwear unless the blemish was covered or heavily disguised with makeup. And once she'd had an impacted wisdom tooth pulled. But she'd never been sick. "Oh . . . I haven't seen anyone this year," she compromised smoothly.

The nurse smiled. "You're not afraid of doctors and needles, are you?"

Christine grimaced, recapturing some of her spirit. "No, I'm not."

"Then you have nothing to worry about. Besides, Dr. Chandler is a very gentle and understanding man."

Christine could only stare at the woman as she left her alone. She wondered how they could possibly be talking about the same man.

When the door closed Christine sat on the edge of the examining table in annoyance. There was nothing wrong with her. She didn't need D. Maxwell Chandler to examine her. She wanted him to look at her. She wanted to get in his face and question his abilities. She wanted him to realize what a mistake he'd made treating her so lightly.

Christine frowned at the folded gown on the table. She lifted it carelessly and let the fabric hang. It was short, and meant to be worn so that the opening was in the back. It was blue, which was a terrible color for her. But slowly she began to smile and she laid out the gown so she could see the shape of it completely. She put her purse on the low stool and draped her light sweater on top of it.

She began to undress.

"Dammit!" D. Maxwell Chandler murmured irritably when he read the name on the medical history forms. Tightening his jaw and narrowing his gaze, he quickly scanned through the information, but his mind was already on how to get this Christine Morrow out of his office. He wasn't interested in seeing her. "Joyce!" he called out to his assistant.

Joyce Milner stuck her head in the open door of her office. "Yes?"

"Did Miss . . . *Morrow* say why she's here? What's the problem?"

"Nothing, as far as I can tell," the assistant said wryly. "But she said something about last night. She said you'd seen to her when she fainted."

"She didn't faint," he corrected. "Her body was simply reacting to too much . . ." he stopped his diagnosis.

"When she called she seemed determined to see you today."

"In other words, she buffaloed her way into an appointment."

"That's about it," Joyce chuckled. "Look, I couldn't take the chance that something might have been really wrong. And she did say she'd already met you . . ."

He sighed. "All right. Don't worry about it. Where is she?"

"In examining room three."

"Thanks . . ." he muttered, his annoyance not abating one bit.

Joyce returned to her desk in the reception area, but D. Maxwell continued to sit at his desk, staring at the pages. Christine Renee Morrow. Almost twenty-eight. Five feet, ten inches . . . and one hundred and twenty-five pounds. Mother deceased and father suffering from heart disease, high blood pressure . . . and glaucoma . . .

He stopped reading and sat for a long moment. He let his mind drift back to the night before as he'd stepped forward to catch Christine Morrow's falling body. Even that she had done gracefully as only a soft sigh of distress had whispered past her lips. His frown deepened at the memory because he could remember everything. Every damned detail about her.

She was unreal. Made up. People like Christine Morrow didn't really exist. Certainly not in his life. She was a teenage boy's fantasy. But he was a grown man and he knew better. But that didn't stop the peculiar tightness Maxwell felt in the center of his chest, or the persistent reenactment in his memory of his encounter with Christine Morrow at the Sheraton Hotel. Worse still, that she reminded him of someone who'd taken his love . . . and given nothing in return.

Abruptly Maxwell pushed away from the desk, snatched up the papers, and headed out of the office. He wanted to get this over with as quickly as possible. He didn't want to have anything to do with Christine Morrow.

When the door opened and he finally came into the examining room, Christine pretended not to notice. She was sitting demurely on the edge of the examining table, her long legs hanging over the side and crossed at the ankles. Her hands rested in her lap. Her eyes were studying a framed certificate on the opposite wall with the name of a Dr. Frances Mary Grimes. Holding her head at an angle, she appeared quiet and thoughtful.

But D. Maxwell was not fooled. As a matter of fact, seeing her again just confirmed his earlier opinion. She wasn't waiting to see him, concerned with some medical problem for which she needed consultation. Christine Morrow had come to posture and pose.

"What seems to be the problem?" he asked officiously without a greeting.

Christine blinked innocently, her green eyes wide and bright. "That's what I want you to tell me. Since you're the doctor. You're the one who said I should find out why I almost passed out last night. Well . . . here I am."

He resorted to looking at the information sheets again, leaning against the edge of the sink as he read. Christine silently watched him, taking the opportunity to try and find out more about him. The doctor was a big man, not at all fat or even muscular, but tall and broad. Everything about him seemed large. His hands and feet certainly, but also his face, which was very angular with high cheekbones. To die for, Christine thought irrelevantly. A prominent nose, but not broad or flattened. His mouth was, relatively speaking, thin, but wide. And he had the kind of jawline that automatically tightened in a provocatively masculine way. It suggested intensity and seriousness.

Christine's gaze quickly assessed the rest of him. He was fit and trim, but not with the kind of hard body of a male model or actor. Not like Keith's. His skin was dark, and it was most noticeable in his hands, where the palms were an ochre color, contrasting to the oak color on the back. But his hands were strong-looking and clean . . . and she wondered suddenly if . . .

"I don't know what I can tell you," he said flatly.

Christine focused her attention on his face. She braced her hands on the examining table and leaned forward beseechingly. Her expression was humble . . . and challenging. "Maybe you should examine me first," she said smoothly, not blinking as she held his gaze. "Your nurse said you'd have to."

His frown became a scowl. "Don't you have your own family doctor?"

"Yes. In D.C. I just don't happen to be in D.C. at the moment." She kept her voice calm and quiet. She knew he was displeased that she was there . . . which was exactly why she'd come.

He placed the form on top of a cabinet and finally looked directly at Christine. He tried not to see that she wore almost no makeup and still she seemed beautiful. There was just a light lipstick coating her full mouth, and he wondered if the long lashes were hers. Her hair was fluffed out and full, attractively framing her face. He couldn't help staring at her skin. It was flawless, its tone even and smooth.

For a moment his hands clenched into fists before finally relaxing. He reached out slowly and placed them on either side of her neck. He could feel her surprise at his touch, but she held still and looked into his face as his fingers probed gently along the sides of her neck. Placing his thumbs lightly under her jaw, he tilted her head as the examination began.

"Tell me about your father."

Christine blinked and frowned. "My . . . father?"

"That's right."

"Why do you want to know about my father?"

"Family history. How's he doing? You listed a number of health problems."

She blinked again, confused. "Well . . . he's sixty-three years old. Retired. He . . . he's been sick for the last few years . . ."

"Yes, you mentioned heart problems." His hands moved to her throat and shoulders, continuing to get a sense of her body. Her skin was smooth and soft. He let his hands drag down her arms, feeling all the way until he grabbed her hands and began to massage and rotate his fingers on her palms and wrists, as if trying to detect every bone and muscle. "What else?"

Christine felt impatient. She shrugged. "I don't know. He loves to play the piano but he can't see very well anymore. He likes to drink scotch or beer, but my sister won't let him."

"What about your sister?" He took a pocket flash-light from his shirt pocket and flicked it on. Resting his whole hand atop her head he tilted it, using his thumb to carefully pull one eyelid open and peer in with the light. Then he did the other eye.

Christine forgot the question. The doctor had to lean in close in order to peer into her eye, and she felt herself stiffen as she tried to cooperate. But she was acutely aware of his nearness, of the way he seemed to overwhelm her physical being with his own. His hand, splayed on her head, felt like a hat, but he was again remarkably gentle. As he'd been the night before. As his nurse said he would be.

"Ah . . . my . . . my sister Alexandra is really the head of the family. At least she used to be before she got married. My mother died when I was still very young and Alex sort of took care of me and

Daddy. But, she just had a baby. This week, as a matter of fact."

"Congratulations . . ." he murmured.

The sound came from the middle of his chest and was rough. The edge of his voice rasped over her nerves, and Christine felt the warm wave of his breath against her cheek.

"Then, you're the baby of the family?"

"Not anymore," she responded wryly, clearly remembering how that position had held certain privileges . . . and drawbacks. "Lauren Shani Harrison is now the reigning queen."

He stepped back for a moment to change instruments and reach for the one to examine her ears. As he did so he glanced briefly into her eyes. "Jealous?"

Christine grimaced and snorted. "Of a baby? Give me a break."

"I take it you're not interested in having kids . . . getting married," he said, again pressing close to look into her ear.

"I didn't say that," she murmured.

He looked at her again as he switched to the other ear. "But you're used to being the center of attraction, aren't you?"

Christine felt he was baiting her. She arched a brow and glared at him. "What has all this to do with me fainting last night? Have you found anything?"

"Nothing unusual," he said and shook his head. He put the instrument down on the table. With his back to her he began to rearrange the items. "Lie down, please."

Christine hesitated. It was only then that she realized the gown didn't leave many options for grace or discretion. With nothing but her bikini panties between her and total embarrassment, she quickly tried to recline on the hard leather surface so that she'd appear relaxed but not foolish. She smoothed the fabric of the gown over her thighs and tilted her pelvis upward so her chest wouldn't thrust out quite so obviously. But when he turned around to approach the table Christine found herself staring at his stern expression and wondering what he was thinking. She knew what *she* was thinking . . . that he wasn't like the men she was used to. She thought he was arrogant and full of himself, but she found herself caring about what he thought of her.

He loomed over her but she didn't feel threatened. Just a peculiar sort of vulnerability . . . like being helpless and curious. It occurred to Christine, for no particular reason, that he didn't look like a doctor. More like a football player or construction worker. Extremely physical.

"What does the D stand for?" she found herself questioning softly.

He just stared at her, lying there with her hair thick and loose around her face, her emerald eyes staring openly at him, unlike the vamp who strutted her stuff the night before. He watched her breathing, and the way her breasts rose against the blue material . . . the way her nipples indented the gown into tiny mountains. He straightened his shoulders.

"Dangerous."

Christine thought he was trying to be funny at first, but then realized she was wrong. It was sarcasm. "I'm serious."

"People who know me call me Maxwell."

Christine tucked her chin in. "Come on," she coaxed in as charming a manner as she could muster. "It can't be that horrible. Delbert? Dweezil?"

He narrowed his eyes and she had the momentary

satisfaction of seeing the ghost of a smile quiver his chin, but it was gone so quickly she could just as easily have been mistaken.

He suddenly touched her leg, and her humor quickly faded. Her nerves quivered and her skin felt hot where his hand rested just above the knee. She tried not to move or even to react. His fingers slid upward and Christine held her breath. He wouldn't dare . . .

His fingertip found the raised, rough nodule. "What is this?"

"A . . . a mole," Christine answered. "It's always been there."

He leaned over her thigh and rubbed over the dark brown spot. "It looks like a keloid. It's probably benign."

Christine heard what he said, but she also felt his hand moving. "Benign . . ." she repeated in a thin voice.

"You don't have to worry about skin cancer," he added gruffly. "You can have it removed. It's not a painful procedure."

"Yes, doctor," she demurred playfully, hoping to break through the outer shell of his demeanor.

But it didn't work.

The next few minutes of the exam were conducted in silence. All the while Christine just watched Maxwell Chandler, waiting patiently for him to loosen up. Waiting for him to notice her and be appropriately impressed.

It didn't happen.

She wasn't prepared for him to rest his hand on her stomach and when he did she found herself suddenly catching her breath. He pressed, as before, with his fingers, and rotated them gently but firmly around her abdomen and groin area.

"Are you pregnant?" he asked suddenly.

She was beginning to experience a certain languid fascination with the movement and feel of his hands, but Christine nearly bounded up from her prone position at his words. "What?"

"Or have you ever been pregnant?"

She slapped his hands away and tried to sit up. *"No,* I'm not pregnant," she said indignantly, as if the question was somehow perverted. "Not ever. What kind of question is that?"

"It's one that I'm supposed to ask. It's on the medical history you were supposed to fill out. You left that one blank. Freudian slip?"

"You're getting fresh," she muttered.

"Like I said, you could have gone to your own doctor."

His hands suddenly and unexpectedly moved to rest over her breast. Christine tried not to gasp audibly, but drew in a deep breath and held it. Her gaze widened as his large hands began to press and palpate around first one breast and then the other. He never looked her in the face, but his brows were drawn together in concentration. If he was getting off on feeling her breast he certainly didn't show it. She, on the other hand, wondered if he could feel the way her heart was beating, or detect the tightening in her groin muscles as she lay still under his touch. There wasn't much to the gown, but now she was grateful that the opening was to the back.

Maxwell finally looked into her eyes, unmoved by her indignation but intrigued by the way she was breathing and the way her body moved. He stopped abruptly and slid his hands away. Her long legs swung forward as she sat up, hugging her arms around her ribcage to hold the gown in place.

"Look, the only thing that's wrong is that I get

headaches. The *only* reason I'm here is because you told me to check it out. I've never fainted before, I've never been pregnant, and I don't have wax in my ears!" She hopped off the table and stood confronting him, even though he was still nearly five inches taller than she was in her bare feet. "I thought you were a doctor, but you're really an obnoxious jerk. You'd make a perfect veterinarian. You wouldn't have to talk to your patients or worry about them liking you. You could poke and probe and be mean and it won't matter. But I don't happen to be a horse or a cat and would appreciate more than a grunt from you, *doctor.*"

His expression never changed. He simply stared at her with mild indifference. He stood with his arms crossed over his chest and was conscious of the vein standing out in her neck and the way her fuzzy hairdo trembled with each annoyed swivel of her head. When she stopped talking she was out of breath, and her nostrils flared and her incredible green eyes flashed.

"Are you finished?" he asked calmly.

"Yes," Christine said through clenched teeth, infuriated by his distance, wanting to punch him but afraid of how he'd retaliate if she did. Besides, it was childish. It had been a mistake to come. The man was catatonic.

He turned away and headed for the door. "Get dressed and come into my office." He left her gaping after him.

Christine couldn't get dressed fast enough. It no longer mattered that he wasn't responsive to her. She just wanted to get out of there and forget she'd ever met D . . . as in dreadful . . . Maxwell Chandler. She jerked on her tan gabardine slacks and the short cropped white sweater. She hastily finger-fluffed her hair as she pulled the door open. Christine had no intention of going to his office, but headed instead toward the exit. She nearly bumped into the assistant, who smiled at her.

"Oh, you're ready. Quick . . . Dr. Chandler has about ten minutes before he has to see the next patient. He's in there."

She pointed to yet another door. The slight delay in her progress was just enough to make Christine realize she was losing control. "Thank you," she muttered, and reluctantly went into the office.

Dr. D. Maxwell Chandler was seated behind a cluttered desk making notes and didn't even acknowledge her presence. Christine stopped abruptly on the threshold and stood staring. The room was unlike any of the other offices. Not any bigger, but more comfortable and almost homey. Dozens of framed photographs decorated the walls and the edge of his desk. A basket of toys lay on the floor next to a chair and a stack of children's books filled a bookshelf. Near it was another jar of candy, and assorted items of children's clothing. A tiny sweater or a hat. A sock . . . a pacifier.

"Sit down," the doctor said flatly, pointing to a chair in front of his desk.

But Christine ignored him, drawn to the pictures on the wall. She came closer and peered closely at the Kodak color images. Maxwell was in some of the pictures, but mostly they were shots of children at play in a park or other outdoor setting, at birthday celebrations. One picture had obviously been taken right in that very office, one in front of the building as the doctor stood holding hands with a set of twins . . . little girls about the age of four.

"I have other patients waiting, Miss Morrow. If

you don't mind . . ." he said again, with that hard tone she was coming to recognize.

Silently, Christine turned away from the photo gallery. She took a lollipop out of one of the apothecary jars and took a seat as directed. She didn't bother opening the candy, but sat twirling the stick between her fingers. He was leaning over a folder that had been created for her with her name on the tab. Her medical history forms had been stapled to the inside, and the doctor was writing additional notes on a new sheet of paper. Christine could only make out the date, reading upside down, but she did notice that like the stereotypical doctor, Maxwell Chandler's handwriting was indecipherable.

When she looked at him now, however, she saw a little bit more than she'd seen before, than she'd even imagined. Her first impression was that he was decidedly two dimensional, but entering this office made Christine recognize there was much more to the doctor than met the eye.

"So . . . am I going to live?" she asked, calmer now.

His jaw went into a spasm of reflexive tightening. He sat back in his chair, tossed the pen on top of her case file, and regarded her with studied interest, taking his time to casually scan her features before he spoke.

"You're too thin for your age and height."

She bristled all over again. "I'm a model. I'm the perfect weight for what I do. What does my age have to do with it?"

"You're going to get too old for what you're doing, sooner or later, and your body and organs are going to pay a price for the deprivation necessary for you to wear clothes well. You must be pretty close to the peak of your career."

Despite herself, Christine felt the sting of his words. It was all true, of course, but his bluntness only irritated her and she found herself resisting the logic and good sense. "I could have another ten years of modeling if I want. There are models over forty who still get work. I'm very good at what I do."

He frowned and gestured impatiently. "Is that what you want to be? A model who makes it to forty? What you do is an anomaly. It's not normal. If God hadn't given you a pretty face and perfect body what would you have done with your life? Do you have any other ambition besides being beautiful and admired?"

"Don't you find me attractive?" she taunted him archly. "I happen to make a very good living doing what I do. I probably make more than you do. At least I'm gainfully employed and can take care of myself."

"That's debatable," he said sharply.

Christine frowned. "What do you mean?"

He sat forward and braced his elbows on the desk. "You don't eat right and you're not getting enough sleep. Both are contributing to your headaches. I don't suggest you continue to make aspirin part of your daily diet—it isn't a cure-all. You have to be careful with any medication you take. All of them have toxic side effects if taken in excess."

That was *definitely* the doctor talking. Christine decided not to argue his points.

"Anything else?" she asked impatiently, anxious to leave. She was already putting her sweater back on and checking that she had everything in her purse. She pulled out a checkbook.

"I suggest you see an eye doctor as soon as you can. You should be checked for glaucoma."

"There's nothing wrong with my eyes."

"Not now, perhaps. But your father has it, according to what you wrote down. That makes you a suspect for two reasons: heredity and being African-American. We're prone to that disease. Don't fool around with it. You can go blind."

His words struck a nerve. She thought of her father, who loved to play his old beat-up piano, but who couldn't see the keys so well anymore. "Thank you," she murmured, not sure what she was actually thanking him for. "Is that all?"

He handed her her folder across the desk. "That's it. Give this to Mrs. Milner out front."

Christine took the folder. "How much do I owe you?" she asked stiffly, not looking at him.

He stood up, looming over her, ready to dismiss her again. "My assistant will tell you."

He came around the desk and headed for the door. He brushed past Christine but didn't look at her. He wasn't even going to say goodbye.

"These children . . . are they yours?" she asked.

He stopped with his hand on the doorknob and glanced at her over his shoulder. "Yes."

She frowned in astonishment. "All of them?"

"They're my patients."

Christine looked at him more closely. More things became clear through the armor of his personality. "What kind of doctor are you?"

"A pediatrician." He had a wry smile on his face.

A rush of blood made her face, neck, and arms feel hot. She wondered if her face looked strange as embarrassment washed over her. "Why . . . why didn't you say something?"

"Why didn't you ask? My credentials are framed and on the walls." He gestured behind him to the half-dozen certificates with gold leaf lettering and seals. "But I don't think it would have mattered if

I'd told you," he said with a careless shrug. "You seemed determined to come here, get in my face, and make me sit up and pay attention to you. You weren't thinking about me or anyone else. Certainly not my other patients since you were so set on coming here today.

"Okay. You came, you saw . . . but you didn't conquer. I don't have time for your games, Miss Morrow. My patients don't have the time, money, or determination you have to get your own way."

"You're not being fair," she said weakly, totally taken aback and unprepared for this attack on her character. He stared at her and Christine watched as his face grew harder and more remote, if that was possible. He looked like he wanted to throttle her.

"There's no such thing as fair. What would you know about it anyway?"

She shook her head. "I don't understand you. Why are you a doctor if you dislike people so much?"

"I don't dislike people at all. But I don't have time for people like you. You're spoiled and self-centered. And what you do with your life . . . is irrelevant."

Christine could only stare at him. She didn't even feel angry anymore, just stunned. He took one more look at her, and then grimacing almost in disgust, he went through the door.

Christine didn't move. His words echoed in her head. She decided he was cruel and that some woman had done him wrong and he hadn't gotten over it. She looked around the office again. It was warm and kind of fun. She couldn't imagine how he could take himself so seriously when he kept an office that looked like a playroom. But she decided it didn't matter. She really didn't care to know any more about Dr. Chandler. His children may love him, but he had a hell of a lot to learn about people his own size.

The waiting area was just as crowded as when she'd first come in. Every seat was taken, and there were still children all over the place, only now Christine understood why. One boy, about twelve or so, was in a wheelchair. As before, nearly everyone turned their attention to her when she came back to the reception desk. Only this time, she didn't welcome the stares and felt out of place.

The assistant smiled at Christine and took the folder. "Well, I hope everything was okay."

"Fine," Christine murmured. She opened her checkbook. "How much?"

"Oh, the doctor said not to charge you for the visit. It was a consultation."

His largess annoyed her and she gestured impatiently. "I have to give you something."

The nurse shrugged. "If you really want to."

"Should I make this out to D. Maxwell Chandler?"

"Make it out to LIFELINE."

"The amount?"

"Anything you feel you want to give."

Christine frowned and glanced at the nurse. "What's LIFELINE? A charity?"

"Well, not really. It's an organization the doctor is part of that works with terminally ill patients and does research."

"He does all of that besides take care of children here in his practice?" Christine asked in surprise.

"LIFELINE is part of his practice. It's a pediatric AIDS care group."

* * *

Maxwell brooded over the open folder and the few sheets of information, but his clinically objective opinions of the data blurred with the image of the woman he'd just examined. And that image superseded everything else. He closed the folder angrily and chucked it carelessly across the desk. Never in his life had he expected Christine Morrow to appear in his life again. Even meeting her to begin with, having her fall literally at his feet, had been bad timing . . . an apparition. He might have forgotten all about her and that fortuitous encounter in the hotel eventually. He might have gone over the details once or twice to make sure he hadn't made a snap decision and that Christine Morrow was no more than what she appeared to be. Capricious and vain.

But he *had* seen her again. And he had held her and touched her. Maxwell knew she was different. Even more than the obvious attributes, which were considerable. Christine Morrow was confident and strong. And not the least intimidated by him. She had a lot of ego . . . and she could back it up.

Reluctantly Maxwell retrieved her newly created medical records and began looking over the facts once more. She was not even remotely the kind of woman he'd ever been involved with—or would even want to be.

Now . . . he wasn't so sure anymore.

But even if that was true, he still had no intention of doing a thing about it.

Four

Christine looked at her watch and then glanced up into the mirror at her reflection as her hair was being combed and styled by Miguel Piña. She sighed. "Miguel, I was supposed to be out of here an hour ago."

"Relax, I'm almost done. What's up with you anyway? Aren't you having fun yet?" he asked with a chuckle.

"I just have someplace else I have to be, that's all," she responded, not willing to admit that no, she wasn't having a particularly good time.

"Have you heard from Keith? What's happening in L.A.?"

Christine conjured up the phone conversation she'd had with Keith the morning before. He'd been about to do lunch with a couple of producers. He sounded excited, and his speech was already sprinkled with West Coast jargon and the idea that Hollywood was the center of the country. He was meeting lots of people, dropping some pretty impressive names.

"So . . . are you coming out?" Keith had asked halfway through the conversation.

Christine had responded immediately as she'd walked aimlessly about with the phone in one hand and coffee in the other. She hadn't even thought about it. "Keith, I don't think I can right now. I have a shoot tomorrow and next Wednesday I think a client is flying me to Bermuda because there's a particular shot he wants."

"Maybe it's just as well. It's crazy out here. I'm busy all the time. I don't know if we could really spend a lot of time together. I'd feel really bad if you came out and then we couldn't see each other."

Christine thoughtfully gnawed the inside of her bottom lip. "I agree," she said smoothly, listening to the tone of Keith's words, and the explanation. It made sense and she didn't doubt him. But he'd said nothing about when *he* was coming back east.

Christine blinked and looked at Miguel's image in the mirror. "California seems to be working for him," she finally responded. "He's already finished the role he went out for, and was asked to read for a film about these two black guys who used to play hockey."

Miguel shook his head with a smile. "That's pretty cool. We can say we knew him when. Maybe you'll go out there and start a film career, too. Cybill Shepard did it."

Christine chuckled silently. "I don't think so," she drawled.

Suddenly she felt impatient with the routine of the shoot. The music on the CD was too loud, and although she'd asked to have it turned down, the volume seemed to inspire creativity in the temperamental photographer. Christine was tired of the wind blower blasting at her full throttle. She was tired of being told to turn to the side and tilt back her head, or moisten her lips and pout. She didn't want to arch her back or look sultry or play to the camera. And she didn't like any of the outfits. She wanted out of there.

Christine sighed in annoyance and her attention strayed to the curled copy of *Ebony* magazine lying open to the unfinished article on prominent African-Americans. She'd only gotten halfway through the segment on one Dr. D. Maxwell Chandler, pediatrician and AIDS advocate, when Miguel had pulled the magazine out of her hand complaining that she wasn't holding her head right as he restyled her hair for the final setup. Christine had tried to concentrate on the current assignment for which she was being paid an obscene amount of money, but she would have preferred to have finished reading the article.

Maxwell Chandler, the article had outlined, had been the first black doctor to devote his skills to treating pediatric AIDS patients. He'd started a foundation to raise money not only for research but for the purchase of the few existing FDA approved medications that helped to stabilize the virus in infants and toddlers, making it freely available to those families unable to afford the high costs. He spent most of his spare time at a clinic in Harlem offering free medical care to children who were HIV positive.

The article went on to hint at Dr. Chandler's deeply personal interest in this area of medicine without being specific as to why. It also didn't mention if he was married or had children of his own, and only indicated that he lived in the metropolitan New York area. He was a graduate of Howard University and Yale Medical School.

The picture accompanying the piece was black and white. Christine had studied it long and hard, seeing clearly in the image the man as she'd come to know him. Serious and thoughtful. Quietly self-contained. Deeply private. He was seated in a high-backed chair, probably the one in his office. His right elbow was braced on the arm of the chair, and

Maxwell's fist was curled and lay pressed against his chin. He stared directly into the camera, but his eyes were guarded, shielding all of his inner thoughts and feelings. It gave nothing away.

But as she'd stared at the photo Christine realized, first from her own encounter with Dr. Chandler and now secondhand from the article about him, that there was much more to him than she'd thought. The first thing that occurred to her was the sense of stalwart strength about him. And although she had never seen much of his humor, she wondered how his face might change if he laughed. Or even smiled. The last thing that finally settled into her consciousness, almost as an afterthought, was that D. Maxwell Chandler was a handsome man in a solid, dependable, primal way. She hadn't noticed it at first, but now it seemed so obvious.

The only thing that irritated Christine about the article was that there was still no mention of what the D in his name stood for.

"Okay, finis . . ." Miguel said with a flourish. "You can get into your last outfit. I'll spray your hair before Rafe poses you."

"Great," Christine said and sighed as she got up from her chair. She couldn't wait to finish. She glanced anxiously at the wall clock. If she hurried she could still make it to the LIFELINE Clinic in Harlem.

She cooperated fully for the last rolls of film, not dallying or wasting time on unusable shots or joking with the stylist and photographer. Christine stayed focused and got the job done.

"I think that's it," Rafe murmured at last, rewinding the film. "But I'd like to do one more roll, just in . . ."

"No," Christine said, stepping away from the klieg

lights and starting to pull off the costume jewelry that went with the outfit.

"Come on, it'll only take another five minutes."

"No." She turned her back to the stylist to have the dress unzipped. "I have another . . . appointment and I'm already late. It's . . . personal."

Christine sat in Miguel's chair again and while he combed out the elaborate hairdo she began to remove her makeup.

"What if all the shots don't work?" Rafe asked anxiously. "We always shoot extra."

"I know, but I just can't stay any longer," Christine murmured smoothly, carefully swabbing her eye area with oil. "Look," she said, glancing at Rafe's reflection in the mirror. "If you need more shots later, just call. I'll give you and the client the extra time at no cost, okay?"

The bell to the studio suddenly pealed and Rafe went to answer. "I appreciate that, Christine," he said, talking over his shoulder as he reached the door and opened it. "I'll make it up to you later." He turned to the door as Tonee Holiday stepped in. Rafe quickly looked her over, assessed the possibilities, and grinned cheerfully at her. "Hi. Did Eileen send you over? She hasn't called yet."

Christine, along with everyone else in the studio, turned to see who had arrived. She raised her brows in surprise when she saw the young model. Tonee was dressed in black leggings and cowboy boots. She wore a long fitted red sports jacket, the hem of which stopped just below her butt, exposing the incredible length of her well-shaped legs. The outfit was calculated to emphasize her height and thinness, plus the proportions of her body which made her ideal for modeling. Her hair was haphazardly stuffed under a cute short-brimmed straw hat, giving her a carefree appearance. She had her tote slung over one shoulder, and she was carrying a picture portfolio.

Christine had to admit the girl had the potential for being really eye-catching, but with summer officially a few weeks away, the outfit made Christine feel hot, and made Tonee seem overdressed.

"Hi," Tonee drawled once she knew that every pair of eyes in the room was focused on her. She adopted a pose of bewilderment and uncertainty, as if she didn't have a clue as to how she'd come to be there. "You mean Eileen Ford?" she asked Rafe.

He nodded. "She's always sending over her newest discoveries. If you aren't one, you should be."

Tonee accepted the compliment graciously. "Thank you. But I'm looking for Christine Morrow. I thought she was going to be here."

Christine swiveled in the chair to face Tonee. "I am," she responded.

Tonee glanced briefly at her, then looked to Rafe silently for permission to enter his studio. When he waved a hand, she slowly made her way across the room to where Christine sat waiting. Everyone else went back to what they'd been doing. They'd all seen a model or two before.

This better be good . . . Christine thought and looked expectantly at Tonee. "What is it?"

Tonee was looking around as she approached Christine. "I've never been to a studio like this before." She noticed the rack of designer outfits and briefly riffled through the items. "I have something that belongs to you," she said.

"Oh?" Christine said, walking over to a screen that had been set up so she could slip behind it to change. She began to get into her street clothing, a pair of tan linen slacks and a red and ecru printed silk top cropped short at the waist. "How did you know where to find me?"

"From your appointment book." With that, Tonee put down the portfolio and reached into her tote. She pulled the fat daily calendar out and handed it to Christine.

But Christine didn't take it right away. As she put on her dangling silver earrings she stared at the book for a long moment, and then looked at Tonee. The girl's expression was pleased. And something else. Triumphant? "Where did you find it?" Christine asked softly, still not taking the book.

"It was on the floor near where you were dressing that night at the fashion show. I found it when me and the other models came to change after the show. Here . . ."

Christine finally took the book from the girl. But she didn't say thank you. Instead, she silently and slowly began leafing through the pages, searching through the various scraps of papers and cards, tickets and receipts. As far as she could tell, everything was there. But she felt uneasy . . . and suspicious.

"I tried to call you about it, but you weren't home Saturday morning, and I was busy Sunday and yesterday," Tonee said, answering one of Christine's unasked questions. "What if you couldn't remember what shows or sittings you had this week?" Tonee said, voicing the unthinkable.

"It would have been very difficult," Christine admitted. "It's almost impossible to duplicate the kind of information you jot down in these things . . . details you've been collecting for a long time," she said quietly. She closed the book and secured the snap fastener. "Thank you. I appreciate you returning it to me."

"No problem," Tonee shrugged.

It was on the tip of Christine's tongue to offer some sort of reward, but thought that might seem condescending. She was beginning to feel charitable toward the young model, who at least seemed to have the thoughtfulness to try and get in touch with her about the date book.

"I'm almost finished here. Can I take you to lunch or something?"

Tonee grimaced. "Thanks, but I already ate. I ran into this musician I know and he took me out. I had Chicken Parmesan."

Christine raised her brows and shook her head. "That's got a lot of fat."

"Oh, I don't have to worry about my weight. I can eat anything," Tonee said with all the confidence of an eighteen-year-old.

Christine pursed her lips and remained silent. She'd heard that before and it just wasn't so. She slipped her book into her bag, happy to have it back. "Did you have an assignment today?" she asked, referring to the fact that Tonee had her book with her.

Tonee shrugged. "I always carry it with me. You never know when you're going to meet someone who's interested in what you do, and who might help, you know?"

Christine pursed her lips. "That's right. One never knows . . . do one?" she mimicked, quoting the Fats Waller line.

Rafe finally wandered over, having given Tonee and Christine a chance to chat. "Are you a friend of Christine's?" he asked the girl. "A protégé?"

Christine could see from Tonee's frown that she was about to ask an obvious question. She quickly forestalled it. "Tonee is an up and coming model.

Calvin's been pushing her and sending her around. I did a show with her last Friday night."

"Great," Rafe said, pointing to Tonee's portfolio. "Are those your pictures?"

Tonee giggled girlishly. "They're not very good. A friend of mine did them. I can't afford to have new ones done yet."

"Let's have a look . . ." Rafe said, unzipping the portfolio. Miguel wandered up behind them, leaning over Rafe's shoulder for a better look.

Christine turned away to gather her things and add a bit of lipstick and some blusher. She took a brush and raked it once more through her hair, pulling out the rest of the curls and letting it fall naturally into a straight, unstyled blunt cut. Behind her she could hear the critical analysis of Tonee Holiday's book.

"This one's not bad, but those clothes are awful . . ."

"They're mine," Tonee admitted guilelessly.

Christine smiled to herself. She put on a headband and squirted some *Egoeste* behind her ears.

"You've got great skin. Nice shade of brown. Not too dark . . . no offense, but dark skin is harder to photograph," Rafe said.

"Yeah, and you should smile more in your pictures. It makes you look youthful," Miguel added.

"Okay," Tonee readily agreed, accepting the expert opinions.

"I've got to go," Christine said to the room at large, drawing everyone's attention.

Rafe and Miguel left Tonee to walk her to the door. Tonee stayed where she was, thoughtfully considering her own images.

"You were great, darling," Miguel gushed.

"Stunning," Rafe added, kissing her on the cheek. "There's no one like you."

Christine stopped at the door and faced them. "You have anything else planned for this afternoon?"

"Just developing those rolls we shot and seeing what's good."

"I'm doing a show tonight in Philadelphia," Miguel said.

"Good. Then you both have time to do some shots of Tonee. I think she needs a more professional looking portfolio."

"Christine . . ." Rafe said slowly, not wanting to mention the delicate subject of how he was going to be paid for his time and equipment.

"Let her wear some of those things I modeled this morning. The client doesn't have to know."

"Christine," Rafe tried again.

She smiled at him. "You can leave me a message on my answering machine if you need me to do another sitting," she said clearly. She air-kissed them both. "Thanks, guys. You made me look beautiful."

Miguel chortled. "That wasn't hard. We had good stuff to work with."

"So . . ." she said, arching a brow at Rafe as she opened the door. "Do we have a deal?"

"How come you want us to help the girl? Do you have any idea how many would-be stars come through that door?" Miguel questioned quietly, inclining his head briefly in Tonee's direction.

Christine sighed. "I owe her."

"But I don't," Rafe informed her.

"Then, do it for me?"

"Christine, has anyone ever refused you anything?" Rafe asked wryly.

"Not yet," she grinned, pivoting gracefully out the door.

It wasn't at all what Christine was expecting.

Actually, she had no idea what she would find once she reached the clinic. She thought perhaps it would be some sort of storefront walk-in place, like so many around the city, mostly in neighborhoods where the residents were too poor to afford good hospital care. But LIFELINE was a modern, three-story building, an annex to an existing neighborhood public hospital. Both were right in the middle of a community where other buildings were graffiti-covered and, in some cases, boarded up. But the LIFELINE structure was red brick and pristine.

It was brightly lit and more cheerful looking than Christine would have imagined, and the staff was pleasant and helpful . . . but cautious. The receptionist would not let her past the information desk until she'd explained her presence. Was she from one of the network stations, or a reporter from a newspaper? Was she from one of the other city agencies? Finally assured that Christine was none of those things, the woman relaxed.

"Well . . . you sure look like one of those news people."

"Don't trust them?" Christine asked sympathetically.

"It's not that. But our patients and their families have plenty of problems without nosy people poking around in their business. If you know what I mean."

Christine nodded, not sure that she did. What was it that outside people would want to know? "I think so."

"What can I do for you? You here to see a patient

or are you one of the new volunteers?" Her eyes grew mischievous and speculative. "You Dr. Chandler's girlfriend?"

The idea was so ridiculous under the circumstances that Christine nearly burst out laughing. "Why would you ask that?"

"Well, you *sure* don't look like you're from around here! And we've been teasing the doctor about not having a life outside of this clinic."

Christine smiled, unwilling to deny or confirm the woman's theory, and unable to come up with a plausible excuse. So she lied.

"Joyce Milner, Dr. Chandler's assistant, told me about the center when I made a donation last week. She said I really should come over and see for myself what goes on here. But if you think I shouldn't be here, I'll just . . ."

"No, no, that's okay," the woman said, flustered. "If Joyce sent you over that's good enough for me. I'll call Dr. Chandler and let him know you're here." She picked up the phone and began to dial. "What's your name?"

Christine quickly raised a hand. "Please don't bother the doctor. He's probably with his patients and I don't want to interrupt."

The woman hung up the phone and nodded. "All right. Do you know where to go?"

Christine smiled. "I'll go to the volunteer office."

The woman wrote out a visitor's pass and buzzed her through the security gate, pointing out the way to the volunteers' office. On the spur of the moment Christine changed direction and decided to explore a bit. She placed the self-stick visitor's tag over her left breast, unmindful of what the adhesive backing might do to the delicate silk fabric of her blouse. Feeling thus protected, she began to look around.

It was clear that the first floor housed administrative offices. There were offices for a director and assistant director, but neither door bore the name of D. Maxwell Chandler. There were also a small pharmacy, two rooms marked Classrooms A and B, and a kind of waiting room area with TV and a small library of books and magazines. There were several people seated around the room, poorly clothed and with blank, sorrowful expressions. Christine wondered if they were waiting for friends or family who had appointments . . . or if they simply had no place else to be. There was a certain lethargy about them, as if they were lost, and it was extremely hard to judge their ages because they appeared so worn out and tired. Christine also came across a room marked EMERGENCY: MEDICAL PERSONNEL ONLY. There was an empty gurney outside the closed door, and a wheelchair.

After another ten minutes of walking around the main floor and reading the various notices pinned to a bulletin board, Christine boarded the elevator and took it to the second floor.

This floor was different.

There were more people around. And lots of children. There was a nurses' station, just like in a large hospital facility, and there were several medical staff people seated behind the counter at desks—two women and one man, all in white hospital garb. She saw medical carts with supplies, and from one room somewhere down a hallway could be heard the sounds of a Saturday children's TV program.

Any possible solemnity was dispelled by Mylar balloons clustered in bunches, like bouquets of flowers, and tied to doorknobs or taped to the counter of the nurses' station. Some had floated free and languished, half-filled with helium, near the ceiling, their strings dangling. There was children's artwork taped to the walls. Every now and then Christine caught a glimpse of a child in hospital pajamas . . . all printed with Disney characters . . . sitting on laps of visiting family, or being carried from one room to another.

"Oh!" Christine uttered in startled surprise as something crashed into her side, jostling her, then dropped momentarily to the floor and then scrambled up again. She had to stop short in her tracks as the chubby little youngster of about five tried to hide behind a linen wagon. In hot pursuit was another little boy, moving equally fast even though he was attached to an IV stand, the plastic bag of nutriments swinging precariously back and forth as he wheeled it along the corridor in search of his playmate.

Christine couldn't help smiling at their impish behavior. She stared after the children realizing, suddenly, that she never had any contact with children at all in her day-to-day life. All of her friends were busy professionals with hectic lives. Although a few were married, only one couple had a child, but they lived in New Jersey and commuted into the city. Christine never saw the little boy. Now there was her sister Alexandra, of course, with Lauren Shani . . . but she hadn't been introduced to her niece yet.

It still bothered Christine that the reality of her sister having had a baby made her feel oddly left out. In a way she also felt that by becoming a mother Alex somehow put a distance between them, and Christine knew she hadn't been able to bridge the gap yet. But it was not her sister's fault. Christine didn't know if she was actually jealous of Alex and Parker's happiness. But it felt like it.

She'd put off going home to see her new niece because she was a little afraid, actually, of how she'd react to the baby. But she'd eased her guilt by sending a huge UPS package of baby things and toys from Bergdorf Goodman's. Yet, as Christine stood absorbing the atmosphere of the clinic, she felt no hesitancy about being around these kids.

She found herself curious and interested in these little specimens of future men and women.

"Hi, can I help you?"

Christine turned at the sound of the voice. It belonged to a very thin young woman dressed in jeans and a sweater. Her brown face looked drawn and her cheeks hollow. She was certainly not hospital staff, and Christine wondered if she was the newer, more urban variety of a candy-striper. She didn't know what to say. She couldn't imagine this woman being able to help her with anything. The clinic photo I.D. pinned to her sweater read, simply, 'Delores.'

"I was just looking around," Christine said carefully, not prepared to justify herself to this woman.

"We don't let people just look around. You have a kid here?" Delores asked suspiciously.

Christine frowned at her. The question was so pointed, but so unexpected. "No. I don't have a . . . child. And who are you?" she asked, looking the woman up and down.

"I work here," the response came back with a slight haughtiness. "I don't get paid or nothin', but I come every day."

"Are you a volunteer?" Christine asked.

"Yeah, that's right. My name is Delores," she suddenly added, as if remembering how she was taught to greet people. She held out her hand awkwardly.

Christine looked at the hand, noting the roughness and lack of care. The bitten nails and dry, ashy skin. She took the woman's hand but it was limp, as if she wasn't used to shaking anyone's hand and wasn't sure how to do it.

"My name is Christine."

"I bet people tell you all the time you're pretty," Delores said in simple observation. There was no judgment attached.

Christine grimaced. "Sometimes."

She became distracted when she heard the sudden chorus of 'yeas' and applause from a group of children in a room somewhere down the corridor. She turned briefly in that direction before giving her attention back to Delores.

"I just wanted to see what the clinic was like," Christine said in her most persuasive tone.

"It's a nice place . . . considering what goes on here," the woman said with surprising awareness. "I guess I can show you around."

The woman turned away to begin strolling slowly down a hall. Two of the staff people glanced up at them as they passed the central station, but otherwise did not say anything to Christine. She was well aware that she hadn't seen Dr. D. Maxwell Chandler, but she'd already devised several things to say to him should she encounter him. But just as quickly Christine experienced an emotional swing in the opposite direction, hoping she didn't see him after all. Even though he was part of the reason she'd wanted to come.

"What does go on here?" Christine asked.

Delores stared blankly down the hall, into space. "We take care of children. And we talk to parents about how to protect themselves so the children won't be born with AIDS. They get you medicine and deal with the people from welfare and even sometimes help you find a place to live.

"When things get bad for the kids they can come

here and Dr. Chandler does what he can to stabilize them so they can go home again with their families. Sometimes the kids have to stay here, or sometimes they have to come back every week or every month for checkups. We do other things for them, too, like take them on trips or have people come here. Last Christmas we took a busload to Radio City, and then we had a private room at McDonald's for lunch. It was great."

Christine was mesmerized by the woman's recitation. And she was aware that Delores made no clear distinction between the doctors and nurses who actually cared for the kids' medical needs, and people like herself who volunteered to help out. But also there was a sense that all this was routine for Delores, part of her life and what she did. There was neither particular joy nor sorrow in that fact . . . merely acceptance. They stopped in front of a door.

"This is the Power Ranger Ward. There's room for four boys."

"The Power Ranger Ward?" Christine asked, confused.

"Yeah. You know who they are, don't you?"

Christine didn't have a clue, but she never had a chance to respond since Delores just assumed she did know.

"That's their favorite show. For Halloween last year we had eight boys dressed as Power Rangers running around the ward saving people and karate-chopping each other." Delores shook her head in reflection. "They were so funny. But two of the boys are dead now."

She said it so matter-of-factly. Christine didn't know what to say . . . or if she should say anything at all. Just like that. *Two of the boys are dead.* The mere voicing of those words sent a peculiar wave of apprehension through her.

Delores was moving down the hall toward another room. "This is the Sleeping Beauty Ward . . ."

Christine raised her brows. "Why do you have names for the different wards?"

Delores looked at her directly, her eyes so old and suddenly seeming to hold so much pain and memories. "We don't want the kids to think they're in a hospital or that there's anything really wrong with them. We tell them all the rooms are special places and they're like magic." Delores shook her head in disbelief and shrugged. "That's what Dr. Chandler tells the kids"

Delores moved on, but Christine didn't follow, walking instead into the nearest ward room where three children in bed were reading or napping or watching their own TV. It was impossible to tell what was wrong with them just by looking at them. It didn't seem to be much, but Christine knew that they had to be here for a reason.

"Over here . . ." Delores pointed to the last room on the floor.

It was the room where all the laughter and sudden applause had come from moments earlier.

"This is the playroom. Kids get their transfusions here, too."

"Transfusion . . ." Christine repeated blankly, and peered into the room.

About eight children of varying ages were seated at the small tables coloring or playing with puzzles. But the rest were on the floor playing with wooden blocks as they constructed a tower-like building. Helping them was Dr. D. Maxwell Chandler. Except . . . he wasn't anything like the man Christine had encountered twice before.

The man sitting cross-legged on the floor was like a gentle giant. There was no concern about getting dirty or creased. His white shirt sleeves had been rolled up to the elbows, exposing muscular forearms. His tie was pulled loose, and there were kids hanging all over him. One little girl was attempting to use Maxwell's stethoscope . . . on his forehead. A little boy crawled across his lap trying to reach a particular block. Another little boy stood behind the doctor, hugging him around the throat and leaning over his shoulder to ask questions. And in a quiet, patient voice, the doctor was replying.

Christine stood and stared.

A transformation began to take place, slowly. Whatever she had been thinking about D. Maxwell Chandler, whatever she thought his personality was lacking, was suddenly irrelevant. This man was not hard or cold or remote or unfeeling. At least not to these children. And this was obviously more important to him than many other things. In a way, Christine felt envious of the children. It was an unfamiliar sensation. Not that she would in any way deny them the attention or time that Maxwell was giving so willingly . . . and with so much affection. But that he didn't have enough of himself left to share with anyone else. Nor, if her experience was typical, did Maxwell necessarily want to.

It made her feel odd. Like she really wasn't important, and her concerns didn't matter. Of course they did, but not when compared to children a third her age and size.

Christine blinked rapidly realizing, to her annoyance, that her throat was closing up and tears were quickly forming in her eyes. She was on alien ground. She felt suddenly bewildered and surreal. She had flashbacks of herself surrounded by friends and admirers, laughing and carefree and generally having the time of their lives. There had been lots of professionals in the industry who'd died of AIDS, but no one she'd known personally. This was not the same because these were children. She frowned, making a contrast of her life . . . and theirs.

She simply didn't know about being ill. She knew even less about being terminally ill, and dying.

"You going in to say hello to Dr. Chandler?" Delores asked.

Her voice startled Christine, reminding her where she was and with whom. She shook her head and withdrew from the room quickly, feeling confused . . . and more than a little embarrassed.

"I thought you said you knew Dr. Chandler," Delores reminded her.

Christine was further embarrassed. After all, she'd played a little fast and loose with the truth. "I don't want to bother him. He's with the children and they look like they're having a good time."

"Dr. Chandler, he's real good with the kids. He don't mind when they jump all over him like that."

"None of them looks like they . . . you know."

"Have AIDS?" Delores gestured vaguely toward the playroom. "The kids in there are not so bad right now. They come here for checkups, transfusions and stuff, but they don't have to stay."

"So they live with their families?"

Delores shrugged. "Most of them don't have families. They go to foster care."

As more of the realization sank in, Christine began to feel like she was suffocating. She was also feeling overwhelmed by the amount of information she was trying to absorb. She felt the tension beginning to pull at the base of her neck, squeezing behind her eyelids until the annoying throb of a headache took hold. She wondered if maybe she should leave now . . . and then she was afraid to.

The growing tension and awareness within her told her that she could leave . . . she could walk out the door and go back where she came from. But she knew, with a kind of finality that was frightening and disorienting, that she was never going to be the same again. Two thoughts came quickly to her mind. That champagne dinner she'd indulged in with her friends after returning from Europe, and the announcement of the birth of Lauren. The contrast between the two events . . . and this center . . . were physically jarring.

"You mean . . . these kids don't have families? Or mothers?"

Delores looked at Christine again with those eyes that had seen too much. But again, there was more reality than feeling behind her response. "Most of these kids' mamas gone. Died of AIDS. If they have family they either too sick to take care of them, or don't want them 'cause they afraid of getting it, too."

"Oh," Christine said almost inaudibly. A totally inadequate response, she realized, but she didn't know what else to say.

Delores made a sweeping gesture with her arm. "This floor here we call the *safe zone*. Like, maybe you stand a chance of getting better, even though most of them won't. Upstairs is the worst," she said with the first sign of emotion Christine had witnessed.

"What do you call *upstairs?*" Christine asked, feeling very tired, all at once . . . and very dispirited.

"Heaven," Delores said without a trace of irony. "We don't tell the kids that . . . but sometimes they know anyway."

Christine didn't have to ask Delores what she

meant by that. She at least knew about the odds of surviving AIDS or being HIV positive. There were none.

"Delores?" one of the workers at the nurses' station called. "I need you to go downstairs for me. Darryl Peters was just brought in by his grandmother. Dr. Jeffreys is checking him out but he's going to have to stay."

"Pneumonia?" Delores asked.

When the nurse merely nodded, Delores shook her head. "That's bad . . ." she said, turning away without saying anything else.

Christine silently watched Delores leave, and knew that she should, too. But something Delores had said kept repeating in Christine's mind. About the third floor. It was the last floor of the clinic and she wanted to see it. She took the elevator up, expecting alarms to go off and lights to flash because she was venturing beyond the boundaries allowed to visitors. But no one stopped her.

There was a distinct difference in the top floor from the other two in the center. This last floor had no bright decorations or visuals to distract from the environment. There was the same nurses' station with three personnel. But the atmosphere was decidedly different. It was not so much quiet as hushed. There were no kids running around in their cartoon sleepwear, no welcoming greeting from staff or volunteers. The people up here were occupied with charts and monitor screens and telephones and low, serious conversation.

They all looked up when she walked off the elevator. There was a silent question in the air. Their silent stares asked who she was. Christine told her second lie.

"I'm . . . a new volunteer. I'm just getting acclimated," she said with quiet confidence. They accepted that and went back to their work.

Christine felt the cheerfulness of the second floor echoing in her head in sharp contrast to the somberness of this level. She remembered the sight of Dr. Chandler sitting on the playroom floor earnestly engaged in activity with those children . . . and began to understand. The heaviness she'd been feeling before stayed with her . . . and intensified. Christine felt like a vessel filling slowly with liquid. When it reached the rim, she didn't know what was going to happen. Was it going to stop because it had reached the top? Or was it going to spill over . . . and make a mess.

She began walking around the floor.

The wards up here had no cute names. The walls were glass, so the staff could see inside. The beds seemed larger and more complicated with cranks and knobs and monitors and tubes and coils and attachments, all going to a child . . . who all seemed so much smaller than the kids on the floor below. And so still.

The first thing Christine noticed, besides the deep quiet, was the thin, limp lethargy of the children. Some may have been sitting up in bed, or attempting to read, but they looked like it took every ounce of energy to move. Eyes seemed oversized in faces that were pinched and narrow. Hair was flat and dull and so sparse the children's scalp could be detected.

"Oh, my God . . ." Christine heard herself say. It didn't sound exactly like her voice. But then . . . she didn't exactly feel like herself anymore.

She stood outside one of the glass-enclosed wards and looked poignantly at the occupants. One little boy looked to be about six, and there was a girl possibly as old as eleven or twelve.

They had made it this far.

Christine quickly turned away, feeling the tightening continue in her chest and throat. She walked on down the hall and came to another ward where there were several cribs. Two of them were occupied by sleeping children, tiny little lumps under white blankets, one sucking a thumb and the other breathing audibly through the nose. At the last moment Christine noticed a young woman in a chair next to another crib, cradling a baby in her arms. Christine could only see the top of the child's head, with almost no hair. The rest of the baby was swathed in a pale blue hospital blanket. The woman holding her appeared to be nursing her from a bottle. But then Christine realized that it wasn't a bottle but some sort of plastic tube about an inch and a half wide and about a foot long. She had no idea what the woman was doing to the child, except that it seemed a practice that was routine and one that was necessary.

The woman looked up suddenly and caught Christine's gaze. A faint smile came to her mouth, although it didn't quite reach her dark eyes. Christine felt grateful for the signal so that she felt less an intruder. She tentatively returned the smile and continued to stand and watch.

"What are you doing here?"

Christine gasped and jumped so violently her heart thudded in her chest. She dropped her purse and whirled around at the sound of Maxwell Chandler's voice.

"For God's sake," she uttered, caught between annoyance and shame. "You scared me."

"How did you get up here?" Maxwell asked again, just as sharply.

Christine gave him a baleful glare and bent to

pick up her purse. It gave her a moment to try and recover from the surprise. The shock. It was more than just having Maxwell Chandler jump on her so harshly. It was also noticing the strong column of his neck through the open collar of his shirt, and the dark tuft of curling black hair. It was noticing that his voice had a rich quality that was commanding, even as he was yelling at her. It was experiencing an odd weakening and awareness that this man could be equally strong . . . and gentle, although she had only known one side. Christine knew her reaction was completely out of the blue and inappropriate. And suddenly, it changed everything.

"I was just looking around. I . . ."

"We don't allow anyone but family on this floor. And volunteers."

She could feel the rush of blood to her face and she remained silent through the censure, not knowing quite what to say to justify her curiosity. "I wanted to see what LIFELINE was all about," she said, raising her chin defiantly. "Your receptionist mentioned it."

"You're not interested in what we do here," he said tightly.

Christine blinked at him. He had changed again. Back into the man she'd first met. Back into the man of steel who held her in such contempt. But why? What had she done that was so terrible that he couldn't show her the warm, playful man she'd caught a glimpse of on the second floor? That he *must* be for parents to trust their children to his care. Why didn't she rate a soft voice, a welcome? She lifted her chin and narrowed her gaze on him, having no intention of cowering just because she had invaded his territory.

"Don't tell me what I'm not interested in. I made

a donation. I've read about the clinic and the good work that you and everyone does with the children."

He narrowed his eyes, too, his jaw working reflexively. "There is no such thing as *good* work here," he murmured softly between clenched teeth.

Christine took a step back and blinked at him again. He was furious. Livid. But why at her? What had she done? *What had she done?*

"This is a place where children die. And there's not a damn thing I can do about it."

Christine clamped her mouth shut. She was afraid to try and speak. She had guessed that, of course, but she didn't need to have it thrown in her face. She didn't have to be told that these children were playing a waiting game. She could finish looking around . . . to see what goes on . . . and then she could go home. Healthy. Back to . . .

"I'm sorry," was all she could say. She could barely get it out, her throat was so tight. She bit her tongue to keep her chin from starting to quiver.

Maxwell sighed, trying to control himself. "I don't want you to be sorry. It doesn't help. And these kids don't need your pity. They don't feel sorry for themselves so why should you? I don't want you playing tourist here, Miss Morrow, or looking for a publicity opportunity . . ."

She felt defeated. She could feel her brows tilt up on the inside, the way they did when she was close to tears, and the water began to flood around her eyes. The way it used to happen when she was a very little girl . . . when she was being chastised for something and she knew she'd been wrong. It hadn't happened in years. "I'm not insensitive and cruel," she said tightly. "I haven't done anything to you, or to hurt anyone else. Why . . . why are you so awful to me?"

Maxwell stared at her for a long moment, as if trying to decide what to say . . . and how much. He looked into her face and for a fleeting moment saw genuine confusion. Her green eyes aided in the impression of open vulnerability. He noted that her hair was different today. Not full and sensuously wild, but without any curls. A simple headband held it from her face, which was totally clear of any makeup beyond lipstick. And yet, she still managed to be noticeable. Striking.

Maxwell tightened his jaw, and the muscles corded just beneath his ears. He leaned a fraction of an inch closer to Christine. "You don't do anything that helps a living soul . . . except yourself. I have no patience with that."

Christine's eyes widened. She was so stunned at his words she wasn't even sure she'd heard right. And then they began repeating in her head.

"You want to see what goes on here? Let me show you . . ."

With that he took hold of her arm and turned her into the ward right behind them both. She tried to resist, and then realized how utterly foolish she would appear to be struggling with a doctor on the ward of a children's clinic. She let Maxwell lead her to the foot of one of the cribs where the child—a little boy, Christine could discern—lay. She could see that he wasn't sleeping as she'd first assumed, but was staring blankly into the space between the bars of his bed. He was a little black child, but his hair, not the natural kinkiness of his race, was straight as a pin.

"Nathan is seven years old," Maxwell said in a low, clear voice. "He's had pneumonia three times since the start of the year. We've been giving him blood transfusions but they no longer make a difference. His count is very bad—plus we have to give him inhalation therapy twice a day. He can't sit up by himself anymore . . ."

"Stop it . . ." Christine hissed at the doctor, trying to turn away. She jerked her arm. Maxwell held her fast.

"It's just a matter of time," he said, and moved her to the next bed. "This is Katie. She's eighteen months old. She was born HIV positive, but we're hoping she'll be in the small percentage of kids who simply outgrow the virus before they reach the age of two. We're watching her closely."

"Then why is she here?"

Maxwell looked down on Christine. "Because no one wants her. She's been in four different foster homes since she was born. Taking care of her properly takes a lot of time and patience. And there are risks. There aren't that many people who have both and are willing to give it to children who aren't their own."

The blood that had made her overly warm five minutes ago now seemed to drain from her body as Christine blinked down at the little girl, with her rounded brown cheeks and tangle of uncombed hair. She looked so sweet and lovely. So healthy. "She must have *some* family?"

"What family?" he asked rhetorically. "Her mother died of AIDS four months after she was born. We don't know about the father. Katie had an older brother. He's gone, too."

Christine finally freed her arm and turned to head out of the ward. The woman in the chair was still there, holding the baby. She didn't seem to have paid any attention to what was going on between herself and Dr. Chandler. She slowed her footsteps as she passed the woman, who didn't look up from the child. Christine continued out into the hallway.

Maxwell was right behind her. She faced him abruptly, swallowing back any show of emotion.

"What about her? What's she doing to that baby?"

Maxwell turned, crossed his arms over his chest, and stared through the glass at the woman and child. "That's Wendy," he said in a sudden quiet tone of reverence. "That's not her real name, but we call her that. We like to think of her as the little girl in Peter Pan. We wish that our Wendy could fly away to never-never land where she could always be a kid, and not be sick, and not . . ."

He turned his head to glance at her, and Christine could see that his eyes were filled with . . . helplessness.

"Die?" she supplied.

"That would be preferable to what she's going through right now. But Wendy's a fighter. That's her aunt. She's giving inhalation therapy to Wendy. Children with AIDS don't get Kaposi's sarcoma. They get L.I.P and have trouble breathing, as if they have asthma." Maxwell gave his attention back to the girl and her aunt. His voice dropped even lower. "She keeps holding on. She's not a baby, Miss Morrow. She's four years old."

Christine didn't understand at first. And then it hit her. Hard. She drew in her breath, looked once more into the room at the waste and inevitability, and tried to escape. Without another word she headed briskly toward the elevator. But she knew she didn't want to wait for it. She chose the stairwell instead.

Christine pushed through the exit door so hard that it banged gently against the wall. She started down so fast she nearly fell. The door swished closed behind her, but in a moment opened again.

"Miss Morrow . . ."

She kept going, but the sound of him calling her made Christine angry, and then hurt . . . and then terribly sad. It was that which caused the tears to finally spill and a quiet short sound to escape from her.

Christine got to the second level and saw that there was no reentry from the staircase. She jerked on the doorknob but it was locked.

"Christine," Maxwell said, reaching out to touch her.

"No!" she sobbed, evading his hand and heading down the next flight. The strap of her purse slipped from her shoulder and the weight of her bag caused it to pull awkwardly on the inside of her elbow. She was breathing heavily now and just the surprise and stress of trying to hold her reactions inside caused the tears to fall in jagged trails down her cheeks.

The first floor door was locked as well. She uttered an oath under her breath in frustration and slammed a fist against the door. He had caught up to her. Christine whirled and opened her hand. She swung and slapped him soundly. It took him by surprise and he stopped to stare at her.

Christine glared at him. "How dare you! Just who do you think you are? So you're a doctor and you care. That doesn't give you moral superiority over the rest of us." The welling inside seemed to be approaching tidal wave dimensions. She tried to brush the tears away with shaky fingers.

"Look," he began.

"No, *you* look! You don't know enough about me to judge me. I am *not* selfish. I am *not* unaware. I . . . I . . ."

He just stared at her, his gaze sweeping over her distressed features, noting that the way she cried made Christine Morrow seem so young. And he didn't feel angry with her anymore. At the moment his reasons didn't seem relevant. He had cut to the bone and he wasn't sure that's what he'd wanted to do to her.

Christine sobbed again once. She brought her hands up to her face to cover her trembling mouth. Her eyes were swimming in tears as she tried to look Maxwell in the face. She slowly shook her head.

"My God . . . she . . . she was so tiny," Christine got out in a thin, anguished voice. She buried her face in her hands and cried harder.

She felt strong fingers and hands on her arms. She felt herself being pulled forward as masculine arms wound firmly around her. Her forehead was pressed into Maxwell Chandler's chest. One hand held her around the waist, and the other slid to Christine's nape and massaged the soft column of her neck. Her tears soaked into his shirt and seemed to release a kind of steamy warmth that was male and strong. Her spine loosened and she let her weight rest against him, her body causing his to shake with her crying.

Maxwell didn't say anything. He wanted to use her name, but somehow it seemed too personal. He frowned to himself at the irony of holding Christine Morrow in an attempt to comfort her. It was his turn to say he was sorry . . . but he couldn't. Instead, he held her, rediscovering all the nuances of her feminine form, recalling the shape and feel from the first time they'd met. He was speechless at her response, and sensed the sincerity of it seep into him, along with the tears that soaked the front of his shirt near the opening at the throat. He could still feel the sharp sting of her hand. And he wondered how he would have felt if she'd really used the full force he knew she was capable of.

She was taller than any woman he'd ever met . . . or held. And there was something intriguing about the way her head just reached the level of his nose, and the rest of her body could fit correctly against his own. Thigh to thigh . . . stomach to stomach almost, although she was incredibly slender and light. He knew exactly where her breasts touched him, and Maxwell drew in a sudden quiet breath as he remembered the feel of her under his hands. He found himself holding her loosely, afraid he could hurt her more than he already had. But he'd *wanted* to hurt her. Perhaps he'd been confusing Christine with the other *her.*

Her name was Rachel.

She wasn't as tall as Christine Morrow, or as delicately built. She wasn't as beautiful, either. But what Rachel had in common with Christine was the single attribute that Maxwell was impatient with: the need to be at the center of everyone else's life. Only now, holding Christine . . . who had a different feel in his arms, could he sense something else he might have been wrong about. Christine Morrow was *not* without feelings or awareness. Or a conscience. But that did not make it easier for Maxwell to feel contrite. It only made it that much more difficult to forget her.

And Rachel had never cried. About anything. She threw tantrums. She teased. She made love with him with a wanton passion that had held him a willing but tortured prisoner. She had been demanding and impossible. But none of that had stopped Maxwell from loving her . . . or *her* from breaking his heart.

He reflected on the comparison for about half a second. And then imperceptibly tightened his arms around Christine Morrow. Maxwell wasn't sure if he was actually comforting her . . . or reassuring himself.

Maxwell silently held Christine and listened to the purging of emotions. He felt stiff and awkward because he hadn't been prepared to switch gears with her. And he certainly wasn't prepared to treat Christine Morrow as if he might really have made a mistake about her.

Still, holding her seemed the least he could do for having forced some nasty but compelling realities onto her. Maxwell closed his eyes briefly, listening to her sounds of . . . he wasn't sure. Despair? Shock? Embarrassment? He turned his head a little and inadvertently pressed his lips against her temple. He quickly moved his mouth from the appealing softness and scent of her skin to letting his cheek rest against hers. He decided not to say anything. The hand which had been around her small waist slid comfortingly up her back.

Christine went silent and still. And she stopped crying. No hiccups. No sniffling. She came back from the awful jolt of her trip through the clinic and was herself again. Except that she was in Maxwell Chandler's arms and somehow that made things very strange between them. The first thing that occurred to Christine was the memory of having slapped him. She winced slightly at the mindless spontaneity with which she'd lashed out. But the second thing that happened was her acute awareness of being touched by the doctor. Like that night at the fundraiser. Like the day of her visit to his office. And now . . . there was something startling and familiar about his strong arms, his large, well-shaped hands, the solid wall of his chest.

Christine sighed quietly, but then braced her

hands against his chest and gently pushed herself away. They looked into one another's eyes and simply stared, very much as if they'd never seen each other before, and couldn't understand how they'd ended up in an embrace. But neither were they embarrassed.

Maxwell allowed Christine to step back, but he kept his hands lightly on her waist. He was rather fascinated by the fact that her eyes didn't turn red when she cried. They just seemed to sparkle brightly with that interesting green light. It suddenly seemed very quiet, and he was aware of her as if she'd left some part of herself still leaning against him. He lifted his hand and held it aloft for a moment, near her face. But her eyes never blinked, never shifted from looking deeply into his own. Maxwell lightly touched her cheek and jaw, his thumb brushing just at the corner of her mouth.

That broke the spell.

Christine took another step back, completely out of his reach. Maxwell put his hands into his pockets. They were almost back to where they had been before.

"Are you all right now?" he asked.

Christine raised her chin. Out came the third lie. "I'm fine."

He nodded and squared back his shoulders. "Good," he said, although his voice seemed a bit hoarse. "I have to get back upstairs."

Maxwell reached past her to push a button next to the crash bar across the door. There was a click, and he could then push the door open without setting off the emergency alarms. He held it and gestured for Christine to precede him.

She found herself back on the first floor, in a small passageway to the left of the main entrance and reception area. Christine hastily wiped her hand across her face, removing the last of her tears. She headed toward the door, but his voice stopped her.

"I hope you've satisfied your curiosity," he said in that familiar flat voice that kept her at arm's length.

It irritated her. But she merely looked at him, her feelings and expression now well hidden. She was back in control. "I found out quite a lot. I'm sorry there's a need for a place like LIFELINE, but I'm glad that it exists. And I'm sorry about you," Christine said on a quiet note.

He frowned in surprise. "What?"

She shook her head and pursed her lips, her spirit quickly rejuvenating. Neither of them made any reference to those moments spent together in the stairwell. "I bet you were a top student. Being black, you probably worked harder than anyone in your class to prove how smart you are." She tilted her head and regarded him closely. "I bet you did everything right, never had any doubts about your abilities, and graduated in the top ten percent of your class . . ."

He raised his brows suspiciously.

Christine grimaced cynically. "You probably didn't think I'd know about things like class percentages or standing. My sister graduated from Georgetown magna cum laude." She leaned very close to him, causing the suspicious expression to deepen in his dark face, and his jaw to clench. "The only problem is, doctor, you don't know the first thing about really caring about people. They forgot to teach you how to be fair. And understanding." Christine took several steps toward the exit and then turned quickly to face him again. "And another thing . . . you need to get over yourself real fast. Being a doctor does not make up for being a bastard!"

He stared as she turned and walked out the door of the clinic. This time he didn't go after her.

Christine walked several yards down the street and stopped, feeling her bravado desert her as she began to tremble. Despite the warm spring day she shivered and tried to catch her breath. She couldn't believe what she'd been through, or what she'd seen. She couldn't believe that what went on in the clinic really existed. Why didn't people know about these children? Why wasn't more being done to help them?

How could parents *let* it happen?

"Hi. I wondered where you went."

Christine came out of her reverie and glanced up. It was the volunteer, Delores. She had her arms crossed over her thin chest and was looking at her almost shyly, like she wasn't sure if they knew each other well enough to speak. Christine tried to smile. This woman knew things that she didn't.

"I'm just leaving."

"Me, too. I'm finished for the day." She hesitated. "You don't live around here, do you?" she asked, as if the idea was ridiculous.

Christine shook her head, again aware of a contradiction about the woman. There was tremendous strength as well as obvious frailty housed in the same body. "No, I don't. I live . . . downtown."

"I thought so," Delores nodded.

Christine frowned thoughtfully at the woman, looking her over again carefully but doubtfully, as if she was considering something that would never have happened before.

"Is there someplace around here to eat?" Christine suddenly asked.

Delores blinked and squinted. "You mean like a place to sit down?"

"That's right."

"Well . . ." Delores glanced around. "There's a Burger King a few blocks away. But, you don't want to go there."

"Why not?"

Delores pulled the corners of her mouth down. "Wrong kind of people hang around there. You have to be careful."

Christine sighed and glanced around the street. It was certainly not a pleasant area. Poor people lived here. Poor and sick children. She wasn't used to this. Even before she'd moved to New York and made lots of money, she never wanted for anything. She got love and attention from her family, a safe and clean home. She thought of the child, Wendy, up on the third floor, and a wave of sorrow coursed through Christine. She saw again that small wrapped little body lying in the woman's arms on the third floor . . . simply disappearing, little by little. Christine could feel the possibility of more tears just waiting to spill out. "Why not? Will you join me? I'd like a chance to talk with you."

"Me? About what?"

"I want to know about being a volunteer. I want to know why you became one."

Delores took several moments to answer. Then she shrugged. "Okay . . ." she responded, still reluctant. She turned in the direction of the restaurant with Christine falling into step next to her.

Five

"Hey, girlfriend. I wondered if you were going to stand me up."

Christine smiled vaguely as she stepped into Cynthia's apartment. She could hear conversation and light laughter from the living room. And the low-volume jazz of Wynton Marsalis playing from the CD unit. She didn't want to confess that the thought had crossed her mind. She was not feeling particularly sociable. Keith had called just as she was leaving, and their conversation had escalated into a fight. And it was her fault.

Keith had asked for her advice and she'd felt annoyed that he couldn't work out his choices on his own. It was as if he not only needed her guidance but her approval as well.

She'd hung up on him, and now she was feeling sorry. And annoyed that she was feeling sorry.

"I had the devil of a time catching a cab."

"Why didn't you drive?" Cynthia asked, closing the door and taking Christine's lightweight silk jacket, a match for her short, smoke-grey, sleeveless tank dress.

Christine pouted. "Because finding a cab is only marginally easier than finding a parking space in this city. Besides, my car has 'steal me' stamped all over it."

Cynthia laughed as she led the way into the center of the apartment. "Not that that stopped you from buying it. You have to be crazy to own a car in Manhattan, but only you would do it anyway and get an expensive, showy car to boot. Girl, I have no sympathy for you."

Christine sighed. "I like the freedom it gives me. I can just get in and go."

The conversation came to a halt when the two of them entered the living room. Cynthia went right over to a middle-aged black man and slipped her arm through his. Christine lost her focus and her attention immediately wandered as she became aware that Maxwell Chandler was among the guests. She didn't have to look at him to know he was there. He stood taller than anyone else in the room, with an aura that was electric. She could feel his presence as if it was a living thing. Her stomach muscles curled when she briefly considered their last meeting and the powerful effect he'd had on her. His dark skin contrasted against a collarless cream shirt under a sports jacket. Christine didn't deign to acknowledge him right away, even as she wondered if she was going to be able to keep her reactions to herself.

"James, I want you to meet Christine Morrow. You remember—I told you about her. Fabulous model . . . the woman is all over the place," Cynthia said affectionately. She glanced with dreamy eyes at the man whose arm she hugged to her body. "And this is James Weston, cardiologist and handsome devil . . ."

Everyone laughed.

James Weston held out his hand to Christine and smiled at her graciously. He was a stout man with round, pleasant features. He wore glasses and sported a mustache, although his face was rather boyish looking.

"It's a pleasure. Cynthia has talked quite a lot about you."

Christine arched a brow. "Oh, oh . . ." she murmured, causing more laughter. "Please don't repeat any of it. I have enough trouble with my image as it is," she said quietly but pointedly. "Congratulation on your engagement. Cynthia's one of the nicest people in our business."

James put an arm around Cynthia's back and winked at her. "I don't know about the business. How about the *world?*"

Christine continued to smile at their gentle bantering, feeling a curious stab of envy as she watched them—and feeling, again, a terrible isolation. But also, hearing in her head Maxwell Chandler's summation of her life and her character. Her cheeks and neck were infused with a rush of warm blood as Christine recalled how his words had really dug pretty deep. Deeper than she would have imagined. And more hurtful.

Cynthia pushed at James in embarrassment and stepped out of her fiancé's embrace as he quickly planted a kiss on her brown cheek. She took hold of Christine's hand. "Come meet everybody else."

Christine allowed Cynthia to introduce her to the ten guests, professional men and woman who knew either Cynthia or James. But as quickly as she was introduced, she forgot their names. Not out of arrogance, but because she felt as if her entire being was zeroed in on one soul, one person, and his very existence seemed so absolute.

"Christine, this is a friend of James's, Dr. D. Maxwell Chandler. He's a pediatrician."

Christine didn't extend her hand . . . and neither did he.

But for a quick, intense moment they stared at one another. The cool appraisal was back in his eyes, but not as distant as Christine first remembered. There was a history between them now, and he couldn't ignore her . . . nor plead ignorance. Christine felt like she was squaring off with him, but she also felt a peculiar sensation that seemed almost intimate. If she could, she realized that she would have blushed.

"And this is Dr. Frances Grimes. She's an OB/GYN and shares offices with Maxwell."

Christine heard the woman say hello. She knew she was of average height, and rather pretty.

"We've met," Christine spoke up, her tone ironic, although she didn't think anyone detected it but Maxwell.

Cynthia looked confused. "You know Fran?"

Frances Grimes laughed. "No. She means she's already met Maxwell. So . . . you're the one," she said with thoughtful interest.

"Excuse me?" Cynthia asked.

Frances looked up at Maxwell briefly. "Joyce, the office assistant, kept going on about this famous model who came to see Maxwell. Are congratulations in order, Miss Morrow?"

Christine quirked a corner of her mouth. She was sure that Frances Grimes already knew the answer to that. "Please call me Christine. No, I'm not pregnant. And I don't have any children."

"Miss Morrow came to me by mistake," Maxwell finally spoke up.

"It wasn't a mistake," Christine countered, challenging him with her eyes. "Dr. Chandler turned out to be just what I expected."

The corner of his mouth and one brow slowly rose. He nodded perceptibly at her jab.

"Well, I'm glad you know each other. James, Maxwell, and Frances all went to Howard together, and Frances did her residency under Maxwell in Chicago."

Frances smiled at Christine. "Yes, Maxwell and I got along so well that going into practice together made sense."

Christine allowed her gaze to touch on him. "How convenient."

"Okay, you're on your own," Cynthia said, walking away. "I have to go play hostess . . ."

For just the merest second, Christine was shocked to feel panic sweep through her. She felt outnumbered as she glanced back to Maxwell and Frances. She was going to excuse herself and circulate among the other guests when Frances stepped forward and touched her arm, looking up into her face with open curiosity.

"Tell me about being a model. How did you get started?"

Christine blinked at the doctor. She felt awkward and unnatural, towering over this woman with her friendly, open face. She didn't want to talk about being a model. She didn't want to talk about herself at all. After having witnessed what Maxwell Chandler and Frances Grimes did for a living, Christine was beginning to feel like her life was a fraud. Pointless.

"Did you just walk into an agency one day and they fell all over you?"

Christine shook her head. She was aware of Maxwell quietly excusing himself as he left the two women to talk. She continued to ignore him, as he did her. "No. Actually it was my brother-in-law who pointed me in the right direction and gave me some contacts. I was studying fashion design for a while and did internships with Eileen Fisher and Karl Lagerfeld. Someone suggested I model instead. *Then* everyone fell all over me," Christine said dryly. She was surprised when Dr. Frances Grimes laughed in delight.

Dinner might have been more enjoyable, Christine felt, if she hadn't been seated right next to Maxwell Chandler. She considered that Cynthia might have done it on purpose, except that Frances Grimes was placed on the other side of him. But she couldn't relax, couldn't enjoy the food prepared by Cynthia herself who certainly hadn't forgotten her lessons learned in her mother's kitchen in Missouri. She picked at everything, moving the lima beans and saffron rice and baked chicken around on her plate until everyone else was finished and the dishes could be cleared.

The conversation was mostly about health and medicine . . . and children, everyone utterly fascinated and impressed with the work Maxwell was doing at LIFELINE. They talked glowingly of the article in *Ebony*, and how important it was to get that kind of coverage. And it was clear that Maxwell and Frances worked well together. In their joint practice, she started out with the health care even before a child was born, seeing many of them through infancy. Then Maxwell took over when they were toddlers.

Christine felt almost invisible, and it was a strange, dispiriting sensation. She had nothing to add to the conversation, and that brought back the encounters with Maxwell. Especially that afternoon at the clinic. She hazarded a look at his profile and found him utterly focused on the table talk, making contributions and rebutting comments—asking insightful questions or answering them.

He was very smart, she realized. He was dedicated. And Maxwell Chandler, it was extremely clear to Christine, was doing work that was very important. She noticed again the way his jaw muscles worked when he talked, the way his face was so focused and intense. She saw that he didn't use that expression just with her, but that it was an inherent part of him. He was intense because he did care. And because, she realized, time was not on his side.

"Anyway, I think the camp experience would do you all some good," Maxwell was concluding. There was obviously a great deal of skepticism around the table.

Christine glanced around and tried to pick up the threads of the conversation.

"My ego doesn't fit into tents or sleeping bags anymore," James chuckled.

"Not to mention the rest of him," Cynthia teased.

"It's a wonderful experience," Frances said, sitting forward eagerly. "Maxwell and I feel strongly that the children shouldn't just see doctors in hospitals. They should know that there are things they can do that other children do. Like go to camp."

"And we don't just have doctors coming to be with the children," Maxwell added. "We have actors and musicians and craftspeople and even a baker, who comes up for the week and lends a hand. Everyone has something to offer."

"Except Cynthia and me," Christine said clearly. All heads turned to her. "We're virtually useless," she said with self-deprecating humor. It worked. Everyone laughed lightly and demurred that that wasn't so. Except Maxwell.

"Oh, I don't think I could go," Cynthia said, shaking her head.

James took hold of her hand and nodded. "Cynthia is a marshmallow when it comes to children. She can't stand to see them sick or hurt."

"I'd probably embarrass myself and cry all the time," Cynthia said softly. "To think that all of those babies . . ."

"You can cook for them, Cynthia," Christine quickly interjected. "I remember that you make the most indecent fudge brownies. And a mean macaroni and cheese. The kids would love that."

"What would you remember about that?" Cynthia said, getting into the lighter mood quickly. "You're always complaining that all that stuff is fattening."

Christine grinned playfully. "Fond memories. If I ever give up modeling I think I'm going to *love* gaining ten pounds on foods I haven't eaten for years." Again she drew chuckles from the other guests. Only Maxwell seemed to remain stubbornly unmoved or charmed by her attempts to be part of the evening.

"What about you, Christine? Why don't you come up to camp? I'm sure there's something you can do with the children," Cynthia suggested.

Christine grimaced prettily. "Honey, I'm afraid of insects and snakes," she said. "I'm suspicious of anything that has more than two legs."

"Well, maybe you could help the children keep journals the way you do. Oooops!" Cynthia said, covering her mouth with her hand.

Christine winced. It was one of the few secrets she'd shared with people she knew in her industry. Usually the less said, the less there was to gossip about. But she didn't get mad at Cynthia, only embarrassed because keeping diaries is something adolescent girls usually did.

"Oh, really?" Frances asked. "So do I. I started when I was in medical school."

Someone else at the table nodded. "Yeah, me too. It's a great way to get your feelings out."

Christine felt relief that no one took her pastime lightly. She sensed Maxwell looking at her, but refused to meet his gaze, wondering what he was thinking.

"Well, you must have some interesting observations to make," another woman said to Christine. "Especially since you've met so many rich and famous people. Cynthia has told us some of the stories. Maybe you should publish your writing some day."

Christine smiled pleasantly. "I don't think so. I could get sued."

"Anyway . . ." Maxwell began so that he gained everyone's attention. "We're always looking for volunteers, so there's still time to sign up and come along."

"Well, while you all talk about it, I'm going to get dessert . . ." Cynthia said, excusing herself from the table.

"I'll help," Christine said, getting up and following her friend into the kitchen.

"So, what do you think of James?" Cynthia asked the moment they were alone.

Christine sighed and leaned back against the refrigerator, her hands braced behind the small of her back. "I think he's the one."

"Girl, I can't believe how lucky I was to find him."

"I'd say James Weston is the one who's lucky."

"Thank you," Cynthia said graciously. "Now all we need to do is find a good man for you. What do

you think of Dr. D. Maxwell Chandler? I have a
thing for big men. He's certainly tall enough for
you."

Christine pursed her lips and shook her head,
but the question made her stomach muscles tighten
for a moment. "Forget it. He's too serious for me.
What does the D stand for?"

Cynthia turned to Christine with a puzzled frown.
"D?"

"As in Dr. D. Maxwell Chandler."

"Oh. Honey, I haven't a clue. Everyone calls him
Maxwell. I don't think I've ever heard him say what
it stands for. James says he's one of the best pediatricians in the country."

Deep in thought, Christine took out cups and sau-
cers for the coffee, then took the liberty of finding
dessert plates in the overhead cabinet. "What does
he do for fun? Or does he know what that is?"

"He and James belong to the same health club.
You can see which one of them works at it," she
laughed, and then turned her attention to Christine.
"Why'd you go to see him?"

Christine shrugged. "It was a mistake. I . . . sort
of met him that night I saw you at the fashion show.
I've been having a lot of headaches lately and . . .
well, my sister insisted I see someone about it. I
didn't know Maxwell was a children's doctor."

"I was only teasing about matchmaking with you
two. Maxwell is an interesting man. He doesn't talk
about himself very much. He could have a string of
women if he wanted to but he's not a womanizer. I
don't think he's ever been married."

"That's good," Christine murmured softly.
"What's Frances Grimes's story?"

But Cynthia didn't get a chance to answer as

James came into the kitchen looking for her. "Anything I can do?"

They snuggled and nibbled at each other until Christine quietly slipped out of the way and wandered back toward the living room. Someone had slid open the doors leading to the terrace. People had gotten up from the table and made themselves comfortable once more around the living room, talking in small clusters. Frances was among them, but Christine didn't see Maxwell. Sighing, she walked through the terrace door, letting the slightly cool evening air blow gently over her. She leaned over the railing and glanced thoughtfully out over the city.

Her own apartment was only on the sixth floor, but way up here Christine felt disoriented, almost floating above the city as she knew it. And it was odd to be with this mix of people. She wasn't sure, yet, how she felt about it. For one thing, this was a much more adult group than she was used to. For the first time she could draw a comparison between these people and the models, actors and actresses, photographers, writers, and restaurant owners that seemed to comprise her list of friends and acquaintances. Her side didn't come off looking very good. On the other hand, what was really wrong with being an actress or actor, model or photographer, if you were good at it? Not everyone could be a diplomat or brain surgeon. Not everyone was cut out for leadership or responsibility on the level of Cynthia's guests. But they hadn't made her feel small and useless. Only Maxwell Chandler had succeeded in that. Christine realized she wasn't indignant or angry about it anymore. Only surprisingly thoughtful . . . and concerned.

She was twenty-seven years old. Almost twenty-eight. Despite her heated defense to Maxwell, she wasn't interested in being a forty-year-old model . . . a mannequin for other people to display and manipulate. Yet, for the first time since she'd begun modeling at the age of twenty, Christine wondered what she was going to do with her life . . . when she grew up. What was there that she *could* actually do that was significant . . . besides look elegant in someone else's clothes?

"I hope you're not planning on jumping."

She didn't turn around right away, although she couldn't help smiling to herself. Maxwell's voice was quiet, but deep and clear and without any particular emotion. The sound of it grabbed at her, jolted her, made her aware again.

"Are you hoping that I will, so I can stop showing up like a bad penny?" she responded caustically.

He didn't answer right away, and Christine thought that maybe he'd just gone back into the apartment without hearing her question. But then Maxwell did speak.

"No."

He sounded different, and she frowned as she turned around to face him, the breeze blowing at her hair and clothing. But she couldn't see the details of Maxwell's face. He was silhouetted against the light from inside the room. He only appeared large and solid—rather than invincible. Christine drew a slow, deep breath, wondering when she'd begun to realize that Dr. D. Maxwell Chandler was having an effect on her. And it had nothing to do with the animosity between them.

Maxwell couldn't see Christine in any more detail, either. Some of the light from behind him bounced off her face. He could see the gentle swing of her dangling earrings, the soft flutter of her hair which was pulled back from her face and tied with a black and gold scarf. The grey dress had a decolletage that emphasized her neck more than it did her bosom. But the suggestion was enticing and once again recalled to Maxwell her visit to his office. She was looking at him now in such a way that he knew Christine Morrow was also remembering. But she was strong, and still prepared to give as good as she got.

"I'm surprised to see you here."

"I bet you are. You're a bit of a snob, you know that?"

He shrugged lightly. "I've been told."

Christine sighed audibly this time and glanced away briefly. "As if you really care what people think about you."

"No more than you do."

She grinned. "I guess I should apologize for slapping you."

"Not if you really meant to do it."

"I did."

"Then don't. Besides, I might have deserved it."

Christine raised her brows in feigned shock. "Are *you* apologizing?"

He shook his head silently.

She lifted her shoulders. "Then we're even."

He said no more but continued to block the door and the light. Christine wondered why he'd bothered following her to the terrace, and she was aware that her heartbeat was so strong she could feel it in her chest. She blinked at Maxwell and took a step closer to him.

"How is . . . Wendy?" she asked so softly she wasn't sure he'd even hear her. She was afraid to ask any louder, as if in reverence and respect for the sick child.

"She's holding on. Nothing's changed."

She lowered her gaze briefly and nodded. She didn't want to ask how long the little girl could last.

"You've made a friend," Maxwell observed, almost in amazement.

"I have? Where?"

"At LIFELINE. Delores."

"Really?" she asked in genuine surprise, her eyes rounding and momentarily softening her sophisticated demeanor.

"She hasn't stopped talking about you since she met you. You must have made some impression."

Christine recovered quickly. "Well, unlike you she doesn't see me as the devil in the flesh. She doesn't think I'm trying to steal her soul."

"That's not how I see you," Maxwell said suddenly and impatiently.

"I'm afraid to ask you to be specific. I think you've made yourself clear about my character and worth," she said tightly.

He sighed. It was unexpected and it seemed heavy and tired—and confused, coming from him. "I was out of line. My mouth sometimes . . . betrays me."

Christine nodded slowly. "I would say so . . ."

"Oooh, it's so pretty out here."

They both stiffened protectively when Frances appeared to the right of Maxwell, peering around his broad form to gaze out into the night. He immediately turned to offer her his hand. Frances took it.

"Be careful," Maxwell warned her quietly, guiding her out to the terrace.

Christine began to feel cold and she hugged herself, standing aside so there was room for the three of them on the small space. Maxwell didn't release Frances's hand.

"You know, I've always said that New York had the

most dynamic skyline of any city in the world." Frances gasped softly. "Oh, they've made the lights at the top of the Empire State Building red, white, and blue."

"That's because next Monday is Memorial Day," Christine supplied.

"You sound just like a true New Yorker," Frances said and chuckled lightly. "I've lived here for five years and I don't think I ever knew that."

"Christine isn't from New York," Maxwell said authoritatively. "She was born just outside of D.C."

Frances glanced up at Maxwell but didn't say anything. Christine also stared at him, trying to see his face, but he was giving all of his attention to Frances. Still, she slowly began to smile in surprise. "I think I'll go back and see if Cynthia needs any help. Excuse me . . ." she murmured, sidestepping the two of them and going back into the bright light of the living room.

Shortly after dessert the dinner party broke up and people began to leave. Christine was surprised but pleased at the genuine expressions of those who said they enjoyed meeting her and that they would now look for her picture in fashion magazines.

Christine wasn't surprised to see Maxwell help Frances Grimes into her evening jacket and hover near her solicitously. After Frances had made her goodbyes, thanking Cynthia for a lovely evening and also telling Christine she'd enjoyed meeting her, she and Maxwell left. He hadn't said a word to Christine, apparently placing her back in that category where she wasn't worth the time of day. Christine decided it was just too difficult to try and figure out Maxwell Chandler, but she was taken aback by his capacity for indifference. She waited another ten minutes before she also said good night, promising to call Cynthia soon.

Maxwell was sitting in one of the lobby chairs when Christine got off the elevator. He knew he couldn't be seen, and for the moment he didn't want to be. He sat in absolute silence, watching her. The first thing that struck him was that she suddenly didn't seem like a highly paid model or the image of glamour, wealth, and privilege. She looked like a rather beautiful black woman who seemed a bit pensive and tired, but with presence and stature.

He watched her stop for a moment, in silent thought and consideration, and detected a wistfulness that softened her expression. Maxwell raised his brows and began to smile to himself.

Christine couldn't recall the last time she'd left any function when there wasn't a kind of entourage surrounding her and suggesting late-night cappuccino somewhere, or catching the last set at a cabaret. Or when she wasn't going home with Keith, to her place or his. It felt a little strange but on consideration she thought it was just as well. She had so much on her mind. Christine asked the doorman if he would signal for a taxi.

"I'll drive you home."

She turned quickly at the sound of the voice and stared blankly at Maxwell. Christine felt an uncharacteristic excitement and bewilderment at finding him still there . . . and apparently waiting for her. She glanced around the lobby and out the front door.

"Where's Frances?"

"On the way home, I guess."

"I thought . . . I . . ."

"I know. I just walked her to her car to make sure she got in safely." He put his hands into the pockets of his slacks, and stood awkwardly as she continued to appraise him. "I live on Central Park West. I can drop you off unless you'd rather take a cab."

"I'd *never* rather take a cab," Christine said dryly. "The drivers in New York are out of their minds."

He nodded and said good night to the doorman as he placed his hand on her back to guide her out onto the street.

Maxwell had parked his Lexus in a nearby garage. It was what Christine thought of as a moderate luxury car. Not ostentatious, but not the family sedan either. It seemed right for Maxwell, although she could also envision him in a Cherokee Jeep.

He held the door for her as she seated herself, and when he got into the driver's side, Christine was again made aware of his size. But it wasn't intimidating—she was just tuned in to his overwhelming masculinity. He suggested a kind of power that was more than physical, and very different from Keith. Christine frowned and riveted her attention on the windshield and the Upper East Side traffic of Manhattan around midnight.

She didn't want to think about Keith. He was in California finding himself. She was here, going about her business. But so much of what she was going through seemed to involve D. Maxwell Chandler. Her frown deepened as a swirling sensation snaked through her, twisting her stomach muscles. She could feel his body heat. She watched the way he handled the car. Lightly. His long fingers seemed to just touch the steering wheel, not grip it. The streetlights beyond the window flashed on his skin, highlighting his eyes or the chiseled lines of his cheek, mouth, and jaw.

Christine faced forward again. She sighed and finally relaxed in her seat, realizing that she felt perfectly safe with him.

Maxwell was *not* feeling quite the same way.

For one thing, he was still trying to reconcile the Christine Morrow of fashion fame with the woman who'd visited the clinic and fallen apart in his arms . . . and the one who'd sat next to him at dinner. It was disturbing to realize how hard it had been to ignore her all evening. For another thing, two recent episodes kept replaying in his mind: when she'd slapped him, and her interaction with the other guests during dinner. She had been bright, amusing, and charming. But Maxwell didn't think it a good idea to tell Christine that. He grimaced, knowing she would jump all over him for actually behaving . . . how would she put it? . . . like a human being.

And Maxwell also couldn't ignore Delores's reaction to Christine. On basic principle, Delores didn't trust anyone. And if anyone could see through your attitude or intentions, it was likely to be Delores. Life had not given her many skills or breaks, but as a hard core survivor she *knew* how to sniff out sincerity. Maxwell surmised, with some insight, that the one thing the two women had in common was a lack of fear and the ability to get in your face.

He, on the other hand, was seeing other things as well in Christine Morrow. Like the heartbreaking sounds of her crying. That had been real. It had gotten to him.

"Why did you wait for me?" Christine suddenly asked quietly.

Maxwell sighed. He'd hoped she wouldn't ask. Anything he said might seem like too much of an admission of interest. She'd laugh in his face at his turnabout. He shrugged. "I knew you were getting ready to leave. It wasn't going to put me out to drive you home."

Christine thought about it. She arched a brow, recalling the feel of his arms, his body warmth. "Is that all?"

"What else do you think it is?" he countered smoothly, going tit for tat . . . and enjoying it.

She turned her head to appraise him thoroughly. "I think . . . you're having second thoughts about me. Maybe you see I'm not so horrible after all," she speculated in a teasing tone. The idea was new, and *very* exciting. "Although you'd let your fingernails be pulled out before admitting it," she couldn't help adding caustically.

"Maybe," was his offhand reply.

"You're a difficult man, Dr. Chandler," Christine said and sighed, watching him. "You *definitely* need to lighten up. You take yourself too seriously."

His jaw clenched. "What about you?"

"What about me . . . what?"

"Why did you accept the ride?"

Christine faced front again. She wondered about that. She didn't know. Or maybe . . . she didn't *want* to know. But it had never entered her mind to turn Maxwell down. It occurred to her now, and she knew she had chosen to be with him.

"Curiosity," she finally murmured.

The ride to her apartment took only ten minutes. It was too long not to think about being with him and too short to wait for him to ask if she'd like to stop somewhere for coffee or a drink. To pick up the first edition of the Sunday *New York Times*. To walk a bit. He didn't. Maxwell drove onto her block. Just beyond her building a van was pulling out of a space, and Maxwell signaled to pull into it.

Christine didn't question his decision. She knew

it didn't pay to put his car in a garage just to walk her to the door, and double parking was an open invitation to a ticket.

They walked in silence to the building, Christine thinking quickly of a light and flippant way to say good night and thank you. She wondered, however, in a part of her mind, why it mattered. She frowned in apprehension when she realized she was also very nervous.

She nodded when the doorman greeted her and held the door. She was aware that her heart was suddenly beating too fast, and that her breathing made her chest rise and fall. Maxwell still had his hand on her lower back, and she could feel the pressure . . . the warmth, right through the silk jacket and dress. Christine walked, matching her steps with Maxwell's so the contact was maintained. She walked automatically into the center of the lobby, but could only think of his hand.

Christine took a deep breath, wondering why she suddenly felt so lightheaded. She faced Maxwell and composed her features. "I appreciate the ride."

He was watching her very closely. "You're welcome. It's the least I can do."

She blinked. "Are you apologizing for the way you've acted?"

He shrugged lightly, his jaw muscles working furiously, his mouth pursing thoughtfully. "I guess you can say I was rude."

Christine couldn't help smiling. "That's one way to put it."

He arched a brow and a smile played tantalizing around his mouth. "That wasn't an apology. I just admitted I was hard on you."

"God, you're stubborn," she said in annoyance. She turned and walked away toward the elevator, without another word. Maxwell was right behind her.

"You should talk," he commented dryly. "I'll see you upstairs."

"Don't bother. The security is good here. Good night." Christine boarded the waiting elevator.

"How old is that guy?" Maxwell asked, following her onto the elevator nonetheless, and jerking a thumb toward the doorman who sat at a small desk watching a five-inch TV.

"Mario? About sixty, I guess." She pushed her floor button and the doors closed.

"That's my point," Maxwell said, leaning back against the wall and crossing his arms over his chest.

"Your concern for me is touching, but I can take care of myself," she said shortly.

"I know you can," he responded quietly.

The elevator indicator signaled the second floor. It was quiet between them. Then simultaneously they turned their heads to stare openly at each other. Maxwell slowly bent to the side and lightly kissed her, no more than his mouth alighting on hers.

"I know you were expecting that. I didn't want to disappoint you."

Christine chortled skeptically even though her heart lurched in her chest. "Be honest. You mean you couldn't help yourself."

He stood straight and faced the door again.

The elevator stopped on the sixth floor and Christine walked slowly out. She turned to face Maxwell as he continued to stand in the elevator, watching her.

Christine sighed. "Thanks again." She sounded distracted.

The door started to close on him and at the last

possible moment Maxwell stepped easily into the hallway. Christine's eyes widened at his sudden decision. There was just a second of doubt in her eyes, and then no more time to think as she realized she was waiting for him. Maxwell was coming closer . . . and they were in each other's arms.

Christine met his kiss as if this had been the game plan all along. Actually, the sheer spontaneity of it was what lent the moment so much power and intensity. All questions and considerations flew out of her head as she closed her eyes and let Maxwell find a way to hold her comfortably against him. He didn't crush her in desperation but held her in a kind of sensual firmness.

His mouth was mobile, his tongue slow and darting. He rocked his lips to the side, forcing her mouth wider, and the kiss deepened. Maxwell felt as though his arms could wrap around her twice, she was so slender. He wasn't afraid of squeezing her too tightly, just of not being able to get close enough. The silk fabric of her outfit slipped against his hands and he kept moving them trying to get a better hold.

But the movement of his hands was escalating Christine's sensibilities. She let him kiss her thoroughly. It was, to put it simply, wonderful. Her hands rested on his shoulder, and with the fingertips of her right hand she brushed against his cheek and jaw, enjoying the firm, manly feel of his skin, the slightly textured surface where his beard would grow in. The muscles in his neck were rigid as Christine stroked along the column.

Finally realizing they were in the hallway, she pulled away and stared into his face.

"Was . . . was that a . . . good night kiss?" she asked.

Maxwell's gaze swept over her features. Her green eyes were bright but a bit dazed. Her lips glistened with the moisture of their kiss. He shook his head. "No."

Christine closed her eyes and shook her head as if to clear it. "My . . . goodness . . ."

Maxwell reached with a hand to touch her mouth. "Yes," he drawled.

Christine frowned. She blinked her eyes to focus and finally pushed him away. "This isn't happening. Good night, Dr. Chandler." She began walking down the hall toward her apartment, knowing that her steps weren't too steady or straight. She opened her purse for the keys.

Maxwell reached around her and took the key ring from her limp hands. Stepping in front of her, he opened the door as she stood silently and watched.

Christine couldn't think. She was still processing the feel of Maxwell's lips on hers, the way his tongue claimed territory not with force but with seduction and skill. She could still feel the hardness of his chest, the columns of his thighs. It almost seemed like slow motion, the way he reached for her again, the way she was waiting and ready.

His mouth seemed so familiar now. Christine had no trouble finding that place in his arms that gave her pleasure and melted her senses. He turned her so that her back was against the wall just outside the apartment. He pressed her into it and it was impossible not to feel his arousal, or to hear their breathing. Her nose was against his face and the scent of him, like musk and sandalwood, seeped into her. She was getting dizzy. Mindless.

It was Maxwell who ended the kiss this time. It was he who looked uncertain, even as his nostrils flared and he bent forward to let his mouth and the tip of his tongue just brush feather-like over her lips.

"Maxwell . . ." Christine finally said as she stared at his shirt front, "I don't think we even like each other."

He sighed and looked toward the ceiling briefly. "I know."

"Then, we shouldn't be doing this."

"I know."

"I should ask you to leave. Now."

He rubbed his chin against her temple and she groaned quietly, kissing the side of his neck. "But that's not what you want."

Christine bit her lip when he pressed his groin against her as his hands rested on her hips. "I . . . know . . ."

He turned his head and tilted hers with just the pressure of his jaw until he could rest his mouth on hers once more. Slowly, she wound her arms around his neck. She gave up and gave in. She moved, not wanting to let go of his mouth on hers, but trying awkwardly to get them through the door and into her apartment. Maxwell cooperated. With his arms around her waist he lifted her bodily from the floor and walked with her through the door. Christine reached out her hand to slam the door shut.

Maxwell blindly kept walking, banging into a wall once as he tried to figure out where the living room was. But he wasn't willing to let her go to find out.

"To the left . . . the left," Christine groaned against his mouth, giving him directions.

He stopped and she slid down his body until she was once again standing on her own, although her legs felt shaky. Maxwell's hands were searching for the hem of the dress, trying to grab the fabric and pull it up.

Christine twisted her mouth free and gasped. "Don't. It's silk."

They began to take off their clothing right there. A jacket tossed on a chair. Shoes kicked off, buttons undone, zippers lowered. Maxwell smoothly removed a gold foil-wrapped condom from his wallet. It was so surprising and so sensible at the same time that Christine felt herself wanting to giggle nervously. It's just what she would have expected from Dr. Chandler. But she didn't laugh; he never would have forgiven her, and she was, ultimately, thrilled at his thoughtfulness.

She turned and walked through the apartment until she got to the bedroom, turning on the bedside lamp. She was in her bra and panties, and Maxwell in Jockey shorts. But there was something unbelievably sexy about them on him. Christine turned her back to him as she removed her bra and dropped it on the floor. Maxwell came up behind her and slid his arms around her, until her back rested against his chest. His large hands molded over her breasts, completely covering them as her sensitized nipples pressed into his palm. He began to massage her and Christine moaned his name.

He released one breast and let his hand travel in a long caress down her ribcage and stomach, slipping it inside the band of her panties until his fingertips dug gently through the tangle of curly hair and settled, snugly, between her legs.

She gasped and clamped her thighs closed, grabbing hold of his wrist.

He continued to rotate his palm over the one breast. Maxwell kissed the rounded end of her shoulder. "Hasn't a man ever touched you there before?"

"No one who knew what he was doing . . . or what I wanted," she admitted readily, in a soft, almost shy, voice.

He effortlessly shook her hand away as a finger found the sensitive folds of her body. "I know what I'm doing."

He certainly did.

He kept them standing, so that he could take her weight, which Christine relaxed against him more and more as her passion took over. There was something wanton and erotic about having Maxwell stroke and stimulate the very center of her being. The spiraling sensation, heading toward an explosion, gained steady momentum.

Christine's head fell back against his shoulder, jutting her breasts out. His manhood was surging against her buttocks, but she was too far gone, too focused on her own release to reach back and touch Maxwell. The dam burst and the pulsating completely weakened her knees. Christine grabbed at his arm, trying to hold on and not slither to the floor. But she wasn't going anywhere. He had a firm hold on her. When she had gasped out the last of her pleasure, Maxwell bent and lifted her and placed her across the bed. She couldn't move, but lay there in a euphoric stupor as her body gently reverberated. She heard Maxwell strip himself of his shorts, apply protection, and climb on the bed with her. Her eyes were closed and his weight made the mattress dip and rock until she began to feel seasick.

He kissed her breasts, his lips pulling and sucking gently on her nipples. He stroked her thighs until she automatically raised her legs and opened them so that Maxwell could settle between them.

"Max . . . wait," Christine moaned, feeling too sensitive to take him yet. But he was already starting to enter her. He was built large and thick and her body adjusted as he slowly slid deep within her, slowly meshed their bodies until there wasn't an inch of space between them. His skin was incredibly hot and she wanted to curl up in his warmth.

He began to thrust and Christine drew her breath in, clutching at his shoulders, her toes curling tightly. Another internal detonation went off, and she nearly wept with pleasure.

Oh, yes . . . the man *definitely* knew what he was doing.

Once Christine had reached her second climax, Maxwell began the rhythmic dance in earnest. His thrusts were long and steady, and they held on to one another until Christine felt the muscles in his legs and buttocks, arms and neck tighten and he grunted deep in his chest. When the storm was over he lay on top of her, both of them breathing heavily.

Maxwell placed his cheek against her chest. Christine stroked his shoulders and his head, the rough, tightly curled texture of his hair reminding her of terry cloth.

"Is this what you had in mind when you wanted to bring me home?" she whispered.

He was silent for a long moment, then shook his head against her breasts. "No, Christine. It wasn't."

She sighed. She believed him.

"Then . . . what is going on?"

Finally Maxwell lifted his head and gazed into her face. Her legs were still wrapped around his hips. He was still buried within her, although he was starting to go soft. Her hair was loose and the scarf gone. She was looking at him honestly and openly—it was probably the first moment in which they both felt uncertain and without a need to be right. He frowned and shook his head slightly. Then he briefly and lightly kissed her chin, her mouth.

"I don't know."

Maxwell lifted himself from her body, even though he was very comfortable and liked the feel of her beneath him. He knew he was too heavy. He lay on his back, and Christine immediately curled into his side, resting her head on his chest. He put his arm around her and held her to him.

"And that was the easy question," she murmured sleepily, stifling a yawn.

He closed his eyes and just felt the pleasant weight of her near him. But he'd already discovered that Christine Morrow was hardly as delicate as she looked. "Is there another question?"

"Lots."

"Like?"

"What are you going to tell Dr. Frances Grimes?"

He stroked her shoulder and back. "I don't have to tell her anything. Why should I?"

"You're a fool if you don't know the woman's in love with you."

"Fran and I go way back. She's a good friend. An excellent doctor."

"Okay. But she's still in love with you. She coupled her name with yours so much this evening I was waiting for her to say 'Maxwell and I are engaged'."

"I don't want to hurt her. She's a good person."

"There's no reason why she should be hurt if you haven't promised anything."

"I haven't. I never did." He tried to look down on her face. "That doesn't mean that . . . there's anything between you and me."

"That's what you think," Christine murmured, even though his bluntness irritated her. "You're a double fool if you think there's not," she said in irony. She used her fingers to tease through the curly hair on his chest. There was quite a lot of it, and she found that, too, sexy and masculine.

"Whether you like it or not . . . we're attracted to one another."

Maxwell sighed deeply and stared at the ceiling. "I didn't want to . . ."

She covered his mouth with her hand. "You may not like me very much, Maxwell . . . but you *do* want me. So . . . what were the reasons again?"

Maxwell cringed. That certainly had been the way he'd felt upon his first encounter with Christine. And even the second. But something happened at the clinic that got under his skin and forced him to recognize another side of her. He didn't want to know that side, because it might mean changing his mind about a lot of things. But it had appeared, in his face . . . and poignantly real. The way she had suddenly started to cry at the LIFELINE clinic, about what could and could not be done for the children. That image of Christine Morrow in tears seemed to be indelibly imprinted on his consciousness. He was willing to bet almost anything that she was not one to get highly emotional over very much.

"It's not that I don't like you, Christine. It's just that you and I are very different. We have nothing in common. My work is important and time-consuming. And it's very serious. What you do . . . it irritates me because I can't see any point to it. You just seem to be living to have a good time."

Christine listened closely, as she'd done before to Maxwell's opinion of her. Their mutual sexual enjoyment aside, nothing much had changed between them except they'd stopped growling at one another. But she wasn't going to let him get away with thinking he was so right.

"I am having a good time. I certainly work hard enough for it. I know you don't think so, but what I do supports a whole lot of people in an industry that makes other people feel good. Did you like the dress I had on tonight?"

He frowned. "Yeah, I guess so. The color really went well with your eyes."

"That's because I know how to wear clothes so that it makes me look good to myself and other people. You might have had a different reaction if I'd come in a peasant skirt and off-the-shoulder gypsy blouse. Or if I'd worn a kente cloth caftan."

He chuckled silently. "I doubt it. You'd probably look sensational in aluminum foil."

She pinched him lightly. "Someone designed that dress, someone who was talented and artistic. Someone constructed it who had an eye for fabric. Someone marketed it, knowing what other women want to wear . . . and what men want to see women in. This isn't brain surgery, but I'm making an honest living and contributing to the tax base of this city. I'm not useless."

He got impatient. "I didn't say you were useless."

"Not in those words, but the implication was there. You're pompous, Maxwell." She caressingly ran her foot against the hard muscle of his calf. "You're self-righteous and self-important and self-absorbed. I think what you're doing for those children up in Harlem is . . . is heroic," she said, gesturing grandly with her hand. "But, why don't you have a life?"

She raised her head and braced herself over his chest, peering seriously into Maxwell's eyes. They were slumberous as he returned her gaze. She liked the color of his skin. It was like bittersweet chocolate.

"This is my life. I've always wanted to be a doctor. Since I was a kid."

"Was your father a doctor? A brother or sister?"

He shook his head. Maxwell averted his gaze, staring off into space. Christine watched the transformation in his face, the tightening of his mouth. She laid her hand along his cheek and could feel the jaw muscles at work.

"Tell me," she coaxed softly.

"I grew up in foster care, Christine. My natural parents were, to be nice about it, dysfunctional and unable to handle the responsibility of raising kids. I think I'd been passed around to about a dozen different families by the time I was sixteen. Somewhere along the way my natural folks died. I had a sister. We were split up as kids and I lost track of her until I was twenty-one. That was fifteen years ago. She was sick and . . . and dying. Of AIDS." He turned his head to look at her again. "Sexually transmitted. She'd just had a baby and he was infected, too.

"I was so angry that I'd finally found what was left of my real family, and I was going to lose them again. I couldn't do anything to save her. I got lucky and got into a series of homes where people cared, and I was encouraged to work hard and go to college. I did, on a football scholarship. My sister wasn't so lucky and ended up in abusive families and relationships. When she and the baby died I switched my major to pre-med. I lost my football scholarship, but that was okay. I got through."

Christine frowned and ran her index finger delicately back and forth across his bottom lip. "Ever been . . . married?" She felt the way the question had taken him by surprise in the way his body stiffened slightly beneath her. She braced herself, half expecting that he'd push her away and withdraw. Instead, Maxwell looked into her eyes. Christine was amazed at the anger she detected.

"Yes."

Her stomach roiled. "Cynthia said . . . you hadn't been."

It registered that she'd been interested enough to ask. He shook his head. "Cynthia wouldn't know. James doesn't. It was before I'd met him in school." He sighed. "Frances knows."

"Oh . . ." Christine murmured, unreasonably annoyed that his colleague might know so much more about him. "What happened? Did she . . . she didn't die of . . ."

"She left me."

Christine heard him, but repeated it to herself before it made any sense. She blinked at Maxwell. She had only seen a few sides of this man. Even when he was difficult he was attractive. Even when he was being righteous he was also humane. But she wasn't going to ask why his wife had left. The fact of it was enough of an admission. And deeply personal. Christine stroked his lips again wondering what had inspired Maxwell to be so honest and open.

Christine thought it best not to comment about Maxwell's history. It was too stark and real. When she recalled how she used to complain to her father and sister about how provincial their house and neighborhood was, how boring and backward, Christine wanted to bite her tongue. But that didn't excuse Maxwell from trivializing anyone else's life.

"So . . . it's been rough. No one said it was going to be fair, Maxwell."

He raised a brow mockingly. "A philosopher hidden under a layer of Donna Karan."

She grinned easily. "It got *your* attention."

They both grew serious.

He ran his hand up the back of her neck and his fingers into her hair. "Does this mean we're calling a truce?"

Christine shrugged. "What do you think?"

Maxwell's gaze seemed to take a long time to assess her. He took his hand to explore the curve of her neck, down to her collarbone and her breasts. He played momentarily with a nipple and watched in fascination as it quickly grew turgid and Christine drew in a quiet breath. The hand continued to her waist, her buttocks. With a little push Maxwell caused Christine to lie on her back once more, and he rolled himself atop her, adjusting his weight and fitting her against him.

"So I guess we're not going to fight one another anymore?"

Christine arched herself against him, feeling the rising heat of his arousal and his hands under her butt as he positioned her for his entry. "That wasn't fighting. That was foreplay. Look at where we are, how far we've come . . ." She put her arms around his back and sighed as he began to enter her.

Maxwell waited until the journey was completed before whispering against her skin, "Amen . . ."

They slept until seven the next morning. When the phone rang, dragging her from sleep and the comfort of Maxwell's arms, Christine had turned down the ringer and let the answering machine take over. But now awake, she went to the bathroom and returned to sit on a chair in a corner of her room and just stare at Maxwell as he slept. He lay, for the moment, on his stomach, the full length of his back,

from head to toe, bare. Christine let her eyes follow
the lines of his physique, noting the leanness in his
hips, the hard muscles of his calves, and the firmness of his butt. He really did have a beautiful body.
Not like Keith's or many of the male models for
whom achieving a washboard stomach was akin to
a religious experience.

But what also made Christine pensive was realizing that she actually liked D. Maxwell Chandler
more than she was willing to admit. At the moment
she couldn't recall exactly how they'd ended up in
her bed. When had they passed the boundary of
their Mexican standoff and found reconciliation?
And where the devil were they going from here?

She didn't want to think about it yet, either.
Christine recognized that she and Maxwell were still
light years away from agreeing on anything. Except
that they had enjoyed each other sexually. *Well . . .
it's a start,* she said to herself, not realizing the sig-
nificance of the thought.

Christine got dressed in a pair of leggings, an
oversized sweatshirt that said "Paramount Pictures"
on the back, pulled a green canvas baseball cap on,
and quietly left the apartment to get the Sunday
papers and fresh orange juice. She came back and
started the coffeemaker. She gasped violently when
Maxwell came silently behind her in the kitchen,
startling her. He wordlessly began pulling the sweatshirt over her head. She hadn't bothered with a bra
beneath it. He turned her in his arms and kissed
her deeply, his tongue plunging assertively into her
mouth to dance and spar with hers. His warm hands
cupped around her breasts, his thumbs tormenting
her nipples until a small cry of delight was wrenched
from her. Maxwell tried to wiggle the skin-tight leggings down her hips, but was forced to end the kiss

to make it possible. Taking her by the hand, he fairly pulled Christine back into the bedroom. They fell cockeyed across the bed to make slow, lazy love again. Experimenting. Teasing. Driving one another to the brink of ecstasy . . . and starting all over again. Until Maxwell ran out of condoms.

They ordered dinner in and then lay on the bed watching TV until, with a sigh, Maxwell got up to shower, get dressed, and go home. Christine had fallen asleep again by the time he finished in the bathroom, and now it was his turn to study her. But he didn't. It wasn't necessary. He was going to remember everything about her and everything that had happened between them. Maxwell quietly let himself out of the apartment.

He knew, as he began the descent in the elevator, that he'd complicated his life immeasurably. He didn't have time for an involvement. He didn't want to be involved with Christine Morrow. But the last fourteen hours or more with her had been like floating on a magic carpet . . . and then having it pulled out from under him. He hadn't worked her out of his system by going to bed with her. He'd merely implanted her on his senses, melded with her soul. He hadn't slacked his desire, he'd only whetted his appetite. He didn't want to just walk away, but he was going to because Christine Morrow possessed nothing that he thought he needed in a woman . . . and *everything* that he wanted.

Frances Grimes was the kind of woman he knew would be good for him, good to him. It was ironic that Christine Morrow had been able to size that up after a mere few hours. But he was not in love with his colleague and never had been. She was a friend and he valued the friendship too much to raise Frances's expectations falsely.

Maxwell pursed his lips as he compared the two women. And into the mix again came Rachel. It had taken him a long time to get over the hurt of her betrayal, of her finding someone with more means and better standing than a mere medical student. Well, there wasn't anything that Christine Morrow expected from him, or wanted from him. Their coming together last night had been pure and un-adulterated. No agenda. But spending time with her . . . going to bed with her . . . he had forever banished one misconception. She *was* a woman of depth and insight. She *did* have humor and soul. And she was, undeniably, beautiful.

She was perfect, Maxwell thought dispiritedly as he climbed into his car and began the drive through Central Park toward home. There wasn't a thing wrong with Christine Morrow. Not a *damn* thing.

Six

"Hi, Miss Morrow."

"Hi, Delores. Didn't I tell you it was all right to call me Christine?"

"Yeah, but . . ." The young woman shrugged. "I just feel funny doing it. I mean . . . you're famous and important and everything."

Christine opened a locker, put her purse inside, and closed it again with that tinny metallic slam she remembered so well from high school. She turned to the other woman. "I'm not famous and I'm certainly not important."

"But, how come you don't want nobody to know you're here?"

"Because . . . because . . ." Christine struggled for an excuse, knowing full well that in a way, Delores was right. She was well known enough that if word got out she was volunteering in Harlem at a center that treated children with AIDS, the newspapers would get hold of it and unwanted attention would descend on the place. "It would upset the children and staff. Some people would come around just to be nosy. I don't think Dr. Chandler would like that very much. And he might blame me."

"Well," Delores said as she prepared a cart with a stack of children's books, paper, paste, and scissors for craft projects, "he sure can get mad and go off

when reporters come around. He won't even let
them in the door." She started giggling. "He once
grabbed this guy's camera and took the film out.
The man was so mad. But he was a little short guy
and he was afraid to do or say anything. Dr. Chandler would've ripped his heart out."

"I believe it," Christine murmured as a thread of
apprehension snaked through her. She didn't want
to consider what Maxwell would do to her if he
found out about her being at the center. But
Christine reasoned to herself that his proprietary
attitude was out of place. The center, after all, was
not about him . . . but the needs of the children.

Not that she really understood all that they
needed, other than to be treated like kids and be
able to do what most kids do. But she had to find
that out for herself. She'd never been around children before.

She learned what she had to know from Delores
and by watching other volunteers and clinic staff.
Delores seemed to know a lot about it. She was the
same age as herself. Christine had found out that
Delores already had an eleven-year-old daughter
who was being raised by a grandmother in South
Carolina. And she'd had a son who had died. Right
there in LIFELINE. Christine hadn't asked about
the circumstances.

Christine let Delores chatter on as she signed in
and checked which children were due into the clinic
that day and for what treatment. It occurred to her
that until three weeks ago, when she'd first walked
into LIFELINE out of curiosity, she'd never really
paid much attention to children. It had been pretty
enlightening to get close enough over the past few
weeks, to discover their charm and innocence. The
funny and sometimes amazing observations they

made. The questions they formulated based on the simplest logic, but the often startling revelations based on their own history and experiences.

The kids at LIFELINE had gone through a lot in their short lives, and they probably weren't going to last long enough to have memories. When the realization had first hit her, she'd wanted to cry. But tears weren't going to help anything, least of all the children. She *never* saw them crying. There was no time for it.

She would have preferred to tell Maxwell what she was doing but Christine knew intuitively that he would not be pleased or impressed. He would question her motives and throw her good intentions right back at her. And, too, she knew that she was trying to find a way to connect with Maxwell beyond what they'd shared together the night of Cynthia's dinner party. It had been fantastic. And memorable. He had engaged her imagination more than any other man she'd ever been with. She felt tentative, still, but Christine was starting to entertain the fantasy that it might be nice to have more between her and Maxwell than just great sex. Actually, she wasn't even sure they had that, she thought wryly, given the fact that she hadn't heard from him since that Sunday morning when she'd awakened to find him gone. She'd been avoiding him at the clinic, not wanting him to read more into her being there. Thankfully the schedule he maintained didn't allow for their paths to cross.

"What should we do with the kids today?" Delores asked, rolling the supply cart through the door of the volunteer office and heading for the playroom.

Christine wrinkled her brow as she followed, carrying a box of loose toys. "Well, I could read them a story, and then we can have them do their own illustrations. Or we can have them write their own stories."

"The last time you tried to read to them they all wanted to sit in your lap."

Christine groaned to herself. She remembered that a little shoving had gone on as several of the more assertive children had almost started fighting to get her attention. "Well, we can't have that. Maybe I'll sit in a chair this time, and not on the floor."

"Then your clothes won't get all messed up."

"Don't worry about my clothes," Christine said dryly, thinking of her overflowing closet.

"Miss Morrow . . . I mean, Christine, thank you for getting me that job."

"I didn't get you the job. You did. All I did was make a phone call," Christine said smoothly, not wanting to make a big issue of it.

She'd twisted a few arms to get Delores an interview with one of the commercial studios she knew was always short of gopher help. She'd noticed around the center that Delores was good about following orders and smart enough to take the initiative when she saw something that needed doing. And she suspected that the woman needed the money. Delores had pride. She'd made a lot of mistakes and poor decisions early in life, but it was obvious she was trying to get it together and take care of herself.

Five minutes after they'd opened the room and turned on the lights, children started arriving with their guardians, parents, or older siblings. They didn't come rushing noisily into the room, but were quiet and slow, reminding Christine of the basic symptoms of their condition, weakness and anemia. They were wasting away.

The children were allowed to play for an hour or

so before the nurse came in and took them, one by one, behind a screened partition where they were given IV treatments. Christine had never watched one of the procedures, not sure of how she'd react to seeing these little bodies hooked up to tubes and needles.

"I have to go soon," Delores said to Christine after they'd started half a dozen children on projects to keep them busy.

"To work?" Christine asked absently as she crawled on her hands and knees to pick up crayons and chalk under tables and chairs.

"No. Upstairs."

Christine sat back on her heels and looked at Delores. "Oh," she said quietly.

"Are you coming up?"

Christine got to her feet and put the markers in their proper containers. "I don't think so," she said with a shake of her head.

"It's real quiet up there."

"I know. That's why I can't go up."

She knew that Delores was staring at her, waiting for an explanation, but Christine couldn't tell her that the quietness, the children lying listlessly in their beds and cribs, reminded her too much of death. And that they were not going to be leaving the third floor. She hadn't developed the stamina yet to get past her own emotion.

Delores stood next to her. "I'm used to it now."

"I know," Christine nodded, remembering some of the history Delores had shared with her the day they'd gone out to eat. She glanced up at the woman. "Don't forget. You'll let me know how Wendy's doing."

"I will," Delores said, getting up and leaving the room.

Christine prepared to leave herself about an hour later when she checked her watch and saw how late it was. She had a reception at a gallery down in Soho, and early the next morning she was leaving for a two-day shoot in Newfoundland. She signed out of the volunteer office and was headed for the elevators when Maxwell came out of one of the wards with a parent, heading toward the nurses' station.

Christine tried to avoid him. She ducked back into the office, but five minutes later Maxwell was still in conversation. She slipped out of the room and quickly headed for the bank of elevators which could not be seen from Maxwell's position. Christine jabbed at the button, annoyed that she felt she had to be so careful because of Maxwell's feelings.

"Christine, Christine!"

Christine turned to watch the six-year-old running down the corridor in her direction. She knew there was no way Maxwell could not have heard the name, but she ignored the inevitable as the youngster came straight on in her direction.

She laughed and put down her tote, bending to catch the child in her arms and lift him from the floor. Christine whirled him around once, very fast, listening to the delighted childish squeal as he held her neck for dear life. She kissed his cool cheek, enjoying the moment of abandon.

"Where are you going?" the child asked, leaning back trustingly in her arms and playing with the silver pendant around her neck.

"I'm going home."

"Can I come with you?"

It was such a simple question. And so unexpected. The thought came to her quickly that maybe he thought he'd be safe with her. That if he could just change some of the circumstances of his life, maybe he really wouldn't be sick, and wouldn't have to come to the clinic, and wouldn't have to feel different.

Christine hugged him briefly and set him down. "That would make your family very sad. Your mommy and daddy would miss you."

"They're not my real mommy and daddy. Can't you be my mommy for a while?"

She was speechless as the child looked pleadingly at her, putting his thin hand in hers. She glanced up and saw Maxwell standing imperious and stern at the end of the corridor, watching her. Christine smiled down at the little boy. "Tell you what. I can be a pretend mommy to everyone when I'm at the playroom. Is that okay?"

He thought about it and nodded. "Okay."

"Now you better go back inside. I'll see you next week."

"Okay," he said readily, running back the other way.

Christine took a deep breath and stared at Maxwell. She felt a peculiar sensation ripple through her. It was much more than apprehension and nervousness. It was a memory of her response to him physically. It was the answering of a question that had lain unasked in the back of her mind since she'd last seen him. It was an admission that came up out of nowhere to confront her. The night of that fashion show when they'd first met seemed an awfully long time ago. And she was a different person. She wanted Maxwell to know that.

For his part, Maxwell was furious to see Christine Morrow back at the center. But he also felt an indisputable rush of excitement and surprise. And, in truth, he no longer understood what his anger was all about. At the moment it seemed misplaced.

She was dressed in jeans and a white, long-sleeved sweater cropped at the waist, emphasizing her lithe body. Her hair was in a French twist, with a fringe of bangs over her forehead. She wore no jewelry but for a small pair of silver ear studs and the pendant. And no makeup but lipstick. There was nothing the least bit glamorous or special about how she appeared, except that she still managed to look beautiful . . . and to stand out.

Maxwell watched her eyes. He could see that Christine was prepared to greet him warmly, her memories no different from his own of their last time together. But she was also ready to square off. He wasn't sure which he wanted from her.

Christine began walking toward Maxwell, studying the way he stood with his long legs braced apart and his hands in the pockets of a silk windbreaker. He looked serious. He looked unbelievably handsome.

"Hi," Christine said simply when she was about two feet from him. "I . . . was just leaving."

"So . . . you're the new volunteer. Why didn't you tell me?"

"So you can scowl at me like you're doing now?" she said sweetly, keeping her voice down as the staff looked on in curiosity from the nursing station. "So you can be difficult and sanctimonious and tell me I have no right to be here?"

He frowned at her and let his jaw twitch in annoyance. "Can I see you for a moment in my office?"

"We have to be quick. I have an engagement tonight. Would you like to come with me?" She didn't expect an answer.

Maxwell's frown deepened and he turned abruptly and headed for the elevators and the first floor, where his office was located next to that of the center director, an immunologist with the main hospital.

When they reached his office he closed the door and turned to face her, but Christine put up her hand and forestalled his tirade.

"Before you start in on me, I have one question. Do you need volunteers at the center?"

He shook his head, but sighed. "We always need volunteers. People burn out pretty quickly here. It's hard to come every week not knowing if . . . when . . ."

"I know."

"You don't belong here," he said, uncompromisingly.

Christine was determined not to let his rejection get to her. *"Nobody* belongs here. But until someone finds a cure for AIDS or a better way to protect children, this is the deal. I'm here because I have the time and I can help."

"Christine, this is not a matter of playing games with the children or reading them stories once a week. That's the easy stuff."

She put her hands saucily on her hips and glared at him. "What makes you think you're the only one capable of handling these children? They need more than just medication, inhalation therapy, and their blood taken out of their tiny bodies, Maxwell. They need hugs and kisses. They need to be made to feel special."

"I know that."

"So what's wrong with me doing that?"

"Because it's just not that easy. No, I don't think you can handle it. You haven't seen what it can be like later on when there's nothing else we can do. You're tough and you're obstinate but . . ."

She made a sound of disbelief. "Look who's talking . . ."

"And you haven't been trained. I never would have put you on the floor so soon if I'd known what you were up to."

"That's why I asked everyone not to tell you. Now it's too late. The staff likes me, and so do the children. The guardians trust me and . . . and I like what I'm doing." She saw the skepticism, the strain of indecision in his eyes. Christine took a step closer to him, looking beguilingly into his face. She put a hand lightly on his chest. "Give me a chance. I'm not the airhead you'd like to think I am."

"I know that," he said in a low voice, his gaze slowly roaming over her pretty features and the stubborn appeal in her eyes. "I'm just afraid that . . ."

"I'm not."

They were standing very close. Christine blinked at Maxwell, seeing the light change in his eyes, and suddenly seeing beyond the irritation to something more like confusion. And fear. She wondered if it was about her . . . or for her. She smiled slowly at him.

"I've never done anything like this before, Max. But I want to try. I'll be careful with the children. I won't hurt them."

"What about you getting hurt?"

"I'll handle it. Why? Are you planning on hurting me?"

He shook his head and frowned slightly. "I don't know what I want to do with you," he said almost to himself in a whisper.

Christine touched his face. "Well . . . let me suggest a couple of things . . ."

She reached up and kissed him lightly. He kept his mouth firmly closed, feeling the caress of her soft mouth, the teasing pressure. Slowly, Maxwell responded, parting his lips so that inch by inch the possession became complete. He slipped his arms around her waist and pulled her body tightly to his. Maxwell slanted his mouth over hers, and then opened his to take control of the kiss. He captured Christine expertly as his tongue delved into the warm recesses of her mouth, drawing forth an instantaneous pleasure that shot straight to his groin.

Christine tunneled her hands inside his open jacket and wrapped them around his broad back, feeling the muscles and sinew beneath his sweater.

They went with it for a long, delicious moment, Christine loving the gentleness of his embrace and the stalwart strength of his body. But after a moment Maxwell moaned and firmly pushed her away. He turned from her and ran a hand wearily over the back of his neck.

"There are advantages to letting me stay," Christine suggested softly. She'd promised herself she wasn't going to make the first move but it would seem that she needed all the ammunition she could get to make Maxwell listen to her.

He was shaking his head. "No."

She got impatient. "Maxwell, don't you think . . ."

He turned on her. "I said no, Christine. This is too serious. I can't have anyone here who doesn't understand that. The stakes are too high. The loss . . . too great. The pain . . . you don't know about the pain."

"I wish you'd stop talking as if you're the only one who's ever been hurt or lost someone you loved."

"The discussion is over," he said tightly, moving around her and opening the office door.

"No, it isn't," she said, nearly slamming the door

again. "The director was very glad to have me sign on. She said there was always a need for people. I want to be here. I can help."

He turned on her sharply. "So the staff thinks you're wonderful, and you seem to have won over the kids. I'm not surprised. I can't make you leave. But I just don't want you here. Is that clear enough?"

Christine was taken aback. She stared at him, truly at a loss for words. She felt like the blood was draining from her head and face, flooding down through the rest of her body. She felt heavy. And deeply hurt. He was serious. He meant it.

"You'll get bored with this in a month or so, and then leave and go back downtown, but these kids aren't going anywhere. They can't."

"All right. You've made your point," she said lightly, trying not to let her voice quiver. "Your loss. You're not the only one who can care, doctor."

He stared at her a moment more, then hesitated as if he would say something else. But this was like that moment in the stairwell when she'd seen what went on on the third floor. Her eyes seemed stark and huge in her face—Maxwell could see that his knife had cut deeply. He tightened his mouth and jaw.

"You said you have somewhere you have to be tonight."

"Yes," she said tonelessly.

"So do I. I have things to take care of . . . and Frances and I have plans for tonight."

Christine hitched the strap of her purse on her shoulder and swept past Maxwell and out of the office. "Have a nice evening," she said in a quiet, flat voice, walking briskly toward the exit.

Maxwell watched her go, feeling his chest constrict and a panicky urge to reach out to her. But he didn't. And he realized that it was probably the first cowardly thing he'd ever done in his entire life.

"I would never prescribe that medication for any of my patients," Frances said in amazement as she and Maxwell exited the auditorium at New York Hospital. "First of all, it hasn't been approved by the FDA and I don't like the methodology used for their test group. Not to mention that their control group was a completely different age range. I'd wait at least another two to four years to see more research results."

Maxwell nodded silently, and automatically took her arm as they crossed York Avenue heading west.

"It will be interesting to see what the other pediatricians and OB/GYNs think of this when we go to the national convention in October."

"Where did you park your car?" Maxwell asked, frowning.

Frances turned and glanced up at him. "In the usual place, on 72nd Street. But I thought we were going to have some dinner like we always do before heading home."

"I'm a little beat, Fran. I had a tough day."

"Oh, I'm sorry. Are the kids okay at the center? I meant to get over there this afternoon, but I had an emergency."

"About what you'd expect," Maxwell answered as they began walking down the dark residential side street between York and First Avenues.

"Well, it might help to talk about it. That's what we always do. Something might . . ."

"I think I just want to go home."

Frances didn't say anything for a moment. She'd known Maxwell long enough to know when he'd closed the door to her, and anyone else, when there was something on his mind. They'd been friends for almost nine years and professional colleagues for nearly four, and the signals had always been clear; there were certain corners of his life that were absolutely private. She'd always hoped that sooner or later he would recognize her concern . . . and her deep caring, and let her into his heart. But so far it hadn't happened.

Frances sighed as a couple passed them, holding hands and laughing over the details of a movie they'd just seen. She didn't know if she was ready to throw in the towel, however. She knew realistically what she was up against. But she also knew how to deal with it.

"Look, something is on your mind and I may not be able to help, but why don't we just stop and have a drink or some dessert and coffee? You might feel better afterward and I think it's better than going home alone and brooding."

After a moment Maxwell turned his head and smiled down on her. "Maybe you're right. Have anyplace in mind?"

She suggested one of their favorite hangouts and they headed in that direction. But it wasn't until they'd reached Second Avenue that Maxwell realized that he was just blocks from where Christine Morrow lived.

He tried to pay attention to Frances, to her quiet observations about the program they'd just attended or some of the gossip about colleagues they both knew. But his eyes betrayed him, straying around the avenue, imagining that he might see Christine by chance at any moment. He hoped he didn't. He had no idea how he'd react if he suddenly came face-to-face with her. Maxwell thought about that afternoon in his office, but even before then when he'd seen her on the second floor of the center with that little boy in her arms. She *did* have a way with people. She did have a way of getting your attention, and holding on tenaciously. She did get under your skin . . .

"Oh, good," Frances breathed in a delighted tone as they entered the restaurant. "Our favorite table is available."

They were seated and quickly gave their orders, but Maxwell was pensive and silent, still glancing repeatedly out the window at the passersby.

"I hear there's a new volunteer at the clinic," Frances began smoothly.

Maxwell gave her his attention finally, but only saw mild curiosity on her face. "Yes," he confirmed simply. The less said the better.

"Christine Morrow. That striking model we met at Cynthia Mallory's apartment."

"That's right," Maxwell confirmed, playing with his flatware.

"I can't imagine why she's interested in doing that kind of work. It's very hard. I bet she's not used to putting someone else's needs first. In her line of work everyone is so self-absorbed."

Maxwell felt his teeth clamp down hard. "She probably won't stay. Like you said, it's not what she's used to."

But even he knew he couldn't bet on it. Christine had succeeded in proving him wrong about a lot of things. Whenever he thought of her, images and memories of Rachel had a way of holding him at bay. That was how he knew he was still vulnerable to pain and rejection. That was why he was afraid to get too close to Christine. He wanted her. But he couldn't go through that again.

"She is incredibly beautiful," Frances conceded.

Having Frances say so, however, annoyed Maxwell, as if she thought he hadn't noticed. He merely nodded, shifting his gaze to look out the window again.

"Well, I don't think she can be depended on. Someone like that doesn't need to be exposed to the center or its problems. I enjoyed meeting her, though. Now I know what being a model is like. I bet no one takes her seriously about anything but clothes and hairstyles," Frances added and chuckled lightly.

Maxwell arched a brow and sat back as their food was served. "I think Christine Morrow could surprise you," he said without a trace of irony. "I bet she has a lot of hidden talents that no one gives her credit for."

"I'm so glad to see you!" Alexandra Parker said joyfully as she hugged her sister.

Christine chuckled. "I don't know why. I worked real hard to aggravate you when we were growing up."

"I know," Alex said with a grin. "But I remember I always got even."

"Only 'cause you were older."

"And smarter."

Christine made a face at her sister, very much as she used to do when Alex tried to boss her around. She was a good four inches taller than her sister, and she felt funny bending over her. "You don't look like you gained any weight at all from the baby," she observed critically, eyeing Alexandra's slight frame.

Alexandra beamed, the inherited sprinkle of freckles over the bridge of her nose making her look much younger than thirty-five and considerably less sophisticated than Christine. "I didn't. Everything I ate went into making my beautiful little girl."

Christine pursed her mouth and shook her head in mock horror. "Well, you can't use maternity outfits as an excuse anymore. Girl, you have *got* to do something about your clothes. What is that thing you have on? I know designers who would faint if they saw you. They'd *never* believe we were related. You look terrible."

"Parker doesn't think so. Besides, I haven't had time to worry about my clothes."

"I bet all those pretty things I sent you last spring from Europe are still in their boxes."

"That's right. I couldn't wear them now anyway. But next year . . . watch out. I'm going to make Parker drool."

"He does that already. I've never seen a man and woman more in love than you two. It's disgusting," Christine said dryly, drawing laughter from her sister. "So, where is this miracle I keep hearing so much about?"

"You haven't even gotten in the door yet. Come on up and put your things down."

Christine put her leather duffel down by the foot of the stairwell and looked around. It wasn't the home she and Alex had been raised in. This was Alex and Parker's house, bought the year after they'd gotten married more than six years ago, the same year they had insisted that George Morrow come and live with them because of his poor health. It was open and airy, with sunlight coming in through contemporary glass windows. Very unlike the simple Cape Cod she'd known as a little girl, and had grown to dislike as being too small and old-fashioned.

Christine silently glanced around at the good furniture, the rich carpeting, and paintings. The baby

grand in the front parlor, Parker's prize possession
next to his wife and daughter. But looking around
the well-appointed rooms, Christine suddenly felt a
longing for the shabby comfort of the house she
used to know. The corner of her mouth rose in a
sad smile. She remembered when she couldn't wait
to leave it and go to New York. And yet, this morning when she started out on the four-hour drive
south, she couldn't wait to get back.

In New York she led the life she always thought
she'd wanted. But it had been cold comfort in light
of that horrible conversation with Maxwell Chandler. Christine felt herself grow confused all over
again every time she recalled how he had turned
her away. It didn't make sense when she was so sure
he was attracted to her. That night they'd spent together was not an apparition. That kiss in his office
was still branded on her mouth. Maxwell Chandler
said one thing . . . but she wondered if it was possible that he meant something else?

"Daddy is taking a nap," Alexandra volunteered,
smiling as her sister wandered aimlessly, getting re-
acquainted with the house. She did this every single
time she came to D.C, as if the visits were some sort
of reality check.

"Where's Parker?" Christine asked, finally retriev-
ing her weekend case and following her sister up
the stairs. They went past the first bedroom to the
room given to Christine when she visited. Alex sat
on the side of the bed and watched as Christine
began to unpack her things.

"He had a rehearsal. He's doing a special concert
with Herbie Hancock next week and they're going
over the program. I think Nancy Wilson is supposed
to be the soloist."

Christine grinned at her sister. "My, the company you people keep."

Alexandra wrinkled her nose. "Yeah, I guess. I remember when all of that used to seem so important, and now it just isn't."

"Does that mean you've given up on your music now that you're a mother?"

"No. I'm still going to teach. I love doing that, and I don't mind an occasional concert or chorus. But if I never make it to the Grammys it's just not that important."

Christine sighed. "You're so lucky."

"I can't believe I'm hearing this," Alexandra teased. "I remember when you used to get on my case because you didn't think I had enough killer instinct to go all the way to the top. Well, you were right, I didn't. I think you got it all . . . along with all the good genes and beauty."

Christine glanced poignantly at her sister, again recalling Maxwell's parting words. Remembering how he would rather play it safe behind someone like Frances Grimes than admit there could be anything between them. "Alex . . . I think I'd give it all up in a heartbeat to have what you have right now."

Alex looked askance at Christine, detecting the sigh and tone of . . . regret. Her sister was not given to feeling sorry for herself, or even to *being* sorry about anything. Alexandra always envied her sister's ability to throw herself into a situation and let the feathers fly. "Christine, is everything okay?"

"Yeah. It's just that . . . sometimes I feel . . ." she sighed heavily. "I don't know. Sometimes I wonder what I'm doing with my life. Where do I go from here?"

"Does that mean you're tired of modeling and thinking of giving it up?"

"Maybe. I just don't think there's anything else I'm good at."

"There are lots of things you could do."

"Name one," Christine shot back.

Alexandra thought for about a half a second and then shook her head. "I'll get back to you on that," she said lightly and got up.

"I thought so," Christine murmured with a sigh of resignation.

"Come on . . . I want you to meet someone."

They went into a room that connected to the master bedroom. It was small, probably originally intended to be a sitting room but bright and cheerful and filled with the evidence of the presence of a baby. Alexandra had been serious when she'd told her sister that Parker had tried to buy every stuffed animal in the store for his new daughter, but Christine was not interested in fuzzy dinosaurs or cute teddy bears. She approached the crib and her mouth dropped open as she peered down on her niece.

She wasn't asleep, but lay quietly squirming about, her tiny head turning to catch movement and sounds, and appearing to blink in wide-eyed surprise at the adults standing over her. Her mouth made a little "O" of surprise. She was the color of creamy caramel, with a light black swirl of hair that hugged her scalp. Lauren Shani Harrison was dressed in a yellow seersucker one-piece sleeper with a duckling appliqued in the center of her chest.

"Oh . . . Alex!" Christine said in awe. "Look at her. Can I . . ."

"Go ahead," Alexandra nodded.

Christine reached slowly into the crib and put her hands around her niece to lift her from the bed. She was small but heavier than Christine would have thought. She placed the baby against her chest and shoulder, one hand supporting her back and head, the other under her rear.

Alexandra watched with a smile—and a surprised gleam in her eyes. She hadn't expected this reaction from her sister. Christine was not effusive about very much nor had she ever been particularly demonstrative. Alex used to surmise that it was because they'd lost their mother when they were so young, and perhaps Christine was simply being protective of her feelings and emotions. She kept them to herself so she wouldn't be hurt. Alexandra also recalled that not much impressed her sister, either, or held her attention . . . or made her emotional. But her response to her new niece, Alex had to admit, was one of near-reverence.

"She's so quiet . . ."

Alexandra chuckled with a shake of her head. "For the moment. She threw a hissyfit this morning like you wouldn't believe. Reminded me of you when you were a kid and couldn't get your own way. You used to stretch out on the floor and have a tantrum."

"I don't believe you."

"Ask Daddy."

Christine closed her eyes and let the experience seep into her. The weight of Lauren against her was so sweet. Her little body was warm and vibrant . . . and she smelled so different from anything else she'd ever known. New and fresh. A fist waved and rested against Christine's mouth, and the fingers spread out to grab hold. Five incredibly tiny, perfect fingers. They were cool and slightly damp. Christine took hold of a foot and the baby reacted instinctively as she was tickled, wiggling her toes.

Christine opened her eyes, and Alex was stunned to see tears glistening.

"She . . . she's so beautiful," Christine said in a whisper, slowly swaying back and forth with the baby in her arms.

Alexandra could see that Christine was deeply affected by seeing her niece. And the reaction seemed to be so intensely personal that she quietly left the room.

Christine was reluctant to leave the baby, and would have been just as happy to sit watching her for the next several hours. But she finally came downstairs after Lauren had fallen back to sleep. Her father was up and waiting for her with Alexandra in the family room.

"Baby!" he said, holding his emaciated arms out so his younger daughter could hug and greet him.

He'd always called her Baby, and for the moment Christine would have liked nothing better than to be treated like one, letting her family enfold her with love and security.

Alexandra was setting the table for dinner when Parker came in and Christine enjoyed another greeting from her brother-in-law. It was amazing to her that he was so famous and sought after, yet so down to earth. Her father might indulge her out of unconditional parental love, but Parker understood her and was her confidant. He was the first person she couldn't easily impress, and the first who expected her to take responsibilities for her decisions.

"So, I suppose we're going to hear how you have everyone in New York under your spell. How you've taken over Seventh Avenue and are going to launch your own designer line?" Parker teased, hugging her after he'd kissed his wife.

"Not hardly," Christine returned, chuckling nervously as they stood with their arms around one another affectionately. "I don't want to talk about New York. I came to meet my niece and see all of you."

"Oh, yeah?" Parker said and shook his head as he gazed into her face with a slight frown. "You're not going to get away with that." He patted her back and released her. "We'll talk later. Right now I want to go see my little girl."

Everything settled down to a routine Christine was sure went on when she wasn't there. She stood and watched her sister checking what was in the oven. Her father had his feet propped up on a footstool, his glasses perched on the end of his nose while he read the evening papers. She glanced at Parker as he casually whistled a melody under his breath and leafed quickly through the day's pile of mail and magazines. Christine took a deep breath and felt some of the pain ease in her chest. She was going to be okay. New York and Seventh Avenue—and Dr. D. Maxwell Chandler—were far away.

And she was home.

"I think I'm gonna go to bed. I'm not a young man anymore and you folks are wearin' me out," George Morrow muttered as he slowly got up from his favorite chair.

Christine uncurled herself from the sofa and got up to take her father's arm. She kissed him on the top of his head. He grunted in embarrassment. "Good night, Daddy."

"See you all in the morning." He turned momentarily to pat his daughter's cheek. "Glad to see you, Baby."

"Me, too, Daddy. Sleep well."

"I think I hear Lauren. I'd better go on up and feed her before she starts fussing," Alexandra said,

putting aside the pile of thank you notes she was
writing to those who'd sent cards and baby gifts.

Parker grabbed her hand as she passed his chair,
and pulled Alexandra down so he could quickly kiss
her. "I'll be up in a minute."

Christine sighed and slowly returned to the sofa,
sat down, and curled herself into a corner. She
picked up one of the cards and thoughtfully scruti-
nized the design on the front. Cute and colorful,
clever and cheerful. But Christine was really thinking
about earlier in the evening, just before they'd finally
sat down to dinner, when she'd gone up to her room
to get several small gifts she'd brought from recent
travels for the family and more boxes from the trunk
of her car for the baby. She recalled how much fun
she'd had going through the infants' section of a
New York department store, buying all the nice
things she could find. Then she recalled peeking into
the baby's room, seeing Parker sitting in Alexandra's
rocker with his daughter in the crook of his arm. She
was going to say something teasing to her brother-
in-law, but instead her attention had been held by
the look of sheer wonder on his face. And the most
intense smile of pride and joy. He had been so careful of the baby, knowing just how to hold her, just
what to do to make her gurgle and grin. Christine
had quickly backed away before she'd been seen.

That had been endearing, but the moment that
had really grabbed her heart occurred just after dinner. She was telling her father about the commercial
she was going to be filming in July when she decided
to help Alexandra serve dessert. Christine had gone
into the kitchen only to find that Parker had his
wife in a light embrace, and they were whispering
quietly . . . lovingly . . . to one another.

Mush, Christine had grimaced to herself sarcastically. But she also knew that the obvious love that existed so easily between her sister and Parker seemed like something that only a few people ever had. And she didn't think she was going to be one of them. Thoughts of Keith Layton came to mind. But Maxwell Chandler . . .

"How long can you stay with us?" Parker said, breaking into her thoughts.

Christine sighed. "Only until Sunday afternoon. I have an important meeting with my agent on Monday morning, and I'm shooting two new ads in the afternoon."

"You don't sound very excited about it. Is the thrill gone?"

She shrugged. "Maybe. Going, at least." She leaned her head back on the cushion and frowned at her brother-in-law. "Parker, do you . . . like me?"

He raised his brows and chuckled. "Most of the time." Christine grimaced but didn't retaliate. That's the first thing Parker noticed. It had been a real question. His tone changed to match her sudden thoughtfulness. "Anything you want to talk about?"

"No, not really. It's just that . . . sometimes I get sick of posing and having people fool around with my hair. I'm surprised I'm not bald with all the different things they do to it. I know I can't do this forever, but I don't know what I want to do next."

"Well, you've been pretty smart about saving and investing your money . . ."

"Thanks to you . . ."

"So just take your time. Something will come up. How about going back to designing?"

She shook her head. "I'm not really interested anymore." She hesitated and glanced at Parker. "I've started doing some volunteer work."

"Really? Where? At one of the houses? At the agency?"

"It has nothing to do with fashion. It's a children's clinic. The kids all have AIDS."

Parker sat forward, bracing his elbows on his knees as he regarded Christine closely. "I'd like to hear about this."

So she told him everything . . . short of mentioning Maxwell's name or her relationship to him. She couldn't do that because part of her problem was that Christine didn't know what the relationship was. But she thought about him all the time, wondering how she could get his attention and make him take her seriously. How she could convince him that there was a lot she could offer the children.

"That's pretty heavy stuff, Christine," Parker said quietly, concern and surprise in his voice.

"Don't you think I know that? Don't you think I can handle it?"

Parker stared at her for a long moment, seeing a young, incredibly attractive woman who drew attention to herself like a magnet. Who had the stuff of which celebrity was made . . . and who enjoyed it. Parker had always known, from the first moment he'd met Christine and she'd tried to use her feminine wiles on him, that she was used to getting what she wanted . . . and that it didn't always involve thinking about other people. She could be, at times, like an undisciplined force that appears in your life to wreak havoc, then leave you breathless . . . and ultimately forgiving of her egocentrism.

Still, Parker had noticed some changes in Christine in the past year. Fewer boyfriends and less attention in the gossip columns. Not as many frantic phone calls home when things didn't go her way. And every now and then she'd do something surprising. No. More than that. It would blow you away. Like this revelation.

"Honestly? I don't know. The thing is, you can't go in there and change the story for those kids, Christine. There will be no happy endings."

"But there are," she said, leaning toward him eagerly. "There's this one little child who was born with the virus but now he's almost two and it's all gone. He just outgrew it! And they just found out that AZT can be given to a pregnant woman who has AIDS and there's an 18 percent chance the baby won't have it."

Parker was astonished. She had learned an awful lot and was so excited about that little bit of good news. And she certainly seemed involved. "Well, I would say that volunteering is a good thing in general. I'm impressed. I remember when Alex used to give music lessons to poor children from D.C. She loved it. But I would still tell you to be careful."

"I will. When I go back I'm going to have one of the nurses show me how to handle the really sick children . . ."

"Christine . . ."

"I was thinking I'll even go with them when some of the kids go to camp in the fall . . ."

"Whoa . . . slow down. Where did all of this suddenly come from?"

An image of D. Maxwell Chandler went swiftly through her mind. "It just . . . happened," she said with a shrug.

"And you're serious about this?" She nodded. "Well, all I can say is I'm impressed, but I still want you to be careful."

"I'll be okay," she assured him.

"So, why did you want to know if I liked you?"

"Well . . . I'm having a problem with someone at the center who thinks I'm just in the way."

Parker raised his brows but remained silent. He suspected a *he* someone at the clinic. Interesting. Christine never used to care what people thought of her. Her ego was too strong to bother with people who didn't like her. She'd just blow them off.

". . . And I want to show I really care. There are lots of things I can do. I made a donation and they bought a TV and VCR for the children's playroom. Now we can get some cartoons for them to watch while they're waiting for treatment . . ." Christine gasped and sat up straight. She stared totally wide-eyed at Parker. "I got it! I could raise money for the center. I could talk to all my friends."

"That's a huge responsibility. Ask your sister. There's nothing tougher than trying to separate people from their money," he said dryly.

Christine's eyes filled with a light that was soft and thoughtful. "Yes, there is. Watching children die."

Parker sat back again and made a temple of his long, well-shaped fingers, regarding Christine. "I change my mind. I've decided I like you a lot. As a matter of fact, Christine Morrow, you're probably one of my favorite people," Parker commented with feeling.

Christine grinned happily from ear to ear.

Alexandra closed the door softly behind her and approached the bed. Parker turned off the light as she climbed in beside him, and held his arms open so she could settle against him. Over her shoulder he made a final visual check of the monitor, plugged in on top of the dresser across the room. The light was on, indicating that the transmission was working from the baby's room, ready to alert them if anything went wrong during the night. He sighed and relaxed.

"Did you have a chance to talk with Christine?" Alex asked, hugging her arm across Parker's bare chest.

"Ummmm," he rumbled deep in his chest.

"So, tell me. What's going on with her? Does Keith still want to marry her? Is she still planning to buy that house on Martha's Vineyard?"

"Sorry. That's privileged information," he said and smiled in the dark.

Alexandra scoffed. "That's not right. Just because you're the only one she'll open up to . . ."

"Exactly. We didn't talk about Keith or the house. I will say that . . . things are looking up. I think we can expect some major changes in the future."

"What's that supposed to mean?"

Parker turned on his side so he could kiss Alexandra. He knew he'd have to settle for cuddling for a few more weeks but that was okay. He was feeling a little bit smug at the moment, surrounded by people he loved.

"It means that I think Christine is finally maturing. She's figured out there's somewhere else she'd rather be than at the center of the universe."

Seven

"I saw you on TV last night," the woman said in an offhand manner. She was putting her daughter's sneakers back on as the little girl sat listlessly in her lap.

"Did you?" Christine asked absently, trying to distract the little girl from the discomfort of having sat for nearly three hours with a transfusion needle in her arm. She pulled two lollipops from the pocket of her smock and handed them to the child.

"Thank you," the girl said shyly.

"You're welcome." Christine smiled, touching the child's face gently and feeling how unnaturally cool the skin was . . . and thin.

"It was some commercial about stockings. I loved the dress you had on. Do you get to keep the clothes? Do they still pay you?"

Christine finally gave the woman her attention, but began to gather up the toys that had been scattered around the playroom during the day. She turned off the TV and pushed chairs in under the tables. "They *have* to pay me. Sometimes I can keep the clothes, or I can buy them at a discount."

"Man, you must make a lot of money," the woman continued, shaking her head.

"I do," Christine admitted, because it was the truth. But it made her feel awkward to say so because she was so aware of the fact that all the parents with children in the center, in fact, the entire community, would not make as much in a year as she could in a month.

"Well, if you're making so much money, what are you doing here?"

Christine sighed and stood in front of the woman, smiling down at her daughter as she sucked on a yellow lollipop, the size of it bulging out her cheek. "I like being here. I like spending time with the kids and helping out."

"Don't you have any kids of your own?"

Christine continued to focus on the child. She had a vision of her niece just starting out in life . . . and in perfect health. She could still feel the way Lauren felt when she held her, warm and lively. Unlike the children here, many of whom were literally fading away. Christine grinned slowly. "No. Not yet," she answered. Because she'd finally come to a vague decision that it might be nice to have her own baby someday. She hadn't gotten to the details of how it was going to happen, yet. She'd only fantasized about the end result.

"Do you get your nails done every week?" the woman persisted.

"Sometimes twice a week," she said. "Especially if I have a lot of events to go to, or if I'm modeling evening wear. Tell you what. The next time you come I'll do your nails for you."

"For real?" the woman asked, clearly excited and pleased.

"For real," Christine chuckled. She gave the little girl a hug, and watched as mother and child left.

But when she was alone in the room, her smile quickly faded. It was overwhelming to find out, each time she came to the clinic, how much the women and children didn't have. Sometimes even simple pleasures, like a manicure, that she took for granted and did as often as she had her laundry done, Christine mused. She'd already given another donation to buy books for the clinic library and a microwave for the staff lounge.

She remembered the morning she'd stood at her closet, unable to get even one more hanger on the rack, unable even to look through what was already there.

"This is ridiculous . . ." she'd muttered.

Starting at one end of her closet, Christine had begun to go through her clothes, pulling things out and tossing them on her bed. There were things she didn't even remember having, outfits she hadn't worn in a year or no more than once. Soon the bed was piled with garments for every occasion, and not *one* that was classic and could stand up over time.

Christine had called Delores and together they'd organized a rummage sale. They put up posters at the center and invited all the women . . . staff and parents. Nothing was more than ten dollars, and all the money went back to the center. Christine had watched, at one point, as Delores had handled some of the items—gingerly, as if she was afraid to touch anything.

"You can have anything you like," she'd offered, almost indifferently, careful of Delores's response. "For helping me," Christine added so it wouldn't seem like charity. She'd become very sensitive to the need for the women she'd met at LIFELINE to maintain their pride.

Christine felt relief. Now her closet looked reasonable. If she never bought another stitch of clothing she'd still have too many things.

Her one indulgence had been to buy a pretty pink

robe for Wendy. And then, one afternoon after gearing up her courage, she'd gone up to the third floor. Wendy was asleep, the baby doll that Christine had gotten her weeks earlier held tightly in her emaciated arms. She'd left the robe at the foot of the little girl's bed and had reached out to gently stroke her cheek. Christine had been very upset to feel how cool and waxy Wendy's skin felt. Unnatural.

Christine was thoughtful as she sat at one of the children's tables, her long legs bent until her knees were almost level with her neck. She carefully replaced crayons in a box and gathered the many pieces of a jigsaw puzzle. There was so much that was needed at the center, and it was beginning to hit her that just coming for a few hours twice a week was not nearly enough. And while her small donations had helped, money was needed for more substantial things. The center desperately needed a Titmus II machine for visual eye screening, and a video camera and viewing equipment to use for demonstrations and as a teaching aid. Suddenly the idea she'd mentioned to Parker about finding a way to raise money began to seem like the only way to get what was needed.

"Hi."

Christine's insides reacted strongly to the greeting, but she still tried not to jump at the sound of Maxwell Chandler's voice. She did fumble a handful of crayons and they dropped and rolled on the table. She quickly gathered them, sparing him an indifferent glance over her shoulder, as if she was too busy to be interrupted at the moment. Christine's stomach muscles did a tap dance. And she was doubly annoyed to realize she'd been more or less waiting for this moment, wondering how she and Maxwell would respond to each other. She hadn't seen or spoken to him since driving down to D.C. "Hi," she finally answered carefully.

"I thought Mrs. Atkins was here."

"I think she and the other floor nurses had to go over to the main building for a meeting. I told her I would close up the playroom today." She began the unnecessary chore of organizing the crayons into the spectrum of secondary and tertiary colors. She could hear Maxwell slowly advance into the room and could tell how near he was by the way her heartbeat accelerated. He came to stand just behind her, but still she wouldn't acknowledge his presence by looking at him.

"I see you've made a big impression. And I know you've made several donations. I want to thank you for that. The money has helped a lot."

"You still sound so surprised." She felt him move closer, the bottom of his open lab coat brushing against her back.

"I'm not anymore," he said quietly.

His confession was unexpected and threw Christine off for a moment. But she was on guard, nonetheless. She'd tried so hard to reach out to Maxwell Chandler. She'd taken a great risk with him. They'd come together intimately in what had turned out to be a moment of sheer bliss. And hope, Christine realized later. But it had happened much too soon. She hadn't been sure she was willing to try again.

"You'll get over it. I'm sure you'll find some reason to add to the list of things you don't like about me."

"I never said I didn't like you."

"You did," she said and rounded on him. Her heart felt like it was lodged in her throat when she looked into his eyes . . . his face. He seemed huge looming over her. For no reason just then Christine remembered the way his mouth had felt kissing her. She could even evoke the scent of him. Her imagination went into overdrive. "You told me that . . . that night. You know what I mean."

"So . . . you remember that night, too," he said with surprising softness.

Christine got up from the chair and put the box of crayons away in a cabinet. "I don't think we should talk about that night. Maybe that was a mistake."

Maxwell felt his jaw tighten. He didn't know if he should tell Christine that it wasn't, that he'd been thinking about her ever since. And he didn't know how to tell her he'd let his own fears and insecurities betray what he was beginning to feel for her. Maxwell sighed in frustration and jammed his hands in the pocket of the lab coat. "Look, we've been at each other's throats from the start. I don't want to fight with you anymore, Christine. I just want to let you know you were right and I had no business talking to you the way I did. You're doing a good job. Everyone says so. I just want you to know . . . I'm glad you're here."

Christine could hear the sincerity in his voice. And she could tell it was costing him a lot. "Are you trying to apologize again, Max?" she asked quietly, trying to read his expression . . . and his mind.

He sighed. "I'm just trying to say maybe I've been unfair. I never gave you a chance."

Christine faced him squarely and raised her chin stubbornly as she let her gaze wander over him. "And you think that makes everything all right?"

"No," he said honestly. "But I'm hoping it's a start."

Christine continued to stare at him. She had to be very careful this time, not brash and flippant.

She, too, had been doing a lot of thinking about that night with Maxwell. It had been extraordinary. Something about it worked, made sense. But it had been purely physical and Christine had been around long enough to know that kind of sensation simply didn't last. She didn't want a brief encounter with Maxwell Chandler.

Suddenly, Christine recalled something her sister had gone through a number of years ago with Parker. They had met again, after ten years, at the wedding of a friend. Alexandra said she'd known almost immediately that she was in love with Parker Harrison, but that there was a lot of stuff each of them had to work out that had to do with the past. Learning from mistakes. Growing up.

That was it. Parker had said to her again just the week before that it took a long time to grow up. That you had to get to a place where you could say, 'I'm sorry', and 'please', and . . . 'I love you'. He said it took a lot of work.

But Christine knew that she had seen the payoff. She wanted what Alexandra and Parker had. She wanted to be happy. She wanted to be cherished. She wanted someone who could see beyond the glamorous image and straight into her heart. Someone who would treat her as if there was something more going on inside than just a love for fashion and fun. But first Christine knew she had to show there was more. She tilted her head at Maxwell.

"Let me think about it," she responded softly. "Good night, Dr. Chandler," Christine said demurely as she stepped around him to leave.

"It seems we're back where we started," Maxwell said as she reached the door.

Christine stopped and turned to him. She saw a man who was strong, good-looking, very smart, with an integrity and a capacity for caring that was inspiring. She knew only one other man like that whom she had come to trust implicitly, and who she could give her affection to unconditionally. Her brother-in-law, Parker. She found herself smiling at Maxwell.

"Maybe you're in the same place. But I'm not."

Two can play this game, Maxwell thought as he watched her leave. But by the end of the week he found that he was on the losing end because Christine Morrow had changed the rules. She no longer confronted him. She ignored him.

He observed how everyone at the center responded to her, greeting her like she was royalty and waving her off at the end of her shift as if she was family. And she got things done. From a janitorial staff that was programmed to respond 'It's not my job', she got someone to repaint the playroom. She somehow managed to talk a limo service into providing transportation for six of the children, their guardians, and the other volunteers, and took them to see the Big Apple Circus. Of course, she'd also managed to talk someone else into paying for the tickets.

Delores had a birthday in mid-June and Christine got an ice cream cake so there could be a celebration. Maxwell remembered hearing the voices coming from the playroom late one afternoon. Most of the staff was there, having cake and chatting and congratulating Delores for reaching another birthday without any symptoms of the HIV virus. Maxwell had come to stand in the doorway, unaware that this had been planned.

"Hey, Doc," one of the male floor aides had called, beckoning him in.

Maxwell touched Delores's arm and wished her a

happy birthday. And then he had turned his attention to Christine. She was playing hostess—he was not surprised. But she had not allowed herself to be the center of attention. That spot had been reserved solely for Delores. Maxwell had then turned to Christine, steeling himself against the contention that was always between them. She was watching him and Maxwell felt the constriction in his chest as he recognized that Christine Morrow had succeeded in getting thoroughly under his skin. She slowly began walking toward him, through the throng, until she was a few feet away. She was wearing a beige knit skirt that stopped a few inches above her knees and a simple black tunic top. Her hair was in a loose pageboy.

"I suppose you're going to tell me that this is against regulations or something. That I'm disrupting the staff and their work routine."

Maxwell pursed his lips and glanced briefly around the room at the good time everyone seemed to be having. "Actually . . ." he began, bringing his attention back to her, "I was going to ask if I can have a piece of cake."

Christine looked uncertain, blinking at him as she detected the note of ease and even teasing in his tone. "Then, you're not mad at me for doing this?"

Maxwell chuckled silently. "Would it do any good if I was?"

She grinned impishly and shook her head. "No."

"I didn't think so. What kind of ice cream do you have?"

"Everything. Chocolate, vanilla, and strawberry."

Christine carefully cut a slice of the cake for Maxwell, handing him the paper plate and accompanying him to the window ledge where he could put down his things and eat.

"This is very nice of you," he said quietly, casting a sideways glance at her.

Christine sighed. "I don't mind. It's such a little thing. And when I think of everything Delores has been through . . ."

Maxwell could see, however, that Christine had worked her wiles on Delores. She was changing and blossoming into a self-confident, productive adult. She was taking better care of herself physically, had found a decent apartment and moved out of the women's shelter she'd lived in for two years. She'd gotten a new hairstyle . . . and she smiled more frequently.

Maxwell realized that while he may have had his reservations about Christine Morrow, she was quickly and effectively destroying every single misconception he'd had about her. He'd thought she was self-centered and spoiled, frivolous and irresponsible. But he hadn't seen any evidence of that since she'd started working at the center. He'd come to know that if there were sudden bursts of laughter, it was because she was somewhere around. The incredible thing was that her popularity in no way detracted from the needs of the children or the attention the staff gave to them. If anything, she seemed to energize everyone and make them do just a little bit more. The only person she hadn't included in her entourage of worshippers was himself, Maxwell admitted. He was on the outside looking in. He'd perhaps handled things all wrong, Maxwell thought wryly, watching her at a recent meeting of the center volunteers and no longer surprised at the way she worked a room.

Maxwell finally came to the conclusion that if she put her mind to it Christine could charm Tiffany's out of a tiara. And as much as he realized she'd genuinely thrown herself into her work at the center, he wanted to warn her to keep a balance.

"I understand we have you to thank for the new computer in the volunteer's office. It was pretty expensive, Christine."

She shrugged. "It's only money."

"I wasn't going to criticize you," he said, putting up a hand at the slight defensive tightening in her mouth. She was looking at him furtively to see if he meant it. "It's just that . . . there's always something we need here. You can't continue to take care of it all. I won't let you."

Christine suddenly turned to him, her eyes bright. "I know, and I have an idea about how we can maybe make money for the center."

Maxwell finished the cake and tossed the plate into a nearby garbage bin. "I hope you're not going to suggest a cake sale, or something like that," he teased. He felt gratified when she smiled.

"No, I have something much bigger in mind."

He regarded her in fascination. "Why doesn't that surprise me?"

"I'm serious, Maxwell," she said, reaching to grasp his arm. She quickly released it and looked around to see if anyone else had noticed.

"Is it going to take a lot of time or cost money to get started?"

"So, you're interested?"

"I've learned that if I don't pay attention to you you're likely to go off on your own and do it anyway. So, what's the idea?"

Christine just stared at him. He was really going to listen to her. He hadn't summarily dismissed her without hearing her out. She blinked at him thoughtfully, realizing that something had changed in Maxwell. The first thing she noticed was that the caution was gone. And the negative knee-jerk reaction to anything having to do with her. But also, when he looked at her she could see a different kind of light and consideration in his eyes, as if he was really seeing her . . . not through her. Right now he seemed to be probing deeply . . . trying to reach what was inside.

She found herself dropping her gaze for a moment. It astonished Christine to find that she felt shy under Maxwell's intense scrutiny. There was an odd fluttering in her stomach. More than that, however, were the vivid memories of having made love with him. That had been visceral and satisfying. And she wondered if he could possibly read her mind or hear her heart beat with a rush of wistful thinking.

"This is a birthday party. I don't want to talk about it here."

Maxwell stared at the bent head. There was a momentary urge to touch her, but instead he folded his arms across his chest. "All right. What do you have in mind?"

She looked at him swiftly, noting the speculation in his expression and the tension evident in the working of his facial muscles. That had always fascinated her about Maxwell—the way he seemed to experience everything so deeply. Took so much to heart. Except her, of course, but . . . maybe that was changing, too.

"Can we have a meeting or something?"

He raised his brows. "Or something?"

She felt as if she would blush. She studied her hands. "I could make an appointment to come to your office. Or would you care to go out for dinner?"

Maxwell didn't say anything for a while. He wasn't

sure he'd heard right. She provided him with choices—she'd just suggested that they go out. "Dinner . . ." he repeated to himself.

"But if you don't have the time . . ."

"I think I'd better make this sooner rather than later. Otherwise I'll read about what you've gone ahead and done in the Sunday papers."

She shrugged at his assessment of the possibilities. "I know that the privacy of the families and the dignity of the children is more important than making headlines, Max. I have learned a few things."

"Yes, you have. Dinner sounds fine. When?"

"Tonight? When we're finished here."

He checked his watch. "I'm meeting Frances upstairs to check on some of the children soon. Where shall I meet you?"

"In front of the center," she instructed, moving away to circulate with the others again. She smiled at him mischievously. "I figure if I ply you with enough wine you might let me do anything."

To her great surprise, Maxwell laughed. It was transforming. It made him appear surprisingly boyish. She could image Maxwell as a college jock. Football for sure. Baseball, maybe. Christine knew she'd just witnessed a side of him that rarely surfaced.

"I just might," he confirmed with a nod.

She was excited—and nervous—as she waited outside for Maxwell. Christine shook her head, bemused. Parker would die laughing if he could see her now. Fidgety and unsure of herself. Filled with fantasies and daydreams. Wondering, what were the chances of her and Maxwell . . .

"Sorry I kept you waiting."

Christine turned, ready with a flippant response. Except that Frances Grimes was with Maxwell. She tried to keep her expression pleasant, but the thought came to her that Frances was going to join them. "Hi, Frances," she said to the other woman.

Frances returned the smile. "Maxwell and I were just talking about what a great volunteer you're becoming."

"Were you?" Christine said.

"Yes. We could use ten more like you."

"Sorry. I'm one of a kind," Christine said dryly and watched a moment of uncertainty furrow the doctor's brow.

"Yes . . . well, Maxwell said you had some ideas about raising money for the center."

Christine felt her hackles go up, She wondered what else had been discussed between them. But she continued to give Frances her attention. "Only if Max thinks it's appropriate," she deferred, and gained a point when she used her own nickname for Maxwell and watched the surprise in Frances's eyes. "Are you coming, too?" she finally asked, a bit too sharply.

"No," Maxwell answered. "Frances is taking a summer class at Columbia."

"That's too bad," Christine said.

"I'll hear all about it tomorrow."

Maxwell and Christine accepted a ride with Frances to 96th Street, then she headed up to the Columbia campus. They found a small Italian restaurant, the entire front of which was constructed with French doors opening onto Broadway. Christine and Maxwell were seated toward the side, allowing them to talk without having to compete with New York noise. He was not surprised when she declined a glass of wine and ordered iced tea, the house salad with dressing on the side, and grilled fillet of snapper.

They were halfway through dinner before they'd

dispensed with the chitchat and Maxwell reluctantly turned the talk to discussing Christine's plans.

"We're just a small neighborhood clinic. I don't think you could raise more than a few thousand dollars."

Christine arched a brow and smiled at him across the table. "I think we could raise twenty times that amount, maybe more."

"Okay, I'm listening," Maxwell said skeptically.

Christine's eyes brightened. "I think we should hold a charity function complete with food, entertainment, big-name sponsors, programs printed with all the names of the pledges, gifts for everyone who attends . . . for a price, of course."

Maxwell looked stunned. "You're kidding, right?"

"No, why should I be? You've been to those big nights for every not-or-profit organization known to man. You were there at that political thing for what's-his-name . . ."

"And I didn't want to be there."

"But you *were,*" Christine countered. "You bought a ticket."

Maxwell frowned and shook his head. "Not because I believed in the politician, but because he controls the district my hospital is in."

"Whatever. It was a compelling reason, so you bit the bullet and coughed up big bucks. So, why shouldn't we do the same thing for LIFELINE?"

"You mean, buy a ticket to go to an event and the proceeds go to a tiny children's clinic in Harlem?"

"That's right."

Maxwell's curiosity deepened. "Why would anyone want to do that?"

"Because it's a very good cause. And because I ask them to."

Maxwell thought about it for half a minute and began to shake his head. "No."

"Why not?"

"Because it has a carnival ring to it and I'm not sure that's an image I want to project for the center."

"What the center needs and its image are two different things. What we do for a fundraiser is a third. They don't have to overlap."

"I don't see how they can't," he said impatiently.

Christine sighed and reached across the table to lay her hand over his. "Listen to me. I think you're a great doctor. I couldn't do what you do, and I wouldn't want to. It's too hard. But you couldn't do what I do, either."

"What? Look great in clothes and be photogenic? Charm the pants off just about anyone?"

Christine stopped for a moment and blinked. She grinned at him. "Is that what I do to you? If that's a back-door compliment, I'll take it. What I mean is, planning an event that gets people out."

"You have that many friends?"

She grimaced. "I wouldn't call them all friends, exactly. I'm sure some of them would like to plant a knife in my ribs at times, but that's just professional competition. It's not personal."

Maxwell slowly grinned at her in return. He could well believe that people had strong opinions about Christine Morrow. Either you liked her . . . or you didn't. He'd already seen what she was like when she made a commitment—thorough and strong. She was not a hypocrite. She was animated and bright. She had indomitable spirit and he loved watching the way she didn't shrink from anything. Not even him when he was at his worst. Maxwell realized, as her cool hand lay soft and light over his, that he was in serious trouble. He'd already suspected that he was more than a little in love with this impossibly beautiful, sometimes arrogant but incredibly lively woman. His bemusement faded and Maxwell again began shaking his head.

"It's too much work. Frankly, I don't think it can be done."

"Maybe it's too much for you with everything else you're doing. I'll do it."

"Christine, look . . ."

"Max, please . . . don't say no yet."

She sighed and looked off into space, formulating another line of attack, he was sure as he watched her, thoroughly enjoying this one-on-one. She suddenly looked at him, but he wasn't sure Christine was actually seeing him. She was in some far-off place. A memory perhaps . . . or another argument to convince him of the merits of her ideas.

"What?" he asked quietly, turning his hand over to grab hers and hold it.

She curled her fingers around his and then looked down at their joined hands. "When I was younger I used to be so jealous of my sister Alexandra. She has a wonderful singing voice. She used to perform at nightclubs in D.C., and concerts at the Kennedy Center. She's even done Carnegie Hall."

"I'm impressed. Do you have musical talent, too?"

Christine grimaced, her face comical. "Not hardly. I can't play any instruments and I can't carry a tune. Not even in the shower."

He chuckled lightly at her self-deprecating humor. It was very attractive in someone like her.

"And then I found out that Alex had sometimes been jealous of me. She considers me the family beauty. Everyone does. That was nice, but . . . being pretty isn't a talent, Max. It's just the way I was born. I didn't do anything to earn it."

"But you've done something with it."

"You didn't think so when we first met, remember?"

He pursed his lips. "Guilty."

She sighed. "My dad used to say that God gave each of us something we can do very well. It's up to us to recognize it, however, and then run with it. What I do very well is get attention. Now that probably doesn't sound very admirable, but it comes in handy. I can get people to do things. I can make them listen."

He nodded. It was true.

"You don't have to do anything for the fundraiser. The center doesn't have to be directly involved, and the names of the staff, children, and their families don't have to be used at all. The hook is in what people will be given in exchange for their generous donation."

"Christine, if someone wants to have a good meal they can go to one of three thousand restaurants in this city. They don't have to give money to a children's hospital."

"But people *like* to be generous, especially if they have money. You just have to give them a good enough reason. I can do this. I can organize the whole thing."

His gaze traveled over her face, wondering if she had any idea how appealing she looked at the moment as she made her heartfelt plea. He hated to turn her down, but he didn't see how he could do anything else. The hospital board would never agree. It sounded too much like a full-scale Broadway production.

"I'll think about it."

"That means you're going to say no."

He pulled his wallet from his pocket. "Christine, it means what I said—I'll think about it . . ."

She pushed his hands away and took the check. "My treat. My suggestion, remember?"

"I don't see why that . . ."

"You can treat next time," she said smoothly, signaling for the waiter.

Maxwell didn't argue. *Next time.* He could do that.

They left the restaurant and stood awkwardly outside, neither knowing what to say or do next. But it was a beautiful summer evening in New York, and the energy of the city was catching. Christine glanced around her.

"Well, you must not live that far from here."

"Central Park West and 84th."

"Then you can walk home. I'll catch a cab . . ."

"Feel like walking for a while?"

She felt relief. "Yeah, that would be nice."

"Come on. We'll start across the park toward your place."

"That's taking you a bit out of your way."

He grinned as he steered them east across 96th Street. "That's why God invented cabs. I'll hop one back."

"So, how are the children up on the third floor?"

He glanced at her. "Don't you spend any time up there? You can. The kids like to be read to."

"I'm afraid I'll do something wrong. Hurt them."

Christine was reluctant to confess that she'd actually gone up several times to see Wendy. The little girl fascinated her, and she felt like Wendy was, in some ways, even more special than the other children. She never cried or complained. She'd peer with great curiosity at Christine through the bars of her bed, through the glass walls of the ward. She'd smile, but she never said a word. Once, she'd waved weakly to Christine as she'd walked slowly past the open ward door.

Christine had put a music box on Wendy's bed table, the music playing softly while she slept. She'd left a little doll on the girl's pillow when she'd seen that there were fewer toys in that ward than on the second floor. But they never spoke. Christine realized that they seemed to communicate in another way, and that was enough.

"If you like, I'll take you up there sometime and explain what goes one, what condition the kids are in. What each of them needs. And I promise not to yell at you like I did that first time."

She looked away briefly. "You remember that."

"What I remember is that you slapped me. It got my attention."

"Good," she said tartly, and he laughed.

Christine smiled at him. She liked to hear his laugh. She liked being with him. It was so much different now than at the start. She sighed, watching the late afternoon contingent of children with parents or housekeepers, healthy and active on bikes or roller blades. She suddenly noticed the couples holding hands or with their arms around one another, their laughter and conversation private and happy. Christine didn't think she'd ever experienced a relationship that was really romantic. The holding hands and getting bouquets of flowers kind. Even with Keith the most satisfying part of their affair had been the physical. She'd never had conversations with him the way she was with Maxwell.

"How's Wendy?" She was always afraid to ask.

"Good. She's not any better, of course. But she's not any worse, either."

"Is she in a lot of pain?"

"Don't worry. We keep her comfortable."

"It seems so unfair. She hasn't even had a chance to be a kid . . ."

Maxwell heard the note of confusion and despair. He reached out to take her hand. "Don't, Christine. If you start thinking like that, all of it will seem hopeless."

She nodded and took a deep breath, holding on to his hand. "Delores told me about her baby. He died more than three years ago. I don't understand how her child got full-blown AIDS and she didn't."

He shrugged. They had reached Fifth Avenue and he watched the traffic light, waiting for it to change. "It happens. Some women have a very low viral load. Delores may not show any symptoms for years. If you ask her, she doesn't think she's so lucky. She lost a baby who might have gotten help if she'd had prenatal care."

"I know. The nurses talk all the time about trying to get women to be more careful before they get pregnant. Before they have their babies."

They were silent for nearly a full block, simply enjoying a companionship that wasn't fraught with conflict or a test of wills.

"What about you?"

She blinked at him. "What . . . are you talking about?"

"Is there going to be room in your life for children?"

"I don't know. If there is, I'd like to start out with someone I can love, first."

"Anyone in mind?"

She couldn't believe he'd asked that. Did he expect her to make a confession? Was he fishing? Did he want to be in the running? If he was, would she tell him? Christine smiled cryptically at Maxwell.

"Yes," she responded confidently. "I'm still working on the details. Now it's my turn. You haven't gotten over your wife, have you?"

He shrugged uncomfortably, not offended by her bluntness. "It was a long time ago. We were both students."

"I can see it still hurts a lot. Maybe it's more than that," she ventured softly, watching his profile, feeling the way his hand had gripped hers momentarily. "I think . . . you're not sure you won't still lose someone you might love very much."

Maxwell looked closely at Christine, pleased by the thoughtful concern in her eyes. But wondering, nonetheless, how they got onto the subject of love. "You think so?"

"It's not so hard to figure out, Max. You're a doctor because you want to save lives. You couldn't save your sister and her baby, but maybe you'll save someone else. Yet, you put in time at a clinic in which you lose someone all the time. It's hard to take a chance under those circumstances. It's hard to be the one left behind."

He was quiet and didn't answer. He didn't want to let Christine Morrow know that she was dead on target. He understood all of what she'd said. That didn't mean that he'd ever gotten a handle on how to deal with it. Maxwell still didn't answer. They just exchanged silent glances that seemed to say enough between them. And it was a very personal moment.

They got to her building and rode the elevator to her floor. Christine was reliving the last trip they'd taken to her apartment. Suddenly she was filled with a dread that history would repeat itself. She yearned to make love with Maxwell again, but it had to be different the next time. The elevator

stopped; she got off and turned to look at him, still
standing in the car.

"I think this is where the trouble started last
time," she said quietly, trying to decipher his
thoughtful expression.

The door began to close and Maxwell quickly
stepped off. "No. *This* is where it began."

They turned together and made the long journey
down the corridor to Christine's apartment door.
They faced each other. She took out her keys, her
heart already starting to beat fast. He took them out
of her hands, just like the last time, and unlocked
the door. Maxwell handed her the keys again.

"Good night, Christine."

She stared, wide-eyed. "Good night."

"I'm glad we got together for dinner."

"Me, too," she said softly.

"Even though it was a bribe."

She giggled. The doctor had a sense of humor
after all.

His eyes roamed her face. "I'd kiss you good
night, but you'd probably slug me again."

Christine shrugged. "You'll just have to try it and
find out."

Maxwell bent slightly to kiss her. His mouth was
slightly parted, and Christine accommodated him.
She felt his lips purse against her own and felt the
gentle ease of the tip of his tongue. She sighed. It
was the tenderest kiss she'd ever known, and intensely erotic because it was.

So, this is what it's like, she thought. First came the
sex . . . and then you find the real thing. She desperately wanted to jump his bones. But she wasn't
going for the short term anymore. For the same
amount of effort and time Christine realized that
she and Maxwell might actually have a chance at an

honest relationship. She was going to try for the gold ring.

Maxwell ended the kiss so cautiously that Christine laughed lightly. He touched her lip with a finger, glanced at her thoughtfully, and headed back toward the elevator. She watched him walk away, feeling incredibly lonely. It was an interesting experience since she had no desire to be with anyone else at the moment.

"Can I get back to you about your fundraising plan tomorrow?"

She shook her head. "I have a show at Ralph Lauren's. And I'm auditioning for a commercial. I'll be in touch."

He nodded and silently boarded the elevator. Christine waited until the door closed before going into her apartment.

But she wasn't going to wait for Maxwell to make a final decision. She immediately got on the phone and started making inquiries. By eleven o'clock when she'd had her shower and washed her hair and sat on the bed reading mail, Christine was well on her way to having many of the details worked out.

The chirpy theme for "Entertainment Tonight" came on and she absently watched as she prepared her tote for the next day's events. Christine did a double take when one segment came on about a hot new discovery named Keith Layton. Early rushes from the movie he was working on were making the studio people sit up and take notice. There were a few brief clips of Keith on a set, fooling around with some of the crew, and then finally being interviewed by ET. For a second she recognized the man she'd first been so attracted to. But then . . . she couldn't understand what she'd seen in him at all beyond an

incredible body and wonderful looks. Christine
watched Keith now, dispassionately. Analytically. The
end of the segment showed him at the opening of
another Hollywood film. There was a young woman
at his side, clinging coyly to his arm as he was being
photographed.

Christine sighed, clicked off the TV, and sat thinking silently as her life suddenly took another sharp
turn in a new direction. Then she thought of the
past month or so without Keith, and the time she'd
spent at the LIFELINE center. She wished Keith
well, but she felt enormous relief.

Her last thought was of Maxwell holding her hand
as they'd walked across town. Christine sighed con-
tentedly as she fell asleep.

... able body ... and wonder ... ... wanted to ... ... light ... ... appearance. The ... ... one of the women, posed still at the opening of ... ... another of it ... But there was a young woman at the ... ... a chignon ... bar and adjusted as if a ... ... photographer ...

Eight

Christine put aside one list and picked up another. She made some notes, crossed off several names, put it down, and began a new list.

"Christine, we're ready . . ." someone shouted across the cavernous studio.

"Just a sec," she responded absently, trying to stack all of her notes in an orderly way so she'd remember where she was when there was time to get back to it.

"Now, Christine. This is costing the client."

"All right . . . I'm coming." With a sigh of annoyance, Christine finally shoved all the sheets into a leather portfolio and got up from her chair. She was immediately descended upon by the stylist, who sprayed her hair yet again, causing her to squint and cough, and the makeup artist, who added another touch of blusher and a stroke of lip gloss.

She took a deep breath to try and focus herself, and then took her place on the set. She was arranged and positioned as several assistants muttered and complained about the lighting or the color of her eye shadow or the kind of accessories she wore. She got impatient. "Now we're on my dime. Can we hurry? I have a lot to do this afternoon."

The photographer, a lanky, middle-aged man with

a thin, greasy-looking ponytail, took a meter reading around her head.

"What's with you lately? You come to the shoots late, you always have to leave early, and I can't get the pictures I want. How come you're so distracted?"

"Just very busy."

"Can't be more important than doing your job. You make a whole lot of money for a few hours' work not to be here when you're needed."

Christine moistened her lips and took the proper pose. "You're right. How's this?"

"Hey . . . that works. This is more like it. Now just hold it . . ." He ran to take his place behind the camera and the shoot began.

For the next hour she got back into the routine. But Christine realized that the photographer was right—her mind wasn't on her work. Although the motor action of the camera became a lulling, repetitive refrain and she responded by rote to the murmured instructions, Christine became increasingly impatient. She'd rather be somewhere else. Doing something else.

"Rick, I need you to do me a big favor," she began during a brief break.

"Anything," he agreed expansively.

Christine launched into a speech she had put together to explain her project and the fundraiser. She was careful not to name the center, using the main hospital instead since it was public. Rick agreed to be the photographer for the event.

After her shoot Christine called the events coordinator of a large perfume company she'd done ads for and asked for sponsorship.

"Christine . . ." the man sighed over the phone. "Do you have *any* idea how many requests we get to give money or products, or lend our name for one event or another? *Hundreds!*"

"I know, I know. You have to be selective. But I have just two words to say to you. Children. And AIDS."

"That's three words," he responded caustically. "Anyway, there are lots of AIDS foundations raising money."

"But this is for one small facility in Harlem. Now you know as well as I do that that community is generally forgotten. Children are dying up there. They need so much . . ."

"Everybody needs so much," he said, harried.

"Please?" Christine finally asked, pulling her last ace.

After a long pause, the man sighed again. "All right. I guess we can come up with something. Our sales went up the quarter after that ad campaign with you in it. What do you want? A check or some products?"

Christine grinned. "Both . . ."

Although she'd had to be very persuasive and make promises of her own to get cooperation, by the end of two days Christine was well on her way to putting together a major charitable fundraising function.

She called her own legal advisors to check on the tax regulations for not-for-profits, and was told how to set up proper accountant procedures for collecting money. She got a friend who owned a public affairs firm to advertise and promote the event. She made dozens of phone calls and pleaded, bribed, cajoled, and called in favors. Christine got exactly what she'd told Maxwell she could . . . everyone's commitment to pulling off *the* event of the summer.

After her morning assignment Christine arrived

at the offices of a TV producer to find that they were going to keep her waiting for twenty minutes. She used the time to make more phone calls, adding to her growing list of people involved in her venture. That made her fifteen minutes late getting back to the reading.

"I'm sorry," she apologized contritely to the casting director. "That was a very important call."

"Well, *you'll* have to wait now. I'm afraid they've gone ahead and sent in someone else." She looked at her watch and shook her head. "It's going to be at least another half hour. Can you wait?"

Christine sighed impatiently. This had been her own fault. "Sure, I'll wait."

But the wait turned into nearly an hour, cutting into her next appointment. When the office door finally opened she was stunned to see Tonee Holiday emerge, escorted by the producer and a representative of the product client. She watched as the two assured Tonee that she had done a first rate job.

Christine stood and approached the group, wondering how the young model had managed to get a reading. But watching the little exchange made some things clear. The fact of the matter was that Tonee had hustled her way to their attention.

"I hope you can let me know right away if I have the job," Tonee said with the right amount of self-importance and charm.

She learns fast, Christine thought to herself, knowing that in the business you have to be a little assertive. But there were some unspoken rules and ethics; otherwise it became a free-for-all. It was becoming obvious to Christine that Tonee Holiday thought she was above the rules.

"I was asked to do this job in Europe. I might have to leave any day."

The two men looked at one another, and it was apparent from their attempts to think quickly about their schedules that Tonee Holiday was definitely in the running.

"Well, I think we can get back to you in a few days. You'll know one way or another by the end of the week for sure. Thanks for coming in. You did a great job," they said, shaking her hand and assuring her she had a bright future.

Christine found herself smiling. It was a standard script. She'd heard it enough times herself. "I didn't know someone else was reading for this," Christine finally interjected, gaining their attention. "Hello, Tonee. I'd say fancy meeting you here . . . but what's the point?"

"You two know each other?" the producer asked.

Christine's smile was thin and cool. "Not really. But we keep showing up at the same assignments. What a coincidence."

"Sorry we kept you waiting, Christine. Kelly Nash mentioned we were casting. Tonee didn't realize she had to have a formal appointment."

"Apparently not," Christine answered.

"Oh, they were so sweet," Tonee gushed as she smiled girlishly for the two men. "I told them I just didn't know and couldn't they *please* just give me five minutes."

"Five minutes?" Christine asked with raised brows.

"We went over a bit. I know it cut into your time. Thanks for stopping by, Tonee. We'll get back to you. Christine, we're ready for you now."

"I'll be right there," Christine said, turning to

Tonee as the two men returned to their testing room.

"I have to go. I have another appoint . . ."

"How did you know about Kelly Nash?" Christine interrupted, lightly grabbing her arm before the girl could walk away.

"Excuse me?" Tonee asked as if she didn't understand the question.

"Let me tell you something, girlfriend," Christine said in a dangerously calm voice. "Using other people's information and contacts without their knowledge is a strict no-no in this business."

Tonee shrugged, dropping the innocent young thing routine and frowning at Christine. "I don't know what you're talking about."

"I'm talking about my missing appointment book, conveniently found and returned by you. And you . . . surprise . . . showing up at all my assignments."

"That don't prove a thing. You just mad 'cause they liked me."

"I'm not mad at all," Christine said calmly. "You haven't seen me mad, yet. But let me tell you this. You can only run this game for so long. Then the word is going to get out that you can't be trusted. Being cute isn't going to help you then."

"I can't help it if they like me better than you."

Christine shook her head at Tonee's logic and naivete. "Being liked helps. Having integrity and not jerking people around counts for more. You are very pretty and very clever, but the books are filled with clever girls who came and went so fast they're not even a memory."

The receptionist, uncomfortable with the tension between the two women, cleared her throat. "Miss Morrow . . . they're waiting for you."

Christine watched until Tonee turned away before she went in. She did a good reading. The producer complimented her on understanding what angle the client wanted to emphasize and on knowing the targeted audience. Christine had heard that script before, too. They *never* tell you outright when it doesn't have the right feel. But she knew it didn't. The most striking thing, she thought as she finally left the offices, was that it simply didn't matter that much to her whether she did another commercial. She had three that had already been released since the start of the year, and another two due out in the fall when the new season began on the networks.

What was more important, it seemed to Christine, was that she was racking up a list of people to help out with the event. Someone even suggested a theme. . . . "Become A Friend for Life Night."

For a moment she considered calling Maxwell to see if he'd made any headway on getting board approval but decided to wait another day. It occurred to Christine that more and more of her time, energy, and attention were being taken up with LIFE-LINE and Maxwell Chandler. There were worse things she could be doing . . . but nothing, so far, that was any better.

She hadn't thought about it much until the broadcast the night before showing Keith in Hollywood, that now she knew they were not right for each other. Or more to the point, she didn't consider Keith Layton right for her. On the other hand, Christine had known for a long time that having a relationship that was just flash and show wasn't part of her game plan. So what was different?

Suddenly seeing the clear evidence that her sister and Parker were happy in their marriage and that commitment had its up side. The birth of her niece and realizing that miracles can be of our own making. Growing a bit older, perhaps, and learning that nothing lasts forever and that there are bigger things to be excited about than hemlines and makeup tricks. Suddenly meeting children who had taught her about the most important things in life, and a man who was honorable . . . and whom she could love.

In the end it was that last thought that took Christine to the center. It was late, way after closing. But she knew Maxwell's habits. He always stopped by to see the third floor children before leaving for the night. And that was exactly where she found him. And Wendy.

The girl was in bed, curled up on her side and asleep, or so it would seem. She had IV's and monitors attached, but the beeping little noises were regularly spaced, indicating a lack of trauma for the moment. Maxwell was in a chair by the window, making notes on the chart of the child in the nearest bed.

Christine didn't go in. Instead she stood outside the ward's glass viewing window and looked in. Maxwell had said she shouldn't be afraid to visit with these kids just because they were bedridden, but it seemed a sacrilege to Christine not to give them their privacy—or to make them subjects for observation . . . or monitoring. But she had another idea: she would bring them music! Her mind began digging through her resources, trying to figure out who she could tap to donate a CD player. She'd once dated a V.P. with Columbia Records . . .

Maxwell looked up and noticed her. He smiled. As she waved at him, watching him wistfully as if he, too, were in some sort of quarantine, he seemed so tall and solid. And she knew . . . she *knew* . . . that he was the one. Maxwell got up and slowly made his way to the hallway and stood directly in front of her. He didn't say anything, but smiled as if he was surprised but happy to see her. He also looked very tired. She wondered how many hours of sleep he actually got each night, given the amount of time he spent at his practice and here.

Maxwell read the expression in Christine's eyes. He looked in one direction down the hallway, while she looked in the other. It was late and there was no one around. The nurse at the central station was busy making entries on the computer. Maxwell returned his attention to Christine and bent to kiss her briefly. Then he sighed. He'd needed that.

"What are you doing here so late?"

"I came to see you."

"That's nice. But I bet you had another motive."

She blinked and glanced through the window into the ward. "How are they doing?"

"Pretty good. Wendy had a good day." He took hold of her hand and tugged gently. "Come on. I'll introduce you."

She held back, shaking her head. "Not tonight."

"Still afraid?"

She sighed. "Okay, I'm a coward. I don't want to go in there and do something . . . foolish."

Maxwell regarded her thoughtfully. "Lots of words have crossed my mind that I could call you. *Foolish* and *coward* aren't on the list."

She was intrigued. "Like what?" she asked suspiciously.

Maxwell chuckled. "Persistent. I'm finished here for the night. Let's go downstairs to my office."

Once inside the small, cluttered room, Maxwell closed the door. It was like a silent signal to both of them and Christine turned into his arms as he gathered her close. This time the kiss was serious. There was an underlying edge as if this might assuage them for a while . . . but they both wanted much more. They also went one step further toward sharing their feelings instead of the quick, explosive coupling they'd experienced before they'd had a chance to know one another. For Christine, the difference was startling. A revelation. Kissing and being held by Maxwell Chandler made her feel safe. She already knew he wasn't impressed by her looks . . . which then must mean that there was something else about her that he liked.

His tongue swept leisurely inside her mouth, his manipulation languid and utterly stimulating. It was foreplay without the need for immediate consummation.

Maxwell closed his eyes and sighed when the kiss ended. "That was very nice, but I know you have another reason for being here."

"Still don't trust me, eh?" Christine asked, running a finger along his firm jawline.

"I know that you sometimes don't bother with the preliminaries, you just cut to the heart of the matter, Christine. Not a bad way to operate when you have to get things done. The answer to your question is, I'm still thinking about your idea for the fundraiser. I've talked to one or two people at the hospital and there's some interest, but they want to discuss what we're already getting from the city and other agencies. But I think they're leaving the final decision up to me." Christine raised her brows, silently, as if to ask, 'So what's the problem'? He shook his head. "I need to be careful. There's a lot of stigma attached to AIDS. People aren't any more understanding just because the victim happens to be a kid. The other thing is . . . some of the children don't know that the reason they're sick so much is because of AIDS. The families haven't told them, and we're not allowed to."

Christine frowned. "But it's not as if people don't know about this. You know there are AIDS research groups, foundations, and advocacies all over the place. Marches and fundraising all the time. The world's been talking about the virus for fifteen years. There are drugs and treatments, and laws to protect people and . . ."

"Christine," Maxwell said firmly to get her attention. "You're trying to convince someone who already knows that," he added with a chuckle.

"Then you must also know that movie stars and celebrities are always the first ones to get out there and do something, put their money where their mouths are. Our event could be so great. I've already got the Perry Ellis people to donate clothes for a fashion show and sale. And the Sheraton is letting us use the banquet room for free. My brother-in-law said he'd come up and perform, maybe talk some of his friends into coming along."

"Your brother-in-law?" Maxwell frowned, skeptical.

"Why not? You've heard of Parker Harrison, haven't you?"

"Parker Harrison? *The* Parker Harrison?"

She grinned and nodded smugly. "And if you're nice to me maybe I can ask him if he can get Anita Baker."

Maxwell laughed. "I'm afraid to ask what else you have in mind for this shindig."

Her eyes brightened. "Is that a yes?"

"That's a maybe. I'll think on it, like I promised. And if you let me get out of here I can start right away . . ." He got his bulging leather carryall and stuffed a stack of papers into it. He glanced at her with some regret. "You took a lot of time coming all the way up here. I'm sorry I can't give you a definite answer yet."

Christine took a step closer to him and looked into his face. "It wasn't wasted. I got something out of it. And I'm *not* very easy to please."

Maxwell stared at her in amazement. He had to admit that one of the things he liked about Christine was that she was so forthright. It saved him a lot of uncertainty and fear. He was afraid of rejection because he'd never taken the time to learn about courtship and flirtation. But every time she walked into the room and he saw her again, felt the light of her personality warm his soul, Maxwell started to believe that perhaps now he could take another chance. Perhaps he could really love someone and not lose everything again.

He reached out to run his hand down her arm. "Can I take you home?"

Christine lowered her gaze briefly, as if she was thinking it over. Then she looked at him through her lashes. "Yes."

"Fine . . ."

"With you."

He turned back sharply. Maxwell narrowed his eyes and focused on her, trying to gauge her expression. "Are you sure?"

"I hope you have an extra toothbrush. I won't need a nightgown," she whispered.

Wordlessly, he reached out for her hand, threading his fingers with hers. They left the center together, several curious stares from the staff following them out the door. Christine had come to know that Maxwell was a fairly private person. He keep his feelings and his personal business pretty close to the chest.

Which was why Christine felt hopeful and encouraged. It felt so wonderful to know that for the moment Maxwell didn't seem to care what anyone was thinking.

Christine stretched languidly, arching her back and rolling her head against the pile of pillows. She felt the last of sleep release her body, and the sensations of consciousness remind her of where she was . . . and what she'd been doing. Rather, what she and Maxwell had been doing together. The whole night. She giggled quietly. The man was going to be exhausted before the day was over.

On the other hand, Christine knew that she was going to be sore. Her inner thighs felt tender, her groin muscles strained. She knew that if she glanced in a mirror her hair would be a mess, and her mouth a little swollen from deep, intense kissing. But mostly, Christine knew she was going to feel heavenly.

She rolled to the side and buried her face in the warm bed linens. In the background she heard the quiet hissing sound of shower water in the bathroom. Christine grinned to herself. What a wasted effort. When Max came back to bed he would probably start to make love to her again, and only need another shower. Yet, she realized that it was getting late and he had said he had eleven o'clock rounds at the hospital with some of his young patients. Christine moaned, yawned, and slowly sat up. She winced . . . and then smiled dreamily. Maybe it was just as well. Once more would probably kill her.

Christine got out of the bed, dragging the top

sheet with her, and staggered into the small kitchen of Max's apartment. She found the coffeemaker, got it started, and located some English muffins in the refrigerator. There was also a bowl of green seedless grapes. And eggs and sausage, which made Christine shudder as she mentally calculated the fat content. *That* was for Max. She'd rather eat the other stuff and live to love another day.

When Max came out of the shower he immediately followed the scent of coffee and sizzling sausages to the kitchen. He stood for a moment watching Christine as she noisily searched for plates and flatware. The sheet she had so artfully wrapped around her trailed on the kitchen floor. It looked almost chic on her.

Christine detected his presence and turned to face Maxwell. She smiled shyly. Maxwell was stark naked. Well, he *was* using a towel to briskly dry his hair. He finished and wrapped it around his neck, watching her watch him. He looked a bit hesitant, too, which was ridiculous under the circumstances.

"Good morning," he said, his voice still raspy and deep from sleep.

"Hi."

Max slowly walked up to her and kissed her lightly on the mouth. "Thank you for last night," he said against her lips.

Her eyes searched his face. "Me, too."

He glanced over her shoulder into the frying pan and shook his head in wonder. "No one ever made me breakfast before."

"Not even your wife?" she asked with no hesitation.

He grunted. "Least of all my wife. Domestic life wasn't her thing. Rachel was looking for someone to take care of her."

Christine could hear that Maxwell didn't sound so much bitter as resigned. She left it alone.

"Well, I've never made breakfast for anyone before. That doesn't mean you can eat it," Christine cautioned quickly, making him laugh.

"I'll eat it, even if it kills me."

"Very funny," she said, turning away in mock haughtiness.

"I've got to hurry, though . . ." he said, already heading back to the bedroom.

"I know. I'll bring this in. You can eat while you dress." She slid the sausage onto the plate and added the toasted muffins. It was after she had poured the coffee and was preparing to bring him the food that Christine heard Maxwell utter an explicative from the bedroom. It made her jump. She put the tray down and, grabbing up the ends of the trailing sheet, hurried back to the room. "Max, what's wrong?"

Standing in front of the armoire, which housed a color TV, Maxwell was staring at the screen with a thunderous expression on his face. His neck and arms were rigid with anger.

"What's going on?"

He turned away abruptly and began dressing very quickly. "This is exactly what I thought would happen. LIFELINE is going to be paraded before the public like some circus act."

"What are you talking about?" she asked, bewildered, glancing at the screen but only seeing the local morning news anchors. Maxwell had his slacks on and was buttoning a blue oxford shirt.

"Just listen!" he said and pointed to the screen.

Christine looked again. This time she saw an image of herself at a social function, surrounded by people holding drinks and obviously having a grand time. She stood close and listened.

". . . Apparently at a center here in the city for AIDS patients. It's not clear why supermodel Christine Morrow was at the center, but the rumors are flying . . ."

"Oh, my God," Christine breathed in horror.

"This is what I was afraid would happen, Christine," Maxwell said angrily, stuffing a tie in his leather case and sitting on the side of the bed to put on his socks.

She turned on him. "I had nothing to do with that report. Max, you *must* know by now I'd never do anything to bring the wrong kind of attention to the center. I know how important it is and what it's doing for the children . . . and I never mentioned LIFELINE. Besides, the report is about me and never mentions LIFELINE by name."

"By this evening they'll know everything. That's what reporters do."

"Look, I'm sorry. I don't know how . . ."

"*Sorry* doesn't cut it, Christine," Max said. He stood up and braced his hands on his hips and glared at her.

"I know you're upset, but this isn't such a tragedy."

Maxwell made an impatient sound and stormed past her, heading for the door. "You see it as publicity, don't you? Don't forget I haven't given an okay on that fundraiser. And I'm not sure that this kind of news is going to help much."

"We simply turn it into good news. We work with it, Max."

"It would have been a lot easier if I didn't have to deal with this at all."

Christine felt impatience welling up in her. She

pulled on his arm to get his attention. "Max, I think you're overreacting. AIDS is simply not hot news anymore. I mean, I know you're concerned about the privacy of your patients and how people might treat them, but you couldn't possibly expect to keep the center some sort of top secret. It really doesn't make sense. It's a cause for sympathy and compassion, not shame. And I know there are people out there willing to help. I was."

Max sighed heavily and faced her, tucking in his shirt and tightening his belt. "You know, when it got out that I had a sister who'd died of AIDS my teammates at school didn't want to have much to do with me."

"So, this is personal. This isn't about the center, is it? Look . . . that had to have been ten years ago. People know better now."

"Are you willing to take that chance with the children? With Wendy, who's in pretty bad shape? With Delores, who hasn't shown any symptoms yet . . . but she will. And she's just starting to get her life back on track. You want to risk that for her?"

"And what about me? What about the risks I've taken?"

"You can defend yourself. I bet you can make up something. You're good at that." He grabbed up his case, keys, and wallet and pulled open the apartment door.

He hesitated and turned back to her. Christine could see his ambivalence, and felt relief that Maxwell's anger had less to do with her than it did with not trusting that people would ultimately be fair. And, of course, she knew he was reflecting on part of his own past.

"I can't talk about this any more right now."

"Then when? It seems to me that the thing to do

is meet the challenge. If people have anything cruel to say, get in their face and dare everyone to deny that your children need all the help they can get."

Maxwell frowned, slowly shaking his head. "I don't know . . . maybe I understand human nature better than you do. You can let yourself out when you leave," he said shortly. "I'll have the doorman call a cab for you."

Christine stared at him, unable to say anything that would counter the damage and worried that Maxwell's personal spin on the circumstances might prevent something that would be good for his cause and the children. But she sighed, only momentarily defeated. "Don't bother. I can get my own cab," she said quietly.

Maxwell saw the morning newspaper on his doormat in the hall. He bent to retrieve it and glanced briefly at one of the headlines. He grimaced and handed Christine the paper. "I think you can forget about that fundraiser for now."

Christine reluctantly took the paper. Her stomach tightened when she read, "Supermodel Involved at AIDS Clinic" . . .

She didn't even react when the door slammed shut.

"But you must be able to tell me something. That report included my name and picture. It was unsubstantiated. And it's wrong."

"I'm sorry but I can't tell you anything," the nervous woman on the phone said. She'd been repeating the same thing for the last fifteen minutes.

Christine sighed in frustration. "This isn't fair. How do you know the person who told you that story could be trusted? Did you even bother trying to check out any of the information? No one called me to ask questions. This is irresponsible reporting," she said heatedly, getting angrier by the minute, yet knowing there was nothing she could do about the report.

"I could put the news director on. Perhaps if you tell him what's really going on he can do an update on the evening news," the voice offered.

"Sure. Fine," Christine sighed. "I just want to clear up the facts. I work at the center as a volunteer."

She spent another twenty minutes on the phone with an assistant news director, who was only marginally more sympathetic than the person who'd answered the phone, and Christine hung up knowing she hadn't accomplished anything. She put the word out that she wanted to talk to Tonee Holiday, certain that the ambitious girl would not be above resorting to a few tricks if it would serve her own purposes.

She didn't try calling Maxwell at the center and she didn't hear from him. Perhaps, she reasoned, it was just as well. Christine was afraid that she'd get angry at his pig-headedness and they'd start to argue again. She didn't want that. It seemed to her that they were finally making some headway in a relationship . . . *relationship,* she repeated, liking the sound of it . . . and she didn't want to jeopardize it.

Christine then got calls from a number of reporters. Why was she volunteering at an AIDS center? She didn't shrink from answering the questions honestly, but she did keep Maxwell and LIFELINE out of the report. She used the forum to plug continued support for AIDS victims, especially children.

"After all," she told one writer, "I've seen what

happened with designers, models, photographers, writers, and a host of other talented people in my industry when it was first discovered they were HIV positive. But then we galvanized ourselves into action . . ."

Perversely, the report stimulated new interest in her and she was offered a slew of new assignments. The better news was that people finally did want to know what she was doing at the center in Harlem. But best of all, they were coming forward on their own with offers to help.

And then it happened. LIFELINE's name surfaced in print.

Christine finally broke down and tried to call Maxwell, deciding he'd had enough time to get over his objections and see some of the positive press for himself. It had been nearly a week. But he was not available, either by circumstances . . . or design. Still, she knew that in some way maybe she was responsible for what was happening.

She wasn't afraid to face Maxwell, but she was afraid that he might refuse to see her. That would hurt more than anything. She went to his office first, knowing he'd be finished with his patients but not yet on his way to the center. Maxwell wasn't there. But Frances Grimes was.

Christine stood at the receptionist's desk, listening to the standard line. "The doctor isn't available right now. Can I help you?" She was just about to lose her temper when Frances came quietly in.

"Oh, Dr. Grimes, this lady is that new patient of Dr. Chandler's. I told her he wasn't here but . . ."

"Thanks, Joyce. I'll see Miss Morrow in my office."

Christine looked suspiciously at the female doctor, but saw only a vague smile on her lips. And wisdom in her eyes. She braced herself, wondering what Frances Grimes could possibly have to say that would make her feel better. Or make Maxwell see the light.

She silently followed Frances into her office, where the doctor shut the door and took a seat behind her desk. The room was different from Maxwell's. No candy jars or children's pictures here. Everything was excruciatingly neat and orderly . . . like Frances herself. Christine knew that orderliness housed discipline. Enough to see Frances through the rigors of med school, into a comfortable practice, with enough prestige to place her among accomplished black professionals serving as role models for younger students.

Not like me, Christine told herself wryly. She felt compelled to say something first, sure that what was going through the doctor's mind was that she didn't present the proper image for LIFELINE or the work it did. Maxwell had certainly tried to tell her that, too.

"I wanted to speak with Maxwell. Things got so awful with the press but I want him to see that it's beginning to work in our favor."

Frances smiled calmly. "It could have gone the other way, too. I wanted to believe that it was all your fault, but I don't think it was."

"What makes you think that?"

"I've seen you with the children. I've heard the nurses rave about your work. You might be used to drawing a lot of publicity to yourself; after all, you have a pretty high profile in New York. But I don't believe you would do anything that would bring unwarranted attention to these children or their families."

Christine raised her chin. "Thank you," she said stiffly.

"I'm more concerned about Maxwell . . . as you can probably already guess."

Christine blinked at Frances. It was an extraordinary thing to say . . . and just short of a confession of how she felt about her colleague and friend. "Yes, I know. But I wouldn't do anything to hurt him, either."

"You mean, not any more."

"That's right."

Frances glanced down at the papers on her desk and fingered them idly. "Right from the start, I knew Maxwell was attracted to you." She glanced briefly at Christine. "But I knew he didn't want to be."

"And you've been hoping that he'd see you as more than just a friend."

"It might have happened eventually, if you hadn't appeared to gum up the works."

Christine couldn't help laughing. She decided that she liked Frances Grimes after all.

"But I think Maxwell is much more comfortable having me as a friend than as a lover. With you it's probably just the reverse."

Christine shook her head and smiled knowingly. "That wouldn't have been enough for me, either. I want to be both."

"Give him time, Christine. He's never really been in love before."

Again Christine was stunned by Frances's words.

"Not the kind that hurts more than any pleasure it gives. Rachel was a young man's lust. I call her a hormone-induced fantasy that never should have happened. For Maxwell, loving has always meant losing. First his family, his wife, and now, one by one, the kids at the center. You're a double whammy. You're beautiful and sought after. You could have anyone you want. Men probably drop like flies at your feet."

"I don't want Maxwell at my feet," Christine said.

Frances chuckled. "I don't blame you."

"Is that what you wanted to say to me? That you've always been in love with Maxwell?"

"I wanted to say that he's away at camp. You heard us talk about it at Cynthia Mallory's dinner party."

"Oh. Yes."

"We don't call it AIDS camp. Just . . . camp. The kids go for a week, two if there's enough money and room. They do everything that other kids do. Swim, make lariats and potholders, have campfires and roast marshmallows. So . . . I don't think he's deliberately avoiding you. I just think he didn't know what to say when that news thing came out last week. Maxwell is very protective of the children's privacy and dignity. They have so little that's purely their own."

"I know," Christine murmured.

"The other thing I wanted you to know is that I've decided that what we do is not being served if we can't ask for help when we need it for the kids. Raising money means giving people a reason to give.

"I'm holding a press conference in the morning in front of City Hall. It's to emphasize the inadequate funding that comes from the city. We no longer get any from the state or federal government. I want to tell people that we have so many children with desperate needs, and we'd like to do something about it before they all die."

Christine felt her throat closing up. Beautifully said.

"What can I do?"

"For now, just keeping coming for the kids. But don't give up on your plans for the fundraiser. I think it's a wonderful idea and I'll help any way I can." She smiled wryly at Christine. "I bet you can do exactly what you said you can do."

Christine silently pursed her lips.

"And don't give up on Maxwell."

Christine nodded thoughtfully, and then, having heard exactly what she wanted and needed to, she got up to leave. "I don't suppose it helps to say I think Maxwell is lucky to have a friend like you."

Frances didn't look at Christine. And she didn't get up to see her out, or even to acknowledge her leaving. She did shake her head slightly. "You're right . . . not at all."

Christine paid no attention to the passersby staring at her, or the men in particular who tried everything short of breaking into song to get her attention. The best tack was to be indifferent to the whistles and catcalls. It was late in the afternoon, and the bus station was a strange mix of long distance travelers and suburban commuters, runaway teenagers and homeless men and women. There was never a reason in the world for Christine to be in this part of the borough . . . except that she was waiting for Maxwell to come home.

The hospital said that the bus was due in at four. That was optimistic. The reality was it was already almost an hour and a half late. But families were waiting for the children. There was one ambulette, a minivan, and several cars. Christine had spotted them and knew that like her, they had a special mission.

Yet Christine knew her motives were not entirely altruistic. She couldn't stand another day of no word from Maxwell, no way of knowing if their fledgling relationship still had a chance. Or if she'd have to temper the love she was developing for Maxwell Chandler in exchange for protecting her ego and self-esteem. So, she'd decided to get it over with. Face it head-on . . . *him* head-on, so she knew where she stood.

Christine's insides were roiling. So this is what love feels like, she thought, remembering that peculiar dazed look on her sister's face when Parker had materialized in her life again after nearly ten years. Christine knew beyond a doubt that she'd never last that long. And she had no intention of doing so.

Two Port Authority security guards appeared at the doors to open them wide enough to accommodate two wheelchairs coming through. Each held a small child. The bus had arrived and the children were disembarking. A father came forward, dropping to his knees to ask his son how he enjoyed himself. More children came through the door with knapsacks, pillowcases, duffel bags, and shopping bags containing their camp belongings. They looked a little bewildered at being back in the city with all the noise and all the people. In about twenty minutes all the children had been accounted for by someone there to greet them.

Christine waited. She refused to entertain the thought that Maxwell might have made other arrangements for getting home. He wasn't the sort to plan things that way. He had proven to be pretty much a take-it-as-it-comes kind of man, who thought quickly on his feet. She hoped she hadn't been wrong.

She wasn't.

When Maxwell finally came through the exit Christine felt the instinctive tightening in her stomach, a combination of joy and apprehension. He looked exhausted, but oddly peaceful. He was carrying a sleeping bag under one arm and holding a heavy canvas duffel in the other. He stepped out onto the sidewalk and glanced around, as if surveying the land and reacclimating himself before moving on. Christine reacted strongly again the moment he set eyes on her. And they just stared at each other.

For so long, as a matter of fact, that she was sure Maxwell was just going to turn away and whistle for a taxi. But for the life of her, she couldn't move first or say anything. Luckily she didn't have to.

Maxwell started walking toward Christine. He didn't have any particular expression on his face, not even surprise. He'd spent the better part of the week away wondering if he'd finally pushed her away for good, because he was too afraid to admit that he wanted her. That he'd been too stubborn to realize that if she didn't care . . . how much easier it would be to just walk away. The fact that she was there, looking almost as uncertain as he felt, left him unable to say a single thing. Unable even to accept what Christine's presence really meant for both of them.

She didn't move. Just waited to see how close he was going to come. Suddenly Maxwell let go of the duffel and it thumped to the sidewalk. The sleeping bag rolled from his fingers and settled near her feet. And then he just grabbed her, pulled her into a tight embrace and kissed her, fusing his lips to hers as if he drew life from her. Kissing her until Christine was sure her ears rang.

Christine figured he had gotten just close enough.

Nine

Somewhere behind them several passersby started to whistle. Someone yelled, "Go for it, man . . ."

And Maxwell did.

He didn't want to stop holding and kissing Christine, just in case he was wrong about the look in her eyes. In case his eyes showed his need, confessing too much and laying his soul bare. Just in case this was not forgiveness from Christine, but goodbye.

Maxwell finally loosened his hold on her, simply because they both needed air. And for whatever else might happen between him and Christine, he didn't want an audience.

Maxwell didn't ask what she was doing there.

There didn't seem to be any point since he was just so happy to see her. And grateful. When he'd spotted her standing in front of her car, looking so fresh and lovely, the details seemed unimportant.

They stood gazing into each other's eyes.

"I thought I'd pick you up. It's on my way home." She whispered the bald-faced lie, listening to his breathing and feeling the restraint in his arms. "Unless you'd rather take a cab."

Maxwell slowly grinned at her. His gaze swept over her face, taking in the sparkle in her green eyes, the playful curve to her lips. That was *exactly* the line he'd used on her with such astounding results. He felt a surge of longing in his groin and a constriction in his chest. He shook his head. "I *never* would rather take a cab."

Maxwell threw his gear into the trunk of Christine's car and got in on the passenger side. He was afraid to take his eyes from her, as if she might vanish into thin air. He found himself in the peculiar position of thinking he needed to show he didn't care so much, but knowing in his heart he was lost.

"Frances called me," he murmured.

"She did? Why?"

"To tell me about the press conference and to say it went well and that the center got excellent and fair coverage." He turned his head to watch her, wondering abstractedly what someone like Christine Morrow, with her vitality and confidence and beauty, could see in someone like him. "Frances also said you're getting a lot of praise for the work you've been doing at the center."

She shrugged dismissively. "I wish they wouldn't concentrate on me. The center was there long before I happened on it. Children needed help long before I came along."

"But it's happening now because of you. I'm not going to knock it. I hear the Governor called . . ."

"He was embarrassed. People wanted to know why funding was cut off to children in Harlem."

Bemused, Maxwell silently chuckled and shook his head. "You were right. You *can* get people to do what you want."

"Except maybe you," Christine said quietly.

Maxwell reached over and placed his large hand on her thigh. He stroked provocatively through the fabric of her jeans. "Try me again," he said in a hoarse tone.

They pretended, during the drive uptown, that nothing had been amiss between them. That they hadn't parted in anger and frustration, or that while apart they had not individually agonized about how bad things were and whether there was any hope of recovery. Christine talked in the most superficial way about how things had been in the city since he'd left for camp; the weather, the latest political scandals, the home team baseball scores. Maxwell reported that the week had been good. Only one child had gotten sick and had to be sent home. Two trail hikes had to be cancelled because of rain, and they were going to have to think about rebuilding one of the cabins because of wood-rot.

Mostly, Maxwell settled into a kind of stupor of continuing surprise, realizing just how much energy it had taken out of him to get through the week. He had dreamt about Christine every single night, not getting a lot of sleep. And he'd thought about her most days, making him seem distracted to the others. Only now that he was back, and she had been there to meet him, could Maxwell allow himself to relax.

He didn't even bother to ask Christine where she was taking him. It didn't seem to be nearly as important as knowing she intended that they be together. He let her take control.

She drove to his place.

Christine parked her car and they silently boarded the elevator up to Maxwell's floor. He said nothing, merely holding her hand tightly during the ride. Once inside his apartment, the full extent of his weariness became evident.

"Do you want anything to eat?" Christine asked quietly, watching as he put his things down and stretched his shoulders and back.

"I'm too tired. Maybe later."

"Then, I think you should just go to bed and get some sleep."

He nodded, slowly heading into the bedroom. "I think you're right."

"I'm going to turn off the ringer on your phone and tell the doorman that short of an emergency, he's not to buzz you for deliveries or anything else."

"Thanks. That sounds good," he said, his voice muffled from the next room.

Christine could tell that Maxwell was stripping off his clothes, turning on the air conditioner, pulling the coverlet from the bed. She finished with the call to the front door and walked back to the room. He was down to his Jockey shorts and just about to climb into the bed.

"I'm going to go now. I'll let the center and Frances know that you're back."

"They know. I called from the terminal." He grabbed her hand and pulled her closer, looking into her eyes. "And I'm not that tired. Stay with me."

"Maybe I shouldn't."

With a sigh Maxwell began taking off her clothing. It was easy. She had almost nothing on. She was wearing a white cotton camp-shirt with the short sleeves rolled even shorter, and jeans.

The decision was easy then.

They got into the bed and Maxwell settled down heavily on his side, an arm across her waist. Christine was convinced he'd fallen asleep before she'd finished curling up next to him, pressing herself to the near nakedness of Maxwell's large, warm body. She lay awake watching him and smiling peacefully to herself. He was so beautiful.

Not handsome in the same way as Keith or Patrick

or any of the other male models she knew. Those kinds of great looks were an apparition because they weren't typical. But Maxwell's good looks were comfortable and realistic. Christine thought the best part was that it all went much deeper than features and skin color. Dr. D. Maxwell Chandler was a good man. She closed her eyes and placed her hand on his chest, feeling the strong, steady beating of his heart.

For a moment Keith came to mind. Christine felt nothing but a pleasant warmth for him. They'd had a good time together. No more, but no less. That was it. Never once had she even considered that there might have been something more serious between her and Keith, if only they'd worked at it. Christine knew with certainty it was because she'd been looking for something more in a man.

Dr. D. Maxwell Chandler had grabbed her attention without even trying, because he hadn't put her on a pedestal or bought into a persona that was largely a myth. Maxwell had done the single most important thing possible, Christine had discovered, and that was to force her to see she could be more than just pretty. That she had more to offer than style and image. *He* tried forcing it out of her, and with the exposing of her heart and soul Christine had found a man worthy of her respect. Other than Parker she'd never known a man with so much strength of character. She knew she could trust him with her life . . . and her love.

Christine decided that she'd keep Maxwell. She decided she was in love with him.

Maxwell moaned as his dream ended and he pulled himself from sleep. It was another one about

Christine, only this time it didn't torture him. When he reached out she was really there next to him. His hand touched her back, sliding down to her waist and hip. Maxwell moved closer behind her and gently caressed her stomach. He kissed the back of her neck as his hand journeyed upward and stroked a breast.

"Christine . . ." he said in a gravelly whisper.

She sighed and let out a little mewling sound.

Maxwell came up on an elbow and nuzzled beneath her ear and jaw as he found and stimulated a nipple with his finger. He could feel it stiffen. He pressed his hard middle against her buttocks. "Christine . . ."

"Ohhhhh . . ." she said in the back of her throat, finally cooperating by rolling onto her back and turning her head toward him until her mouth connected perfectly with his. Her lips were parted, waiting for his kiss.

The kiss was thorough and passionate. She put her arms around his neck and kissed him back with growing fervor as Maxwell continued to force her nipples into tight little buds that strained toward his touch. Their breathing became labored and heated as their desire grew. Maxwell's hand began further exploration, finding that feminine soul and center of her and making her gasp with longing as his fingers teased along the sensitive folds of flesh.

"Ohhhh . . . my God," Christine uttered in blasphemy as Maxwell's mouth fastened on a swollen breast. She reached out blindly and found him, too. Stiff, and surging warmly against her hand.

Maxwell urged her thighs apart and lifted himself atop Christine. But he did nothing to break the caress between them until they'd kissed a little more, and touched a lot more, and were mindless with the need to meld their bodies and souls. When he found her open and ready and thrust himself home, Maxwell thought that this was as close to heaven as he could get without dying. Their driving union rocked their bodies until the pleasure-pain of their release was like a kind of little death. If nothing else it let them both drift into sated, happy sleep.

At ten o'clock that evening they finally gained enough consciousness to order Szechuan in for dinner. And when they were finished eating and making love again, Maxwell lay pensively beside Christine, her limbs intertwined with his.

"So . . . tell me again what you want to do about this fundraiser?"

Christine was slow to react. She didn't want to show surprise, but she grinned and looked into his eyes. "Changed your mind?"

"No," he said with a sigh of wry defeat. *"You* did."

"Eduardo, please make sure there are flowers on every table. And I need you to help me find someone who can distribute the little gift packages to everyone at the end of the night."

"Yes, Miss Morrow," Eduardo nodded with enthusiasm.

"Now, it all comes down to details and timing. Everything has to be perfect."

"Yes, Miss Morrow," he said again.

"I'm counting on you . . ." Christine said, holding onto the man's arm with a nervous grip.

"Do not worry. Eduardo will never fail you."

Christine suddenly beamed at his loyalty and desire to please her. If only everyone else that she had enlisted for the night did as they'd been instructed, she might actually survive this.

She went about giving orders and making last-minute phone calls, instructing, demanding, and threatening like a commander leading troops into battle. She had her lists, and she was checking them twice.

But all through the final preparation and countdown Christine kept thinking about Maxwell, knowing that although she may have succeeded in allaying some of his qualms about the benefit—to put it bluntly, he didn't like them—he had remained mostly uninvolved in the planning or details. She wasn't concerned, knowing that his time and energy was better spent with the children at the center and his practice. It was actually Frances who had come through in an unexpected way—she had gotten an association of black doctors and physicians to give their official blessings to the fundraiser. And she had managed to get the mayor involved by summarily declaring him grand marshall for the evening. Christine still considered it a victory that Maxwell had been persuaded to make opening remarks before the entertainment program began. And he was going to be introduced by Parker, which seemed to make him uncharacteristically shy.

"Christine, I've been looking all over this hotel for you."

Christine turned and absently regarded her sister. Alex was dressed in black jeans and a tunic top belted at the waist. Christine grinned because she could see that her sister was fast regaining her shape since giving birth. Christine grimaced, realizing that she'd always felt older than Alexandra in some ways. And she still envied her sometimes. But now, as when she was growing up, her sister was there when she needed her.

Christine gave Alex a brief hug and kiss. "Oh, good. You got here. Where's the baby?"

"The hotel is providing a babysitter for the night, but I have to go and feed her when it's time."

"I'm so glad you're here."

Alexandra cast a slight frown at her sister. "You're not nervous, are you?"

"Just a little."

"This means a lot to you, doesn't it?"

"Well, it's for a really good cause and there's so much at stake."

Alexandra nodded. She knew it was about more than the center. "Are we going to get to meet Maxwell before all this begins?"

"I hope so," Christine murmured, gnawing unconsciously on a fingernail.

"Parker feels obligated to check him out and make sure he's not some slight brother."

Christine groaned in mild annoyance. "I know Parker is feeling protective but he can kick that to the curb. I will *kill* him if he says anything to Maxwell that will . . ."

Alexandra started laughing. "Well, he was right about one thing. You got it bad. Okay, what do you want me to do? . . ."

The first time Alex had to take a break to feed Lauren, Christine went with her. They ordered a light lunch from room service and chatted about expectations for the evening, and what numbers Parker was going to play. But Christine couldn't talk her sister into singing.

"I'm not ready. Besides I haven't practiced voice in months and I don't have the right dress. You need the very best for tonight. Parker will do it for you."

When Christine returned to the banquet room

Cynthia had arrived, along with the clothing for the fifteen-minute fashion show. The usual salons had been set up as dressing areas for the models. Christine felt relief at not having to be one of them for a change, but was delighted that so many of her fellow models had agreed to be here.

"Cynthia, I want to end the show with your outfits so they can see that large women are beautiful and stylish. Someone donated the wedding dress for the finale in a large size. Is that okay?"

Cynthia laughed gleefully. "Sounds great. Might as well start getting James used to the idea."

Slowly but surely the afternoon came together. Parker arrived to see the band setup and test the acoustics. But the musical rehearsal was brief because not all the band members showed up.

Christine panicked. Parker told her to calm down, everything was going to work out fine.

At four Christine tried to call Maxwell to give him a progress report only to be told that he'd been called into a hospital board meeting. She began to worry that he wouldn't get out in time to make the start of the evening. On the other hand, half of the professional staff had bought tickets, so it was incumbent upon them to end it in a timely fashion.

Patrick Ferris arrived. He swore to Christine that only for her would he agree to put himself in front of an audience again, attempting to look young, virile and with it. Christine kissed him on the cheek, thanked him, and sent him off to find his outfits.

She glanced around at the dozens of people who had suddenly arrived, efficiently completing their chores as she'd assigned them. Christine smiled in gratification, starting to feel for the first time that she might actually pull this thing off. Her assurance to Maxwell and Frances notwithstanding, she knew

that anything like this had the potential for disaster.
And the evening had not begun yet. She watched
with amusement and confidence as Eduardo, whom
she'd virtually made her second in command, instructed her band of merry workers, coordinating
their efforts with those of the hotel. Christine sighed
and turned away. It *was* going to be okay. If she
could only get through the next four hours. And if
Maxwell kept his word.

"Miss Morrow?"

Christine whirled around to face Delores. She
smiled. "Hi. I wondered what happened to you. We
keep missing each other at the center. How's everything going? Are you still working at the studio?"

Delores nodded but wouldn't look Christine in
the eye. She was nervous. "I got to talk to you."

"Okay. I hope you're planning on staying. I could
use your help. I have just the thing for you. We have
these gift bags . . ."

"It was my fault."

Christine stopped in mid-sentence. "Excuse me?"
she said, puzzled.

"You know that story in the newspapers? They
found out about you working at the center because
of me." She shrugged, looking pained and confused. "I didn't know I was doing anything wrong.
I was just . . . just . . ."

Christine pursed her lips. "Bragging to people
that you knew me. And they wanted to know how."

"Yeah, that's right. Then when everybody told me
about what they saw on the news, I thought, oh,
man . . . she's going to be so mad at me. And you
won't want to have nothing to do with me."

Christine looked at the other woman, seeing
clearly the agony she'd put herself through. She'd
never seen Delores like this. She never seemed to

give a damn what anyone thought of her. And she certainly was not used to apologizing. Christine shook her head, considering the long list of much more serious things that Delores had had to deal with in the last few years. Christine put her hand on her shoulder.

"It's okay. I'm not mad. Nothing bad happened. And you know what? Because you mentioned that I was involved at the center, we got a lot of publicity and help from all kinds of people."

"For real?" Delores asked, skeptical but anxious to believe Christine.

"For real. Now, are you going to stay and help me out? There are lots of things to do and I have a special job for you." Delores nodded vigorously.

She explained to Delores about the distribution of the gifts as guests were leaving, and then she sent her off with one of the models to be fitted for a dress for the evening. Delores looked a little numb as she was led away.

And then, checking her watch, Christine went up to her own room to get ready. She wore a strapless, floor-length silver lamé sheath with a side slit that ended mid-thigh. The shimmering fabric heightened her eye color, making her appear especially exotic and mysterious. Over one breast was pinned a red silk ribbon, the universal symbol of awareness and support for AIDS victims. Each guest would receive one as they came in.

When she reappeared an hour later everyone else was also dressed. Eduardo was in a tux and looking innocently debonair. When Christine complimented him and kissed him on his cheek, he blushed. And when she walked into the banquet hall, Parker whistled . . . and everyone broke into applause.

The first guests started arriving a half hour later,

greeting other guests and accepting drinks from circulating waiters and waitresses. The noise level rose and the laughter resounded. Christine knew exactly how to treat people, and how to move among them. She'd been well trained.

The band played light music and those who recognized Parker, which was just about everyone, introduced themselves and sought autographs. Alexandra came down dressed in a black slip dress with a thin row of rhinestones along the neckline that continued to form the straps. She looked proudly at her sister. Christine had certainly come a long way in the last year. Alexandra realized that Parker was right. It would seem that her little sister had, indeed, grown up.

Christine did one final check of everything. She convinced herself that there was still plenty of time for Maxwell to arrive, be introduced to Parker and the mayor when he, too, arrived, before he'd have to say anything. She took a deep breath, pressing her hand against a defiantly queasy stomach, and stood to greet more guests.

The show had begun . . .

Maxwell frowned at his watch and rushed into his apartment. He dropped the folders and papers from the meeting on the coffee table, and when they slid off the edge he didn't bother to pick them up. He was just going to make it.

He cursed under his breath when the phone rang. He debated letting it ring, but finally snatched it up, standing with his formal shirt still unbuttoned, his lean brown chest and its black curling hair contrasting sharply.

"Dr. Chandler," he answered officiously.

"Maxwell, it's Frances. I'm on my way down to the hotel. Do you need a ride?"

"No, you go on. I'm running late."

"I had a last-minute patient to see. Did I miss anything?"

Maxwell ran his hand across the back of his neck. "There were a couple of other things that really needed to be discussed but I left, too. I can't disappoint Christine tonight, no matter what. I'm going to try and call back before heading to the benefit and see if they scheduled another meeting. We may have to come in early Monday."

"Okay. I'll let you go. See you in a bit."

Maxwell went back to his preparations. He had two more calls, slowing him down even more. One was from the doorman, reminding him that there was a package waiting for him. The other was from a worried parent who launched into a detailed description of her baby's symptoms. Maxwell assured her it was a simple case of colic, and gave her instructions until she brought the child in to see him on Monday.

There was no help for it. He was going to arrive at the hotel a little bit late, but he hoped he'd be in time to make his opening speech for Christine. He didn't want to disappoint her after the incredible job she had done.

Maxwell was locking his apartment door when the phone rang again. He ground his teeth, determined to ignore it. Whoever it was could call back or call his service. He had his beeper and could be reached if absolutely necessary.

He was in traffic headed to the hotel when the beeper went off. Pulling over to the curb, Maxwell found a public phone booth and returned the call. He then made a second call to get a message to

Christine. Finally, he got into his car again . . . and
headed back uptown.

Christine's smile was frozen. She applauded the
mayor's rousing words of praise and enthusiasm, an-
nouncing that he'd found some money in the
budget what would allow LIFELINE to purchase
some much-needed equipment for the pediatric
ward. He introduced Christine and she joined him
on the makeshift stage for more applause and pic-
ture-taking from several reporters in the audience.
Then the mayor had to leave for another function,
waving expansively as his bodyguards closed rank
around him to lead him out to his waiting limo.

Christine added her own words of regret that Dr.
Chandler was apparently detained and couldn't
greet them, but she was sure they'd have a chance
to chat with him later in the evening. With that simple statement, she turned the program over to the
emcee, a popular local news anchor, to start the program.

Christine returned to her table, where Alexandra
was seated. She could see the understanding sympathy in her eyes, which only made her feel worse.
She had no idea what had happened to Maxwell.

"Where's Frances?"

"She said she'd be right back. Her beeper went
off." Alexandra reached out to pat her sister's hand.
"Christine, I'm sure he's on his way."

Christine nodded silently and tried to put aside
her bitter disappointment. Of course something
must have happened. If it was serious, Maxwell
would have gotten a message to her or he would
have indicated something to Frances. But not knowing was nerve-wracking. More than anything,

Christine had wanted Maxwell to be proud of her. She wanted to destroy every misconception he might have had, not only about the wisdom of trying to do an event on this scale and involve LIFELINE, but also to see that she was capable and smart and had much more on the ball than he'd given her credit for. She, in turn, wanted to be worthy of Maxwell's respect.

"If he's the kind of man you described to Parker and me, I suggest keeping your trust in him."

Christine nodded but didn't respond. An unsettling number of insecurities had surfaced inside her. She felt a tap on her shoulder and she turned to face Eduardo.

"Miss Morrow, there is someone here who said she was supposed to be in the show tonight."

Christine frowned, momentarily distracted. "Who?"

"Another model."

Christine got up and did a mental head count. All the models she had asked were already present and accounted for. "Everyone's here, Eduardo."

"Maybe you should talk to her. She is very . . . very . . ."

Pushy was what came to Christine's mind as she followed Eduardo out of the banquet hall and back to the dressing room. She wasn't the least surprised when Tonee Holiday turned to face her.

"Can I help you?" Christine asked calmly.

Bold as brass, Tonee stood her ground. "I came because I heard that there was a show tonight."

Christine knew she couldn't accuse the girl of having gotten *that* information from her appointment book. There had certainly been enough press coverage over the last several weeks. And she realized at once that that was the real reason Tonee Holiday had shown up. To be seen.

Christine arched a brow. "This is a charity event. I'm sure it's a new concept to you . . ."

"So?" She shrugged insolently. "You asked other models to work."

Christine thought a moment and assessed her carefully. "This is *not* The Tonee Holiday Show," she said bluntly. "I don't think I want you here. Things go wrong when you're around, Tonee." She started to walk away, not in the mood to try to second-guess the girl's agenda. If Tonee wanted to grandstand, let her do it on someone else's time.

"I'm not going to be any trouble," Tonee said gruffly behind her, as close to openly pleading as she could come.

Christine turned and looked at her. For a horrifying moment she imagined that she herself must have had a good bit of Tonee Holiday in her when she was starting out. Selfish, persistent, and overconfident. Young. Shallow. Christine shuddered. Thank goodness she'd finally started to grow up. She wondered if Tonee ever would.

She shook her head.

"No, I'm sorry. I can't take the chance. People's reputations are on the line. Children's welfare. You haven't shown me you can be trusted, Tonee. And I don't owe you any more favors. You're on your own."

Christine was not surprised when the model cut her a murderous look and flounced away. Christine watched her leave and sighed in relief. And she wanted to remember to thank her sister and Parker for not giving up on her.

She headed for the ballroom reluctantly, feeling her spirit failing. She was stopped several times along the way to deal with minor problems and questions. Then, just before going into the room, someone grabbed her arm firmly from the side. A strong, masculine hand.

Christine's heart quickened as Maxwell's name came to the tip of her tongue. But when she turned she found herself face-to-face with Keith. She blinked at him for a moment as if he was a total stranger. She wondered how he got in. And . . . what she was going to do with him. Christine thought that if one more unexpected person showed up she was going to have a fit. Keith was dressed in black tie and looked as handsome and striking as ever. It didn't do a thing for her.

She frowned. "What are you doing here?"

Keith chuckled in amazement. "No hello? No welcome back? No kiss . . ."

"Sorry, I don't have time," Christine said evasively.

"You look great. I heard all about what you've been up to. You've been busy while I was away."

"So were you. Congratulations. Things are going great, I take it."

He grinned complacently. "Not bad. I have no complaints."

"You know I can't see you or talk to you right now, Keith. I'm a little busy . . ."

He caught her hand. "Christine, we have to talk. Something's come up."

She sighed and tried to remain patient. "I know. She's about five-feet-three, long, dark hair, young, sweet, and she thinks you're wonderful."

He blinked at her in surprise.

"I saw the ET segment. You looked good. Certainly can't hurt to have that kind of coverage."

"As a matter of fact, I got three new offers because of that."

She shrugged. "Go for it."

"I am. I'm here just to take care of some business, tie up some loose ends . . ."

"Like what to do about us? . . ."

"And then I'm headed back to California. I've just signed a contract for two more films."

Christine looked at Keith, finally focusing, finally feeling less impatient. He was going to do well. She was happy for him. And she was very happy for herself. She wasn't sure when she'd fallen out of "like" with Keith Layton, but she realized by her lack of response to his news that it had happened way before he'd ever left for Hollywood, and before she'd met D. Maxwell Chandler. The timing, actually, had been perfect.

"I wish you all the best, Keith. I really do. So are you here for my little soirée, or are you off to catch up with what's-her-name?"

"Kimberly? She's visiting her folks. She's from New Jersey. I'm going out to meet them tomorrow. But I wanted to be here tonight." He reached into his pocket and withdrew a folded paper. "I want to make a donation to the cause."

Christine stared blankly at him before gingerly taking the check. "How generous."

He smiled wistfully. "It was great with you, Christine. But you don't need me. I'm not even sure what you're looking for."

"I'm sorry, Keith, I didn't mean to build up your hopes."

"Hey, I'm a big boy, I can take care of my own ego. But we sure were a great-looking couple."

With that he kissed her cheek and quickly blended with the crowd in the banquet hall, ready

to work the room. Christine watched him go, surprised . . . and relieved. And then she returned to
the hall. The expression on Alexandra's face told
her that Maxwell had still not shown up. Christine
accepted that, and realized finally that Maxwell was
not going to make it to the program at all.

Maxwell's face was so tight with tension that he
could feel the stress in the sides of his neck. He
came through the revolving door of the hotel and
slowly made his way to the concierge's desk, asking
for directions to the charity event for the LIFELINE
center of Harlem. He was directed to the second
floor. He nodded, remembering how to find it. It
was where he'd first laid eyes on Christine Morrow.
Maxwell waited patiently for the elevator, beyond
being upset, or sorry or anything. He was totally
wrung out, but knew that he had to get to the hotel
because his future . . . his *life* depended on it.
It was pretty quiet when he got off the elevator.
The fundraiser would have ended about an hour
earlier. He could hear the dismantling of tables and
chairs, the clinking of wineglasses being collected,
and musical instruments being packed away. Maxwell stood at the entrance of that very same banquet
room where all of this had begun back in May. He
spotted Christine immediately, astonished at how
beautiful she looked in her elegant dress, the little
red AIDS ribbon standing out against the shimmering fabric. The very sight of it made his throat feel
tight. It stood for so much, and reminded Maxwell
that there was still so much that needed to be done.
But suddenly, he didn't feel quite so hopeless. There
were going to be losses. It was inevitable. But the
gains . . . the present and the future . . . couldn't

be denied either. There was always hope. That's what Christine offered him. He desperately needed it . . . and her.

Christine was sitting on the stage with a very attractive couple. He recognized Parker Harrison—the woman was probably Christine's sister. Maxwell knew they were waiting for him . . . and he dreaded having to go in feeling the way he did.

Christine must have sensed his presence, must have heard his silent plea and felt his pain. She looked up abruptly.

Her heart stopped. There he was. All of her feelings converged and Christine wasn't sure what she was experiencing as he stood silently in the door, watching her. She stood up and made her way from the stage gracefully.

"Christine . . . why don't I . . ." Parker began.

"Shhhh," Alexandra cautioned. "Let her handle this."

Maxwell didn't move, but let Christine make the journey alone across the room, their eyes locked, reading into each other's hearts. It was only when she was within four feet or so that she found her voice.

"Max . . . I was frantic. I thought something awful had happened to you. I got the note about an emergency, and then Frances just disappeared and . . ." She stopped suddenly, her mouth open. She blinked rapidly as her face began to distort and a rush of emotions crossed her startled features. She raised a hand to her mouth as her lips began to tremble. Christine's eyes filled quickly with tears and she began to shake her head. "No . . . oh, no . . ."

He held out a hand and she stepped closer until Maxwell's arms circled her and held her face to his chest. He hadn't said a word. And he didn't have to.

"Oh, Max . . . nooooo," she sobbed. She knew with certainty.

He'd lost Wendy.

Ten

"Good morning. "I'm Dean Whalen . . ."

"And I'm Diana Waters. Welcome back to this segment of 'Wake Up, New York.' In this half-hour we're going to talk with two extraordinary people who've pulled off a coup this summer—they organized and hosted a charity affair that everyone in the city is still talking about. It was a stellar evening to benefit Pediatric AIDS at a small community health center in Harlem.

"We'd like to welcome Dr. D. Maxwell Chandler, attending physician at the center and one of the country's foremost African-American doctors in Pediatrics. And Christine Morrow, a supermodel whom we've all seen many times gracing the covers of such magazines as *Elle, Vogue,* and *Cosmopolitan.*

"We're happy to have you both with us this morning. We'd like to hear how this all came about, and why it seems to have captured the hearts of all New Yorkers. We understand that you managed to raise close to a quarter of a million dollars in one night. That's pretty amazing . . ."

Christine smiled like the professional she was as the two hosts posed their questions to her and Maxwell. She wanted to reach out and take his hand, but knew that it would make him too uncomfortable. But she turned all her attention to him, encouraging him to be the first to speak, to take credit for the work that LIFELINE was doing.

Pain still stabbed in Christine's chest when she remembered that one brief life had just recently slipped beyond the reach of the center's best intentions, and Maxwell's skills as a doctor. Christine hadn't known that it would hurt so much, seem such a personal loss for someone she had never really met, spoken to, or held. She thought that that was the thing she most regretted—not having taken the time to show Wendy that she was loved.

And she'd ached for Maxwell, knowing from his shallow breathing, the tightly controlled way he held himself and didn't say too much, that the occasion had torn deeply into him. When Christine remembered that Maxwell had probably been there before and would be there for another child in the future, she didn't think she could stand it. It was so unfair.

And yet, suddenly . . . everything began to make sense.

For everything there is a season, and things change. While Maxwell had held her the night before, listening to her cry herself to sleep, it dawned on Christine that she was different now. She could never be exactly as she was before. Her eyes had been opened. And so had her heart. She had Wendy to thank for that. And Maxwell, of course . . .

Maxwell glanced briefly at Christine; seeing the encouragement in her eyes, he cleared his throat, knowing the show hosts were waiting for his response. "I guess you could say the fundraiser came about because there is a tremendous need. Good health care in poor communities is generally lacking to begin with. Combine the meager resources with a disease that is one hundred percent deadly, and the community has a lot to deal with. Especially when children are involved."

"How, exactly, did the LIFELINE center come about?" Dean Whalen asked. "We understand you've been operating for close to five years."

While Maxwell continued to be the spokesperson, Christine gazed at him with reverence. She hoped she didn't look sappy, but short of throwing her arms around him on national television, she didn't know how else to demonstrate the love she'd developed . . . almost to bursting . . . for this man.

". . . Serious lack of equipment. When Christine suggested the fundraiser I admit I wasn't hot for the idea. Not because we couldn't use the money, but because of the attention it would bring to the individual children and their families. There's still a lot of fear and ignorance about people who are HIV positive." He looked at Christine again and slyly winked, so she would know it was just for her. "But it's hard to say no to her . . . and ultimately the hospital board realized it was a good idea."

"I understand that some top celebrities came out in support. Parker Harrison performed, as well as several other notable musicians. How did he get involved?" Diana asked.

"He's my brother-in-law," Christine said with a grin. "You can usually get your family to do almost anything."

The anchors laughed. "Tell us, Christine, why you decided to volunteer at the center. It's a far cry from the glamorous life you've led. And that newspaper article a month ago hinted at something far more serious than just visiting once or twice a week to help out . . ."

Maxwell listened to Christine, and watched her with a sense of awe. She deftly skirted the issue of how she'd come to his office and written the check to LIFELINE in lieu of a consultation fee. She spoke of being impressed by the dedication of the clinic staff and other volunteers. She took none of the credit, making no attempt to grandstand because of her high public profile. Perhaps in her other life Christine Morrow might well have made optimum use of an appearance like this one, but the Christine he'd come to know had metamorphosed into a new woman. *That* new woman, Maxwell had already decided, he was seriously in love with.

"Well, what's next on the agenda for you, Christine? Are you headed into an acting career like so many other models?"

Christine smiled peacefully. "I don't think so. I've never been interested in that. I'm thinking of something a little more substantial. And there's still so much to be done at the clinic . . ." She looked at Maxwell. "If I can convince Dr. Chandler to listen to more of my harebrained ideas. I've also been asked by several other children's organizations to help them look at new ways to raise money for their programs."

"It sounds like you're becoming a consultant. Sort of a cottage industry."

"Well . . . I do have some things I'd like to see get done. And I . . . I enjoyed working with Dr. Chandler and his associate, Dr. Frances Grimes. It's been wonderful."

"Can you confirm or deny—we can't reveal our source, of course—that a little romance also came out of Christine's volunteer efforts, Dr. Chandler?"

Christine and Maxwell exchanged glances again and chuckled uncomfortably. "No comment," they said simultaneously.

"Let's try an easier question," Diana Waters began. "We got a little note just before we went on the air that someone out in the TV audience wants to know what the 'D' stands for in your name, doctor."

"I want to know, too," Christine said brightly.

Maxwell shook his head and smiled complacently. "I'll never tell."

"Oh, yes, you will," Christine countered confidently, smiling at Maxwell when he turned a quizzical expression on her.

"Well, let us know when you find out, Christine. Perhaps we can have you both back on the show after you've implemented some of the newly planned programs at LIFELINE.

"We've been talking to Dr. D. Maxwell Chandler and Christine Morrow. Congratulations to both of you on a job well done for a very worthy cause. Thank you for being our guests this morning."

"Thank *you*," they both murmured graciously.

"We'll be right back. It's now 8:15 A.M. Wake Up, New York . . ."

"You didn't like being on camera, did you?"

Maxwell grimaced and shrugged. "I'm better behind the scenes." He took her hand from where it lay between them on the seat in the back of a New York City cab. "But you were great. You fielded some of those personal questions very nicely."

"Practice," Christine said wryly. "One of the disadvantages of being a public figure is that the public wants to know everything about you." She smiled at Maxwell. "There are some things that they just don't need to know."

"I'm glad to hear that. In the future, I think I'll let you be the media contact."

It was not lost on Christine that Maxwell had pointedly mentioned the future. "I'm glad to know that there are some things I'm good at."

Maxwell let his gaze roam over her features slowly, looking into the light of her green eyes. Last night it had been okay for him to feel broken, to be tired and angry and disappointed . . . and defeated because of Wendy. Christine had been there with him—and *for* him. He kissed her forehead. "Some . . ." he confirmed.

Christine sighed. "Maybe it's just as well you never got properly introduced to my sister and Parker last night." She squeezed his hand. "Now that we've had some time to ourselves it will be much more relaxed. You don't mind coming back to the hotel for brunch with them, do you? They have to get back to D.C. because of the baby and my father."

Maxwell frowned. "No, I don't mind. But I would have liked some more time with you . . ."

She smiled lovingly. "Me, too."

He looked at her closely. "I mean . . . more time so I could tell you that . . . I think I'm in love with you, Christine."

Christine blinked, and her expression softened. Gone, for the moment, was her sophisticated persona. In her place was just a woman in love. She placed her hand on Maxwell's face and urged him closer so she could kiss him and feel the gentle pressure of his lips on hers. "Well, it's a good thing," she whispered lightly. "Otherwise, what you and I have been doing together behind closed doors is a sin . . ."

"Max, this is my sister, Alexandra, and her husband, Parker Harrison."

"Pleased to meet you both . . ."

The introductions were quickly dispensed with along with comments about the TV interview as Christine and Maxwell took seats at the table.

"This is a real pleasure," Maxwell began, speaking to Parker. "I've been a fan of yours for a long time."

"And I'm *honored* to meet you," Parker countered. "Ever since Christine told us about your work and the center, I've been reading great things about you. What I do isn't much compared to trying to save children's lives. Alex and I are real sorry about what happened last night."

"Yes," Alexandra nodded with sympathy in her eyes. "I can't imagine anything worse than losing a child."

"There's a loss, but there's also life," Maxwell said, looking at the baby Alexandra held in her arms.

Christine reached over and lifted her niece from Alexandra's lap. "And this little sweetie is the latest addition to the Harrison/Morrow family," she crooned as she positioned Lauren expertly in the crook of her arm. She turned her bright gaze to Maxwell. "This is Lauren Shani Harrison. Isn't she beautiful, Max?" Christine grinned down at the baby again, stroking her soft cheek with the tip of her finger while the infant stared wide-eyed at her.

But Maxwell, for the moment, had eyes only for Christine, watching the way she cooed over the baby. "She sure is," he agreed quietly.

Alexandra and Parker exchanged covert glances.

"Christine, I hope you can come home for another visit before you start your next round of professional obligations," Alexandra suggested to her sister.

Christine nodded. "I'll look at some dates." She reached out a hand to Maxwell and he took it. "Can I bring Maxwell with me?"

"Yeah, that would be great," Parker agreed at once. "So . . . Diana and Dean weren't wrong about the rumors, I take it?"

Christine kept her eyes on Maxwell, waiting for him to respond. She felt the pressure of his hand around hers, the expression of love on his dark face.

"No, they weren't," Maxwell murmured smoothly and was rewarded with a slow, loving smile from Christine.

"Does this mean that you two . . ."

"Parker! That's none of our business," Alexandra fussed at her husband, who didn't look the least bit repentant.

Christine chuckled. "But you're both dying to know, right?"

"If we sit here holding hands, Christine, I think they get the idea," Maxwell said wryly.

Alexandra shook her head and laughed lightly. "I loved it when you told those two hosts that you were going to find out what the letter 'D' stood for in Maxwell's name. Now, just how are you planning on doing that?"

Christine smiled at her sister and brother-in-law. She turned her attention to Maxwell. "He's going to have to make a full disclosure on a marriage license eventually."

Parker laughed outright at Christine's flawless reasoning . . . and her complete confidence that Maxwell would propose.

"And . . ." Christine said, lifting the baby so she could kiss Lauren's face and place her against her shoulder. She could see over the infant's head right into Maxwell's eyes. Christine carefully stroked the back of Lauren's head. "Some day, I want one just like her."

About the Author

Award winning author Sandra Kitt has been writing romances for years and has over a dozen titles published. A native to New York City, Sandra is the Manager of Library Services at the American Museum-Hayden Planetarium. The mediagenic author spends her free time writing articles for various publications as well as lecturing across the country.

Look for these upcoming Arabesque titles:

July 1996

DECEPTION by Donna Hill
INDISCRETION by Margie Walker
AFFAIR OF THE HEART by Janice Sims

August 1996

WHITE DIAMONDS by Shirley Hailstock
SEDUCTION by Felicia Mason
AT FIRST SIGHT by Cheryl Faye

September 1996

WHISPERED PROMISES by Brenda Jackson
AGAINST ALL ODDS by Gwynne Forster
ALL FOR LOVE by Raynetta Manees

PUT SOME FANTASY IN YOUR LIFE— FANTASTIC ROMANCES FROM PINNACLE

TIME STORM (728, $4.99)
by Rosalyn Alsobrook

Modern-day Pennsylvanian physician JoAnn Griffin only believed what she could feel with her five senses. But when, during a freak storm, a blinding flash of lightning sent her back in time to 1889, JoAnn realized she had somehow crossed the threshold into another century and was now gazing into the smoldering eyes of a startlingly handsome stranger. JoAnn had stumbled through a rip in time . . . and into a love affair so intense, it carried her to a point of no return!

SEA TREASURE (790, $4.50)
by Johanna Hailey

When Michael, a dashing sea captain, is rescued from drowning by a beautiful sea siren—he does not know yet that she's actually a mermaid. But her breathtaking beauty stirred irresistible yearnings in Michael. And soon fate would drive them across the treacherous Caribbean, tossing them on surging tides of passion that transcended two worlds!

ONCE UPON FOREVER (883, $4.99)
by Becky Lee Weyrich

A moonstone necklace and a mysterious diary written over a century ago were Clair Summerland's only clued to her true identity. Two men loved her— one, a dashing civil war hero . . . the other, a daring jet pilot. Now Clair must risk her past and future for a passion that spans two worlds—and a love that is stronger than time itself.

SHADOWS IN TIME (892, $4.50)
by Cherlyn Jac

Driving through the sultry New Orleans night, one moment Tori's car spins our of control; the next she is in a horse-drawn carriage with the handsomest man she has ever seen—who calls her wife—but whose eyes blaze with fury. Sent back in time one hundred years, Tori is falling in love with the man she is apparently trying to kill. Now she must race against time to change the tragic past and claim her future with the man she will love through all eternity!

Available wherever paperbacks are sold, or order direct from the Publisher. Send cover price plus 50¢ per copy for mailing and handling to Penguin USA, P.O. Box 999, c/o Dept. 17109, Bergenfield, NJ 07621. Residents of New York and Tennessee must include sales tax. DO NOT SEND CASH.

IF ROMANCE BE THE FRUIT OF LIFE—
READ ON—
BREATH-QUICKENING HISTORICALS FROM PINNACLE

WILDCAT (722, $4.99)
by Rochelle Wayne

No man alive could break Diana Preston's fiery spirit . . . until seductive Vince Gannon galloped onto Diana's sprawling family ranch. Vince, a man with dark secrets, would sweep her into his world of danger and desire. And Diana couldn't deny the powerful yearnings that branded her as his own, for all time!

THE HIGHWAY MAN (765, $4.50)
by Nadine Crenshaw

When a trumped-up murder charge forced beautiful Jane Fitzpatrick to flee her home, she was found and sheltered by the highwayman—a man as dark and dangerous as the secrets that haunted him. As their hiding place became a place of shared dreams—and soaring desires—Jane knew she'd found the love she'd been yearning for!

SILKEN SPURS (756, $4.99)
by Jane Archer

Beautiful Harmony Harper, leader of a notorious outlaw gang, rode the desert plains of New Mexico in search of justice and vengeance. Now she has captured powerful and privileged Thor Clarke-Jargon, who is everything Harmony has ever hated—and all she will ever want. And after Harmony has taken the handsome adventurer hostage, she herself has become a captive—of her own desires!

WYOMING ECSTASY (740, $4.50)
by Gina Robins

Feisty criminal investigator, July MacKenzie, solicits the partnership of the legendary half-breed gunslinger-detective Nacona Blue. After being turned down, July—never one to accept the meaning of the word no—finds a way to convince Nacona to be her partner . . . first in business—then in passion. Across the wilds of Wyoming, and always one step ahead of trouble, July surrenders to passion's searing demands!